A loud, rumbling snort sounded behind her. She turned her head, staring down into the black gorge. She heard the scratch and scrape of huge claws on the stone. Two red points of light were moving upward through the rain.

"Tania!"

She snatched her head around. Edric was leaning over the high lip of rock, reaching his arm down toward her. She threw herself up and caught hold of his hand. It was cold—much colder than before, and the grip of his fingers was fierce and harsh.

"I have you!" The voice sounded wrong.

"Edric?"

There was a snarl of triumphant laughter and at that same moment a blaze of lightning lit up the crouching figure above her.

She let out a scream. It wasn't Edric.

The wild-eyed face that leered down at her was the face of Gabriel Drake.

Also by Frewin Jones

THE FAERIE PATH

THE SEVENTH DAUGHTER
(also published as THE SORCERER KING*)*

The LOST QUEEN

Book Two *of The* FAERIE PATH

FREWIN JONES

An Imprint of HarperCollinsPublishers

Eos is an imprint of HarperCollins Publishers.

The Lost Queen
www.harperteen.com

Library of Congress Cataloging-in-Publication Data
Jones, Frewin.
    The lost queen / Frewin Jones. — 1st ed.
        p. cm.
    Summary: After discovering her true identity as Princess Tania of the Faerie Realm, a
sixteen-year-old British girl returns to the Mortal World, in search of her mother, Queen
Titania, who disappeared 500 years ago.
    ISBN 978-0-06-087107-9 (pbk.)
    [1. Fairies—Fiction. 2. Princesses—Fiction. 3. Identity—Fiction. 4. Fantasy.] I. Title.
PZ7.J71Lo 2007   2006103542
[Fic]—dc22   CIP
                                                                                        AC

Typography by Al Cetta
❖
First paperback edition, 2008
09 10 11 12 13 CG/RRDH 10 9 8 7 6 5 4

For Claudia

Faeries tread the faerie path
One daughter walks between the sundered worlds
Danger haunts her footsteps there
In Mortal Realm a darkness is unfurled

Seek a mother long-time lost
Forge dark jewels that bring forth light
A crystal sword shall show the way
And love shall conquer evil's blight

What Happened Before...

On the eve of Anita Palmer's sixteenth birthday, her boyfriend, Evan Thomas, took her for a speedboat ride on the river Thames. Her birthday surprise turned to terror when they saw a ghostly shape on the river and Evan, swerving to avoid it, sent the boat crashing into a bridge.

Anita woke up in hospital. Her injuries were superficial, but Evan—although otherwise physically unhurt—remained unconscious.

Anita's parents brought her a curious parcel: a birthday present sent with no card and no name. It was an old leather-bound book with blank pages that mysteriously filled with words when Anita started reading.

The book told how Princess Tania, seventh daughter of King Oberon and Queen Titania of the Realm of Faerie, disappeared from the Royal Palace on the eve of her wedding to Lord Gabriel Drake. It was while Anita was reading this story that she learned Evan had vanished from the hospital. Later that same morning, Anita—believing herself to be experiencing a vivid dream inspired by the story in the book—followed a young man in Elizabethan clothes into Faerie.

The young man introduced himself as Gabriel Drake and explained that Evan was in fact his servant Edric Chanticleer, sent into the Mortal World to find and retrieve Anita. Gabriel believed she was his lost bride, Princess Tania—the seventh daughter of Oberon and Titania, with the power to walk between Faerie and the Mortal World. For five hundred years, ever since the disappearance of Princess Tania and the subsequent loss of her mother, Queen Titania, the eternal Realm of Faerie had been plunged into a sad and gloomy twilight.

When Gabriel took Anita to meet Oberon, the king was so overjoyed that his lost daughter had returned that light and life came back into Faerie once more. Soon after, Anita met Princess Tania's six sisters, and as she learned more about this strange world—and *remembered* things she could not possibly have known—her certainty that this was all a dream began to waver. At last she was forced to confront the fact that she was truly Oberon's lost daughter.

Torn between the enchantments of Faerie and the desperate need to get home, Anita—now acknowledging herself to be Tania—learned that the mysterious book sent to her in the Mortal World was her Soul Book, a living diary that chronicled all the days of her Faerie life.

Tania had believed that Edric as Evan loved her,

and full of pain and anger at his betrayal, she grew closer to Lord Gabriel. It was only after Edric told her the true purpose behind Gabriel's dramatic rescue of Tania from the Mortal World that she was saved from falling under his spell. Gabriel Drake had planned to marry Tania and use her unique power to enter the Mortal World and bring back a terrible poison called Isenmort, known to mortals as metal, a substance so deadly in Faerie that its merest touch meant instant death. The Faerie Palace was torn apart with treachery—even Tania's own sister Princess Rathina tried to force Tania to marry Gabriel.

In the end Gabriel's plans were thwarted and the evil lord was banished by Oberon.

Peace returned to the Realm of Faerie but Tania was convinced that her mother, Queen Titania, was still alive, and had sent her the Soul Book. She and Edric returned to the Mortal World to find her.

Part One:

Between the

Worlds

I

Camden, North London

The van's horn blared loudly in the quiet of the early morning London streets: three short bursts followed by a cheery whistle from the driver.

Princess Tania, seventh daughter of Oberon and Titania, King and Queen of the Immortal Realm of Faerie, turned her head to look. The driver of the van was half leaning out of the cab, grinning at Tania and her companion as the vehicle sped by.

Tania laughed. She didn't mind the effect she and Edric were having as they walked along together; it was quite funny, actually, and that driver wasn't the first person to have reacted enthusiastically to their strange clothes. They had already been on the receiving end of several odd looks on their journey from Hampton Court in southwest London to Camden in the north of the city.

Tania knew why they were getting these reactions: Their ornate clothes would have blended in perfectly in an Elizabethan court, but they struck an odd note in twenty-first-century London. Tania was wearing a full-skirted, olive green velvet gown with long sleeves and embroidered panels picked out in leaf green and russet red stitching. Edric's clothes were similarly archaic: a dark gray doublet and hose trimmed with black brocade and with puffed sleeves slashed to show a lining of pearl white silk.

Edric smiled. "He probably thinks we've been to an all-night costume party."

"Probably," Tania agreed. "One thing's for sure: He'd never guess the truth." She paused and gazed into Edric's wide, chestnut brown eyes. A thread of wind caught his dark blonde hair and whipped it around his smiling face—the face of the boy she loved. A seventeen-year-old boy called Evan Thomas, who had turned out to be someone quite different—just as she had turned out to be a different person from the girl she had always thought she was.

Three days ago she had been Anita Palmer, an ordinary girl on the brink of her sixteenth birthday. Three days ago she had known nothing of the enchanted world of Faerie. She smiled to herself. Back then she had been only half alive.

Three days ago she had loved a boy called Evan, but now she knew who he truly was: Edric Chanticleer, a young courtier of the Royal Palace of Faerie.

The sharp click of heels on paving stones brought Tania out of her reverie. A woman was walking toward them, staring at them in amused curiosity.

"Hello, there," Edric said. "We've just come from the Immortal Realm of Faerie." He nodded to Tania. "She's a princess."

"Is she?" the woman said as she passed. "Good for her. The pair of you certainly brighten up the place."

"Thanks," Tania called as the woman walked on and disappeared around a corner.

Edric grinned. "You see? People are okay with the truth."

She looked thoughtfully at him. "So long as they think you're kidding," she said. "But that's not going to work with Mum and Dad."

Edric's face became serious. "No," he said. "I know it won't."

Tania glanced down at herself. "I can't turn up at home dressed like this," she said. "I'm going to have enough explaining to do without these clothes." She had been out of the Mortal World for three days since both she and Edric went missing from hospital following the speedboat accident—three days and nights for her desperate parents to fear the worst. She had to get back to them as soon as possible and let them know she was all right, but not in her Faerie gown.

Edric looked up and down the street. "The shops aren't open yet," he said. "It can't be much past seven o'clock. But even if they were open, we haven't got any money to buy clothes."

Tania frowned, thinking. "There's a charity shop not far from here."

"That won't be open, either."

"It doesn't matter." She gripped Edric's hand. "Come on. I know where we might find some things to wear."

St. Crispin's Hospice Shop, Camden
The charity shop had an assortment of items laid out in the window—everything from books and vinyl LPs to toys and games and ornaments. Deeper into the shop they could see racks of clothing and one shelf that appeared to contain nothing but folded crocheted blankets.

"Just like I said," Edric commented, peering through the glass. "It's closed."

"No problem," Tania said. "Come with me." She led him by the hand into a narrow alley that ran alongside the shop. A doorway was sunk into the wall about ten feet down the alley and up against the door, they found a pile of plastic bags, boxes, and bin liners.

"People leave stuff here for the shop when it's closed," Tania explained. "With any luck we'll find some clothes we can use. We can do a swap."

Edric crouched down and opened the nearest bag. He pulled out a garish green-and-purple knitted sweater. "What do you think? Should I try it on?"

"Over my dead body." She knelt at his side and started working at the knotted string that held closed the neck of another bag, hoping that the clothes inside would turn out to be more wearable than that purple-and-green sweater.

"Okay, I'm decent again," Tania said. She had changed in the shallow confines of the sunken doorway while Edric had turned his back and guarded her from the gaze of anyone passing the end of the alley.

He was already in normal clothes: a pale blue shirt and a pair of blue jeans two sizes too big for him, held up with a black leather belt.

Tania stepped out of cover. "Do I look all right?" The choice of clothing hadn't been ideal, but she had found a pink T-shirt and a calf-length, brown denim skirt. She had discarded her red velvet Faerie shoes in favor of a pair of white sneakers that fit reasonably well.

Edric smiled. "You look lovely," he said.

She raised her eyebrows. "If you say so," she said. She crouched and carefully folded her Faerie gown into one of the bags. "And it's not like we're stealing," she said. "Just making an exchange." She looked up at him. "Imagine their faces when they see this lot."

Edric reached down and she took his hand as she stood up.

"You'll need one of these," she said, opening the fingers of her other hand. She had brought the two small flat gemstones from Faerie in a pocket of her gown. Now they lay in her palm, oval-shaped and glimmering fitfully in the pale morning light: Black amber, the most precious mineral in the Realm of Faerie.

Edric picked one of the jewels out of her hand. "Remember," he told her. "You're as vulnerable to Isenmort now as I am. You have to keep this with you all the time."

"Yes, I know." For several weeks before she had entered Faerie, Tania had been getting electric shocks off anything made from metal. As the Faerie half of her spirit came alive, so had her susceptibility to metal—to the lethal substance known in Faerie as Isenmort. Oberon had given her these two pieces of black amber for protection; unless she kept one of them close by, the touch of metal could be deadly to her. She slipped the jewel into the pocket of her skirt.

"You haven't told me how I look," Edric said. "Am I respectable enough to meet your parents, do you think?"

She adjusted his collar and smoothed the creases on the front of his shirt. "You look just fine," she said. "But you can't come home with me."

Edric frowned. "I'm not leaving you to face them on your own."

"Yes you are," she said firmly. She lifted her fingers to his lips to stop him speaking. "Listen," she went on. "No matter what I say, Mum and Dad are going to blame you for what happened. I need to talk to them on my own—that's the only way this is going to work. If you come with me, it'll only make things worse."

Edric looked at her for a few moments without speaking. Then he nodded. "Perhaps you're right," he said. "But we haven't even decided what you're going to tell them."

"I wish I could tell them the truth," Tania said. "But I can't. They'd think I've gone insane."

"So we have to come up with a plausible reason for why you disappeared from the hospital and where you've been."

"I'm no good at lying," she admitted. "If we make stuff up, we have to keep it really simple otherwise Mum will suss it out in ten seconds flat."

"Okay," Edric said. "Nice and simple. You've already told them the story about my coming from Wales, haven't you?"

"Yes," Tania said. "And I thought it was true at the time. It sounded perfectly reasonable: You didn't get on with your stepfather so you came to London to get away from him."

"You can tell them you went to Wales to try and find me when I left the hospital," Edric said.

Tania nodded. "Yes, Wales is good. It could easily have taken me this long to get there and back. But we have to choose a particular place." She racked her brains—she had never been to Wales but one of her classmates came from a town in the northwest of the country, a small coastal town in Snowdonia. What was the place called? "Criccieth!" she said aloud. "That's it. It's up in the north of Wales. It could easily have taken me a couple of days to find you there. I'll tell them I wasn't thinking straight, that I was frantic with worry about you after you vanished. I went to

Criccieth and found you at your parents' house."

"Tell them I had freaked out because I thought the police were going to prosecute me about the boat crash," Edric suggested. "And you persuaded me to come back."

"Yes."

He looked anxiously at her. "Are you sure you wouldn't rather have me there with you?"

She shook her head. "Trust me, you don't want to be there. Stay with me till we get to the end of my street, then you should go to the hostel and keep your cell phone on. I'll call you as soon as I can." She grabbed his hand. "Let's go." .

Tania and Edric stood at the corner of Lessingham Street and Eddison Terrace. Anita Palmer and her parents lived at number 18, down at the far end of the long residential street.

"I don't want to leave you," Edric said, holding both her hands in his.

"It's only for a little while," Tania said. "We can talk on the phone." She frowned. "What day is it?"

Edric thought for a moment. "Thursday."

"Then I'll see you at school tomorrow," she said. "Keep your fingers crossed for me that everything goes well."

"I will." He looked into her face. "I love you."

"I love you, too. But go, please."

He started to walk away.

"Aren't you going to kiss me good-bye?" she called.

He turned back and suddenly they were in each other's arms.

And then, far, far too quickly, she was alone on the street corner in the early morning light, watching him leave.

He turned and waved. She lifted her hand and waved back. She saw his lips move, mouthing, *I love you*. *I love you*. She formed the words soundlessly.

Then he was gone.

She started to walk down the street. The sun blazed between two buildings, sending her shadow skittering away from her, filling her eyes with dazzling light and wrapping her in the warmth of the early summer morning.

Had it all been a dream, everything she had seen and done in Faerie? Her father the King. Her six sisters: carefree Zara; solemn-eyed Sancha; Cordelia with her beloved animals; Hopie with her stern gaze and healing hands; Eden, her unhappy eldest sister who had believed she was responsible for their mother's death; and poor deluded Rathina, who had done such terrible things for love of Gabriel Drake, who had never loved her in return.

Real? Not real?

Tania walked along the street she had known all her life, gazing amazed at all those strange, familiar houses, knowing as she approached the house she had always called home that the girl she had been was gone forever.

* * *

Tania's hand trembled as she reached for the door-bell; it felt odd to have to ring at her own front door, but then her missing keys were just another part of her old life—the life that had been stripped away from her over the past three days.

A thousand raw emotions churned through her. The pure joy of knowing she was about to see her parents again, and the apprehension over how they would react. The fear that things could never be the same again in her life, and the wonder and delight of knowing who she really was. The overwhelming intensity of her love for Edric, and the desolation of being apart from him. Memories of Faerie, memories of this world. All tumbling together as she stood under the porch and waited for the door to open.

Something in her wanted to run and hide—something stronger kept her there.

She saw a shadow approaching through the glass panels. The blood pounded in her temples.

Be brave! Be brave! Be brave!

The door opened and she saw her father's familiar round, gentle-eyed face. But the change in him was devastating. There were dark bags under his eyes, his skin was gray and his usual cheerful expression was gone, replaced by misery and despair.

Tania's mouth was parched. She swallowed painfully. "Dad . . . ?"

He gave a wordless shout, his eyes lighting up, his face stretching into a huge relieved smile. He jerked the door wide open and almost threw himself at her.

She gasped as the breath was squeezed out of her. She put her arms around him, her eyes shut, clinging on tightly, feeling his stubble against her cheek, smelling the familiar scent of his soap, her face buried in the collar of his dressing gown.

She had no idea of how much time passed as they stood like that on the doorstep.

Finally he let go of her enough to draw her over the threshold and close the door behind her.

"Mary!" he called, his voice shaking. "She's here!"

Tania tried to speak—to apologize—to explain—but her throat felt achingly tight and her voice wouldn't come.

Her father pulled her along the hallway. She saw her mother appear at the head of the stairs. She saw her grip the banister rail, her face a white blur through Tania's tears. She saw her mother's legs buckle under her, so that she sat heavily on the top step, her slender body wrapped in her old blue dressing gown.

Tania pulled loose from her father and scrambled up the stairs. She tumbled onto her knees in front of her mother and buried her face in her lap. She felt her mother's hands trembling as she stroked her hair.

"Oh, Anita!" Her mother's voice was ragged with emotion. "Where have you been? Where have you *been*?"

Tania sat at the kitchen table, her eyes stinging from tears, her chest aching and her head numb. She felt as if she was floating in a bubble of frozen glass, as if everything that was going on around her was happening to someone else. Questions came at her and she heard a voice that sounded like hers giving stumbling answers.

She could smell toast as her dad made her some scrambled eggs.

Her mother was sitting opposite her, her arms folded on the tabletop, her head thrust forward, watching her with bewildered eyes.

Tania was finding it even harder than she had imagined to hold up under her parents' questions. She knew what to say, but she found it desperately hard to repeat the invented story of a journey to Wales to find Edric. And even the strain of remembering to get his name right—to call him Evan—was making her head pound.

"You could have left a note," her mother said. "Or phoned us, or . . . *something*."

"I know," Tania said quietly, her head throbbing with a growing thunder. "I wasn't thinking straight. All I could think about was that I had to find Evan."

"But how did you manage?" her father asked. "How did you get all the way to north Wales? It's two hundred miles away."

"Plenty of trains go there," Tania murmured.

"You got a train from Paddington Station?" her father said.

She nodded.

"How did you pay for the ticket?"

"I had some money."

Her father put the plate of scrambled eggs on toast in front of her.

"So what happened when you got to Wales?" her mother asked.

Tania picked up the fork and mechanically lifted some scrambled egg to her mouth. She wasn't hungry, but eating gave her a chance to gather her thoughts, to delay the lies.

It was horrible that her parents were so willing to believe her story. But why shouldn't they? They loved her and trusted her. . . .

"I had an address," she said, her eyes on her plate, her hands busy with the knife and fork as she cut the toast into small pieces. "People helped me. I caught another train." *Lies! Lies! Lies!* "I don't really remember it all."

"Where did you sleep?" asked her father. "How did you eat?"

"I slept in the railway stations," Tania said. "I had enough money for food."

"Where did you get these clothes?" her mother asked. "We took your own clothes away from the hospital. We were going to bring some fresh."

"I . . . I found them," Tania said. *That sounds so weak! What is wrong with you?*

"In the hospital, you mean?"

Tania nodded and bought herself a few more seconds by putting more food into her mouth and chewing it slowly. She was aware of her parents looking at each other with baffled faces. It would almost have been a relief for one of them to turn and say, "You're lying to us! Tell us the truth!"

She felt so ashamed. More than anything else in the world, she wanted to abandon this ridiculous pretense and tell them what had really happened to her, the wonders she had seen, the things she had discovered, the truth of who she really was.

No! Not now. Not yet. Not like this.

"So you managed to find the place where Evan's family live?" her father said.

"Yes." She swallowed uncomfortably. "And I brought him back with me."

"Where is he now?"

"He's gone to his hostel. I told him that he wouldn't get into trouble with the police." She looked from her mother's face to her father's and back again. "The boat crash was an accident," she said. "They won't prosecute him, will they? They mustn't."

"No, I don't think he'll be prosecuted," her father said. "But he was stupid to run away like that."

Her mother reached out and rested her hand on Tania's arm. "You came back together, yes?"

Tania nodded.

"Have you told us everything that happened between you?"

Tania frowned. "Yes," she said. "What do you mean?" She looked into her mother's anxious eyes and knew exactly what she meant. "Nothing else happened," she promised. At least that was one question she could answer with complete honesty.

"How did you get back to London at this time in the morning?" her father asked. "Surely there aren't any overnight trains from Wales?"

"We got here late last night," Tania said. "We didn't want to wake you so we walked the streets till it got light."

"*Wake* us?" Her mother gasped. "Anita, you wouldn't have woken us up. Neither of us have had any proper sleep since you went missing."

"Of course you haven't," Tania agreed guiltily. "I'm so sorry for what I put you both through. I'll never ever do anything like that again—I promise."

Her mother glanced at the wall clock. "There should be someone at the school by now. I'll phone and let them know you're all right." She stood up and went into the living room.

Tania placed her knife and fork on the plate and pushed it away, still almost full. She looked apologetically at her father. "Sorry, I can't manage any more."

"Don't worry about it," he said. "Is there anything else you fancy?"

She smiled tiredly. "I don't think so. To be honest, I just want to curl up and sleep for a whole week."

"You've had quite a time of it, haven't you, my girl?" he said, sitting beside her and cupping her cheek in his warm hand.

"I've caused so much trouble." She sighed. "You must be sorry you ever had me."

"That's right," he said gently. "We're going to send you back and ask for a replacement. Someone who would know better than to go chasing halfway across the country in search of some idiot boy!"

Exhaustion came down over her like a stifling blanket. "You mustn't blame Evan," she murmured. "It wasn't his fault."

"I'm not concerned with that right now," her father said. "You're home safe and sound, and that's all that matters." His fingers pressed against her cheek, turning her head to face him. His expression had grown serious. "You're an intelligent young woman and you're growing up fast," he said. "But in some ways you still act like a child. Running away like that . . ." He shook his head. "There have to be consequences," he said. "You know that, don't you?"

She nodded, already guessing what was coming next.

"I don't think you should see that boy anymore," her father said. "He has too much influence over you, and it's time for it to stop."

That was it. Right there. That was the axe she had been waiting to fall.

She nodded again without speaking.

A few moments later her mother came back into the room. "I spoke with the school secretary," she said. "She's going to pass the message on to Mr. Cox. I said you're exhausted but you're safe and well. And I said that you'd be back in class tomorrow. Your dad can drive you over there in the morning and help you to explain things."

"I've told her she's not to see Evan Thomas any

more," her father said.

"Yes, that's for the best," said her mother. "I won't ask you to make us any promises, Anita," she added. "Promises are too easily broken, but we are trusting you to do as we ask."

Tania gazed up at her, too tired to argue, and knowing that she was in no position to offer a convincing argument even if she tried. "What about the school play?" she said. "Am I banned from that as well?" She was playing Juliet to Edric's Romeo; they had been in rehearsals for weeks and it was due to be performed in just eight days' time. If her parents agreed to let her continue in the role, at least that would give her a legitimate reason for seeing Edric.

"You're obviously not going to be able to avoid bumping into him at school," her mother said. "And after all the hard work you've put in, I don't think you can let everyone down by not carrying on with the play."

"But if you have rehearsals outside normal school hours, I'll take you there and pick you up," her father added.

"You know what we mean by not seeing him," her mother warned. "Not seeing him as boyfriend and girlfriend, or whatever it is you call it these days. That's what has to stop. And I think you need a curfew, too." She looked at Tania's father. "I think it should be eight o'clock school days and nine o'clock weekends."

"That sounds fair," he said.

Tania swallowed hard. "How long for?" she croaked.

"We'll see," said her mother. "It's too soon to start thinking about things like that. Concentrate on your schoolwork for what's left of the term, and we'll have another talk about it in a month or so."

A month or so. Tania's spirits sank.

She couldn't possibly keep away from Edric for that long—not even if the only problem was the heartache of separation. But that wasn't her only concern, not by a long way.

The last thing she had promised King Oberon before she and Edric left Faerie was that they would seek out Titania, his lost Queen, who had gone through the mystical Oriole Glass in pursuit of her vanished daughter five hundred years ago and who had never returned.

The only clue they had to Titania's whereabouts was Tania's Soul Book. Someone in the Mortal World had sent it to her on the eve of her sixteenth birthday, and Tania was convinced it had come from Queen Titania, the mother of the Faerie half of her nature.

The parcel had been postmarked Richmond in southwest London. That's where the search must begin, but to keep her promise to Oberon, she would have to tell yet more lies to her parents.

I can't think about that now. Too tired. Must sleep.

"You look shattered, my girl." Her father's voice broke into her thoughts. "Why don't you go and catch up on some sleep?"

She nodded. Sleep—that's what she wanted more than anything in the world. A whole day of deep, dreamless sleep.

She opened her bedroom door and frowned. Standing on the floor at the foot of her bed was a large box wrapped in gold paper and tied with red ribbon. There were other, smaller brightly wrapped boxes arranged around it. And a big pile of colored envelopes.

"Happy belated birthday, Anita," came her mother's voice from behind her.

"Did you think you wouldn't get any presents?" her father added.

They had obviously followed her up the stairs.

"I'd totally forgotten!" Tania said, staring at the pile of gifts.

"Come on," said her father. "Surely you've got the strength to open a few things before you crash out. I want to see what you got!"

Laughing through her exhaustion, Tania dropped to her knees on the carpet and reached for the pile of cards.

It was half an hour later. Tania lay fully clothed on her bed, so worn out that she didn't even have the energy to get undressed. Her birthday cards were lined up on shelves and furniture tops all around her. Her new computer stood on her desk. All her other gifts were laid out on her chest of drawers: a backpack from Nan and Granddad, a necklace from Auntie Jenny and Uncle Steve. A CD from her cousin Helena, a couple of books, a red satin scarf. Gift vouchers and some cash.

She gazed drowsily around her room, looking at all her familiar things . . . remembering her bedchamber in the Royal Palace in Faerie, that enchanted room with its living tapestries and windows that overlooked the formal palace gardens.

It had been so different from her bedroom here. And yet she had felt at home there. At home there, at home here. At home in both worlds or neither?

What was it that Gabriel Drake had said to her only moments before Oberon had banished him?

Your spirit is split between the worlds. You shall never find peace!

Tania pushed away the memory of his voice. He was wrong. He had to be wrong.

Her canvas shoulder bag was propped against her bedside table. The last time she had seen it had been in the hospital—her parents must have picked it up for her.

She reached out and dragged the bag toward her. She fumbled into it and found her phone. When she pressed to turn it on, the screen lit up.

HI ANITA!

Still some power left in the battery. Good.

She speed-dialed Evan's number—*Edric's* number—and put the phone to her ear. It was answered after a single tone.

"How did it go?" His voice was full of urgent concern. "I've been waiting ages for you to call. Are you all right?"

"I lied my head off," she said miserably. "And they believed me."

"That's good," Edric said.

"Is it?" Tania replied, her eyes closed, her head swimming. "Is it really *good*? Listen, I'm sorry. I'm too tired to talk right now. We can talk tomorrow at school."

"Is there anything I can do?"

"Not really."

"I love you."

"I love you, too."

She pressed to disconnect. The phone dropped out of her hand and slipped off the side of the bed. She was vaguely aware of a soft thump as it hit the carpet.

Moments later she was asleep.

II

Tania and Edric were stumbling up a steeply sloping, night-dark valley, hand in hand and running for their lives. All around them, the splintered mountains shone like black glass under a deluge of icy rain. The storm clouds were as dense as lead, their swollen bellies torn open by the jagged rocks. Lightning leaped from crag to crag with a sound like the hissing of snakes.

In the gulping darkness at their heels Tania could hear harsh, heavy breathing. She glanced fearfully over her shoulder and felt sure that she saw two red eyes through the falling water.

"Come *on!*" Edric's voice cut through the tumult.

She scrambled along the rising valley floor, only just managing to keep to her feet as she clung to Edric's hand. Sheer black cliffs closed in around them, the shining stone so smooth and sharp-edged that an unwary touch could draw blood. It was like climbing through a snare of broken glass—and all the time the rain beat down on them and the thunder boomed in their ears and the lightning was as fierce as acid in their eyes.

Her foot slipped and she fell onto her knee, crying out with the pain.

"Get up!" Edric shouted down. "It's closing in on us!"

"What is?" she wailed. "Edric? What is this place? How did we get here?"

"Don't you know?" he shouted. "This is Ynis Maw!"

The name sent a shudder through her. But why? She had never heard those strange words before.

"I'll have to let go of you," Edric shouted down. "I need both hands to get up this next bit." His wet hand slid out of hers and she watched as he scrambled up the rock face. She got to her feet. She was deadly cold and soaked to the skin. She clutched her arms around herself, staring up into the vicious rain, her face stinging from a thousand sharp impacts.

A loud, rumbling snort sounded behind her. She turned her head, staring down into the black gorge. She heard the scratch and scrape of huge claws on the stone. Two red points of light were moving upward through the rain.

"Tania!"

She snatched her head around. Edric was leaning over the high lip of rock, reaching his arm down toward her. She threw herself up and caught hold of his hand. It was cold—much colder than before, and the grip of his fingers was fierce and harsh.

"I have you!" The voice sounded wrong.

"Edric?"

There was a snarl of triumphant laughter and at that same moment a blaze of lightning lit up the crouching figure above her.

She let out a scream. It wasn't Edric.

The wild-eyed face that leered down at her was the face of Gabriel Drake.

She tried to wrestle her hand free, but his fingers wouldn't loosen from hers. She stared at their joined hands and saw that they glowed with a dull amber light.

"Let go of me!" she shouted.

"That I shall never do, my lady," he called down. "You will never be free of me! Did you not know? We are bonded for all time!"

His fingers dug into her hand and with a terrifying strength he began to haul her up the rock face. Explosions of lightning revealed the madness in his silver eyes. His laughter howled above the thunder. The rain threw needles into her upturned face.

"No!" Tania writhed helplessly, her feet coming clear of the rock, her legs kicking as he dragged her upward.

"*No!*"

Tania awoke with a jolt that shook the bed. She forced her eyes open, her heart pounding. She stared wildly around. The curtains were open and the room was filled with daylight. Birthday cards danced brightly on the edge of sight.

She let out a relieved groan and ran her hands over her face. She was bathed in sweat, her hair sticking to her forehead and cheeks. She was lying fully clothed on her own bed in her bedroom in London.

It had been a nightmare. That was all.

She lay still for a few minutes. The crashes of thunder that filled her head gradually faded away and the red fire that rimmed her tightly shut eyes dwindled to nothing.

She took her hands away from her face and opened her eyes. She blew her cheeks out in a long breath and then sat up.

Her clothes were sticking uncomfortably to her. She looked around the room, needing to get a fix on reality for fear that she might be sucked back into the dream. She grabbed her shoulder bag and dug out her ID pass. She gazed at the small photo of herself. Long curling red hair framed her heart-shaped face with its wide mouth and high, slanted cheekbones. Smoky green eyes stared out at her.

Anita Palmer.

Princess Tania.

Two people with one face and one heart and only one life to lead.

But which life? And *where*?

Ynis Maw.

She shuddered at the memory of Gabriel Drake's face, his mouth twisted in a horrible smile, his eyes stretched wide so that the whites showed all around the weird silver irises. She clutched her hand to herself, remembering the painfully tight grip of his fingers.

You will never be free of me! Did you not know? We are bonded for all time! She remembered the Hand-Fasting Ceremony that she and Gabriel had gone through in the Hall of Light. It had been against her will—her sister Rathina had tricked her into going there. Gabriel had been waiting. He had poured the liquid amber over their two hands and she had seen him revealed in all his treachery and evil.

His plans had come to nothing. Oberon had come down on him like a thunderbolt; Tania could still remember the moment of Gabriel's banishment. The terror in his eyes as the King pronounced his doom. And then, a split second later, he had been gone, leaving only a thin snake of smoke that coiled for an instant before fading into nothingness.

She knew the Hand-Fasting Ceremony was only the first of many Faerie wedding rituals: The full ceremony took three whole days. She knew she wasn't married to Gabriel in any real sense of the word, but *something* had happened between them—a bond had been forged.

For the first time Tania wondered exactly what had happened to Gabriel. He had vanished but Oberon had not killed him. The punishment for his crimes had been banishment. But banishment to where?

Ynis Maw?

Was it a real place? A terrible land at the far

reaches of the world—a place of exile and torment and horror? Was Gabriel calling to her across the worlds from that place, reminding her of the unbreakable connection between them?

She stood up and walked rapidly to the window. She rested her forehead against the cool glass, staring down into the garden. "No. No. No." she whispered, her breath misting the glass. "He was only able to find me here last time because I was wearing the amber pendant." Her jaw set. "I won't let him do that to me again. I won't!"

But if Ynis Maw was a real place, could someone as powerful as Gabriel Drake find a way to escape?

"Oberon wouldn't let that happen," she said. "He'd have made sure Gabriel could never come back."

She became aware of how uncomfortable her borrowed clothes felt against her skin. She walked to the bed again and looked at the bedside clock.

It was three thirty. She spotted her phone lying on the carpet. Sitting on the edge of the bed, she retrieved it. She had one text message.

It was from her best friend, Jade.

YOU BAD GIRL! WE WANT ALL THE GORY DETAILS! COME TO THE PIZZA PLACE AS SOON AS SCHOOL FINISHES!

Tania smiled. Typical Jade. Word must have gone around the school saying she was okay, and now Jade wanted the inside story.

Tania was suddenly eager to see her friends again, but . . . "Sorry, Jade," she said aloud. "You don't get to know the truth this time." She texted back: I'LL BE THERE.

"What I really need right now is a shower," she decided. As she stood up, she remembered the black amber stone. She fished it out of her pocket and walked to the desk. Sitting down, she took a sharp-pointed nail file out of a drawer. She held the thin stone between her finger and thumb on the desk and began to twist the nail file against its surface. After a few moments she saw that she had made a small circular dent. She worked for the next few minutes, drilling into the stone until she had made two small, neat holes, one at each end of the oval. Then she found a piece of lilac ribbon and threaded it through the holes.

She tied the ribbon firmly around her wrist. She shook her hand a couple of times, making sure that the makeshift bracelet was secure. She picked a metal ruler out of a drawer and held it in her fist. She was aware of the faintest of buzzing in her fingers, as if a tiny fly was trapped in her hand. But that was all. She was safe.

She got up and headed for the bathroom. She'd take a shower—and then it would be time to go and see Jade and the others.

Tania came back into her room, wrapped in a bath sheet and with her wet hair up in a towel turban.

Apart from the fact that this was a Thursday and she ought to be at school, everything else around her was beginning to feel disarmingly ordinary. The posters on her walls, the pile of schoolbooks by the desk, her possessions spread out around her just like they always had been. Her bulletin board with magazine pictures and postcards and old cinema tickets tacked all over it. A picture of her and Jade crammed into a photo booth, pulling faces. A photo of her and Edric—Evan then, of course—in Hyde Park, standing on a bench and making daft theatrical gestures, being Romeo and Juliet for Jade's digital camera.

This was reality. Faerie was . . . what? An illusion? No, not that. But not real—not in the way that this room was real.

Except that she knew that it was.

Almost without thinking about it, Tania made the simple side step that opened the door between the worlds.

She let out a breath as her room melted silently away. Instead of the soft carpet, there were hard wooden boards under her bare feet. Instead of her bedroom she found herself staring at brown walls of smooth stonework. The room into which she had stepped was circular, with a low dark-beamed ceiling and a narrow, unglazed arched window that blazed with golden sunlight.

"You idiot!" she said aloud. "You were upstairs! You could have arrived here in midair!" She laughed at her good fortune: She had come into Faerie inside some kind of building, with a room on the same level as her bedroom in Camden.

She knew from past experience that Faerie and the Mortal World replicated one another—almost as if they were two photographic images one on top of the other, sharing the same space but in quite different worlds. For her, stepping from one world to the other was as simple as moving from one room to another; it was her gift, and no one else in Faerie could do it without the use of powerful and dangerous enchantments.

She padded over to the window. The scent of Faerie air filled her head, sweet as roses, strong as honeysuckle, mysterious as moonflower. Through a veil of slender leafy branches, she found herself gazing over the parkland that sloped gently down toward the Royal Palace.

Was it really only yesterday that she had walked these grassy downs with her sister Cordelia and a pack of racing hounds?

Far away to her left she saw turrets and gatehouses that she recognized, set behind wide formal gardens intertwined with yellow pathways and adorned with fountains and elegant white marble statuary. The tiny shapes of people could be seen walking, no bigger to her than pawns on a distant chessboard. These buildings were the Royal Apartments, home to King Oberon and his daughters. Somewhere in that mass of red-brick gothic buildings, with their steep gray slate roofs and cream-colored stone ornamentations, was her Faerie bedchamber.

The building she was in now was not part of the

main bulk of the palace; it was a small tower set on the hillside among a grove of aspen trees.

A stone spiral staircase clung to the curved wall opposite the window, winding up from the floor below and continuing to a wooden trap door in the ceiling. Part of Tania longed to follow the coiling steps to ground level and to run out into the open, to feel the grass under her naked feet and the warm breeze on her face.

She laughed. "In a towel?" she said. "I don't think so."

Faerie would always be there for her. Just a small side step and she could come back whenever she wished.

She turned with one last wistful glance out the window and sidestepped into the Mortal World.

She came into her bedroom just as her mother was leaving.

Her mother gasped. "Where on earth did you pop up from?"

Tania swallowed hard. *Think!* She pointed behind the bed. "I was down there," she said. "I lost a slipper under the bed."

"Well, you might have said something—I did call."

"Sorry, I didn't hear you." Tania forced a smile. "Did you want something?"

Her mother gave her an odd look. "Just to tell you that I've spoken with the police officer who was in charge of your missing person case."

Tania felt a pang of alarm. "I don't have to talk to

the police, do I? Dad said everything would be all right."

"Everything *is* all right," said her mother. "But I had to let them know you were back. The official line is they don't intend to take any further action."

A wave of relief swept over her. "Thanks, Mum. You've been really good about this."

Her mother gave a wry smile. "Yes, haven't I? I expect we'll all be able to laugh about this in ten years' time."

"Let's hope," Tania said. She looked thoughtfully at her mother; maybe it was time to drop another small bombshell. "Mum? How would you feel if I wanted to change my name?"

Her mother looked puzzled. "What do you mean?"

Tania took a steadying breath. "I'd like to be called Tania."

Her mother stood silently in the doorway for several moments. It was impossible for Tania to tell what she was thinking from the expression on her face. Was she mad at her? Amused? Confused?

"Tania?" her mother said at last, as if getting used to the feel of the name on her lips.

"Yes. Would it bother you?"

Her mother folded her arms and tilted her head to one side. "Tania's a nice enough name, I dare say," she said. "Your dad and I could probably cope with calling you that if it's what you really want. But unless you get it changed officially, you can't sign yourself as Tania Palmer, you know." She raised her eyebrows. "I suppose *Palmer* is still okay, is it?"

Tania smiled, wishing she could tell her mum how much her agreeing meant to her. "Yes," she said, meaning it. "Palmer is absolutely fine!"

As was usual for this time of day, the Pizza Bar was buzzing with young people stopping off for a snack and a chat with friends on their way home from school.

Tania and her girlfriends were occupying a corner table. They each had milkshakes and were picking from a large pizza in the middle of the table. Tania's end of the table was filled with birthday cards and newly opened presents from Jade, Natalie, Rosa, Susheela, and Lily.

Lying unwrapped on the table were lip balm, hand lotion and cotton balls in a chrome tin with CHIK KIT! embossed on it, a pink and white polka-dot notebook with matching pen, a brightly colored photo frame, a box of cosmetics called PAMPERED PRINCESS, which had made Tania smile, and from Jade, a very pretty silver bracelet with green stones set in it.

"Well, I think you're a total deadbeat for not having a birthday party," Rosa said to Tania. "What kind of person is too busy to party?"

Tania shrugged. "The kind of person who has to learn the lines of a really tricky play that she has to perform at the end of next week? Besides, I didn't say I didn't want to have a party at all. I just said not right now."

"Forget the party," Jade said, giving Tania a piercing look. "I want to know what happened with you and Evan."

"Sorry to disappoint you, guys," Tania said as casually as she could manage. "But precisely nothing happened with me and Evan—if you mean what I think you mean."

"Oh, come on!" Lily said with a snort of laughter. "You've got to be kidding. You two have been all over each other for weeks now."

"And then you both vanish for three whole days," Susheela added. "And three whole nights!"

"You can tell us," urged Natalie. "We're your best friends."

"I've already told you the whole story," Tania said. "There's nothing more to tell. Except for the fact that my mum and dad have forbidden me to see him outside school, which is a total pain."

Jade grinned. "Well, what did you expect? I'm surprised they haven't set the police on him for kidnapping you. And as for that curfew you were talking about—that's nothing! My folks would have locked me in my room and thrown away the key if I'd pulled a stunt like that. You were gone for three days, Anita! I can't believe you didn't call me or anything."

"That's right," said Lily. "You could have sent a Wish You Were Here card from wherever the two of you were hiding out."

Tania sighed. "We weren't hiding out anywhere,"

she said. "And can you try to remember I'd like to be called Tania from now on?"

"Okay, *Tania*," Jade said with comic emphasis. "We'll try, *Tania*."

"Why Tania?" asked Natalie. "Apart from the fact that it's an anagram of Anita, what's so great about it?"

Tania frowned. An anagram of her mortal name? She'd never even thought about that. "I just like the name."

"I bet it was Evan's idea," said Lily. "Go on, admit it. Evan wanted you to change your name."

"No he didn't," Tania said.

"Kind of ironic, though, isn't it?" Jade said, gesturing with a floppy wedge of pizza. "You and Evan are playing Romeo and Juliet in a couple of weeks, and your folks have forbidden you to see him—kind of like what happens in the play, isn't it?"

"I hope not," Tania said. "They both end up dead."

Natalie grinned. "You don't want to die for love of him, then?"

"No thanks!"

"Hey, speaking of people dying of love," Susheela said suddenly. "Did you guys see the last episode of *Spindrift*? I mean, is Coral Masters a total dork or what?"

Spindrift was a daily soap that everyone at school watched, but somehow Tania couldn't summon up the enthusiasm to join in the conversation. As they chatted, it felt to her as if she was watching them from behind a glass screen, as if she still had one foot and at least half of her brain in Faerie.

She pictured her Faerie sisters, wondering what Sancha or Hopie would make of pizza and milkshakes. And television and radio and movies—there was nothing like them in Faerie. If you wanted entertainment, you made it for yourself. She was certain that Cordelia would hate the crowds in London, although Zara might think the city was fun. Yes, she could almost imagine music-loving Zara going to a nightclub.

"When are you going?" Lily's voice pierced through Tania's thoughts.

"Tuesday week," Jade said. "Florida, here we come!"

Tania realized her friend was talking about her upcoming family holiday. "Is Dan going with you?" she asked. Dan was Jade's older brother—he was away at university.

"There's a ticket booked for him," Jade said. "But last time I spoke to him he was still trying to make up his mind. Some of his pals from uni are backpacking across India for the summer, and he was talking about tagging along with them."

"Have you got a holiday planned, Anita?" Natalie asked. "Oops! Sorry. Tania, I mean."

"Try Tanita," Rosa suggested. "Or Anitania."

"I think we're going to Cornwall," Tania said, ignoring Rosa.

"Wow!" Jade said with mock awe. "Cornwall again! That's just so exotic." She raised an eyebrow. "How come your folks never go abroad, *Tania*? How come you've never been anywhere exciting in your whole life, ever?"

Tania smiled but said nothing.

Try Faerie for exciting.

III

School on Friday morning was a strange experience. Tania found it embarrassing to be driven to the teachers' parking lot by her dad, and to have to sit with him in the principal's waiting room while people walked past giving her peculiar looks.

The interview with Mr. Cox wasn't so bad; she got the expected lecture on responsible behavior and thinking before acting, but it was tempered by the fact that everyone seemed happy to believe that her apparent brainstorm had been due to the trauma of the accident.

With a final comment that she should report any after-effects—headaches and suchlike—she was let out of the principal's office and, after seeing her father off, she steeled herself to endure the curiosity of her classmates.

It wasn't as bad as she had feared, and as soon as it became clear that she had nothing to say about the lost three days beyond what she had already told Jade and the others, people soon got bored and left her alone.

At morning break she managed to slip away and see Edric. He was waiting for her around the dogleg bend of a staircase that led down to disused storerooms.

He had a similar tale to tell: His interview with the principal had focused on the dangers of overconfidence, especially when his mistakes could lead others into potential danger—a very obvious reference to the boat crash. He was also officially warned to watch his step so far as "Anita" was concerned; the principal told him that Mr. and Mrs. Palmer had forbidden her to have anything to do with him outside school, and asked him to respect their wishes and not make things more difficult than they already were.

As had happened with Tania, questions from his classmates had quickly dried up when he made it clear that there were no secrets to tell.

Tania drew back her sleeve and showed him the ribbon bracelet with the black amber stone on it.

"Snap!" he said, smiling as he pulled up his sleeve and revealed his own stone, threaded on a slender strip of black cord.

"Do you think I'll be permanently sensitive to metal?" she asked. "Or might it wear off now that I'm back?"

"I don't know," Edric said, taking her hand. "But I wouldn't risk it, if I were you. Not unless you like pain."

"No, you're probably right." She squeezed his hand and rested her head on his shoulder. It was good to have him close again, even if only for a few stolen minutes.

"Your parents not wanting us to see each other is going to be tricky," he said thoughtfully.

"Tell me about it." Tania sighed. "You wouldn't think I was a Faerie Princess, would you? They said that if I behave, they'll think about it again in a month or so."

"I'd hoped we could start the search for Queen Titania sooner than that," Edric said.

"So did I, but I don't see how we can," Tania said. "They're going to be watching me like hawks for a while. I'm not going to be able to sneak off without them noticing, and I don't want to have to start telling lies about where I'm going and what I'm doing."

"Of course not," Edric said, lifting his hand to stroke her hair. "It must be really difficult for you. But the trail will go cold if we leave it too long. The only clue we have so far is that your Soul Book was sent from Richmond. I don't think a package of that size could have been put into a postbox, so I'm hoping it had to be mailed from a post office."

Tania nodded, closing her eyes, enjoying the sensation of his hand gently stroking her hair. "Good thinking," she murmured.

"I went into the computer room this morning and

got on to the Internet," Edric continued. "There are only two post offices in Richmond: one north of the Thames, and the other south."

"That narrows it down."

"Exactly. I thought that if we could go there as soon as possible, there's a chance of someone remembering the Queen—after all, she's pretty striking to look at, isn't she?"

Tania lifted her head and looked at him. "She looks exactly the same as me," she said. "Just older, I suppose."

Edric nodded. "And look at you, with your incredible hair and that face and those stunning eyes. No one who saw you would forget you in a hurry."

Tania stifled a self-conscious giggle. "I don't know if I'm that special to look at."

"Yes you are," Edric said. "And I'm not just saying that because of how I feel about you. You're amazing looking!"

"But Titania has been here for five hundred years," Tania said. "I know Faeries live forever, but surely she'd look a bit . . . well, *old*. You know, gray-haired and wrinkly and so on."

Edric smiled and took both her hands. "You don't get it yet, do you? We don't get old—not the way mortals do. There's no reason why the Queen shouldn't still look exactly the same as she did when she first came here." A distant gaze came into his eyes. "I remember the last time I saw her," he said. "At the

Feast of the White Hart—a week before you vanished and everything went wrong." He held Tania's face between his hands. "She was almost as beautiful as you," he said. "Not quite—but almost."

A wave of emotion swept over Tania and she rested her forehead against his. "Oh, Edric," she said. "What am I going to do without you for a whole month?"

"You won't be without me," he said, giving her a quick kiss on the forehead. "I'll be right here, and even if we can't see each other as much as we'd like we can speak on the phone and text and so on. It won't be so bad. Besides, I'm used to being patient—we all had to learn patience in Faerie over the last five hundred years."

She sighed. "I wonder what I've been doing over the last five hundred years? It's very weird, knowing I've been alive for all that time but not having any clue who I was or what I did." Her voice dropped to a whisper. "How I died. Or even how *often* I died."

"You don't need to think about that now," Edric said. "Let's think about the future—about finding Titania."

Tania snapped out of her dark thoughts. "Okay," she said. "So, we hope someone in a Richmond post office will remember her, but even if they do, where does that get us, precisely?"

"It gives us an idea of where in Richmond to start searching," Edric said. "If we assume she'd go to the post office nearest to where she lives or works then we can start asking around in local shops and offices. But if we wait too long before starting the search there'll be less chance of someone remembering her, and then we'll have twice as much work to do."

"Yes, I see that," Tania said. "Tell you what—I'll do my best to get away on Saturday. If I can convince my parents there's a rehearsal without having to tell too many lies, we can meet up and go over there for a few hours."

The bell sounded for the end of morning break.

"See you at rehearsal this afternoon," he said.

She nodded. As she started up the stairs, his voice spoke softly behind her.

"*Good-night, good-night! Parting is such sweet sorrow . . .*"

She turned and smiled at him. "That's Juliet's line," she said.

"I know. I couldn't resist it."

"You know what you are, don't you?" she said as she climbed the stairs.

"Edric Chanticleer, a courtier of the Royal Palace of Faerie, once servant of the traitor Gabriel Drake, now loyal to the Royal Family of Oberon before all others?"

"No, you're just a crazy romantic fool."

The after-school rehearsal in the assembly hall went well.

Tania sat with the play script on her lap, reminding herself of her lines between watching the stage as

Mrs. Wiseman guided Edric and another boy through the tricky actions of one of the big sword fights.

"The important thing is to make it look real," Mrs. Wiseman said, brandishing Romeo's sword. "But without anyone getting their eye poked out! Okay, Evan, you take over now, and remember what I told you about posture and balance."

"I'll try," Edric said, taking the sword.

He practiced a few fencing stances, thrusting the plastic-tipped rapier out at arm's length, then made a swiveling motion of his wrist that sent the blade spinning in a circle. The boy playing Tybalt stared at the whipping blade, his own sword trailing on the floor.

"Oh! Very good, Evan!" Mrs. Wiseman said. "You've had lessons, haven't you?"

Edric gave an apologetic grin. "A while ago. Just a few."

Tania smiled. A few? Like five hundred years' worth. Learning how to use a sword was a perfectly normal part of Faerie education for both boys and girls.

His eyes met Tania's and he winked.

An hour or so later their rehearsal time was up and everyone got ready to leave.

"Next rehearsal is on Monday after school," Mrs. Wiseman called. "That gives you all weekend to polish up those lines. I expect the lot of you to be word perfect when I see you next."

There was no time for Tania and Edric to be alone, and after a brief and frustratingly public good-bye, Edric slipped out of a side entrance to avoid Tania's father, who was parked out front waiting for her.

"How did it go?" her father asked. "Any problems?"

"None at all," Tania said as her father started the car.

He didn't ask about Edric as they drove home, and she didn't offer any comment, either. *Best to let sleeping dogs lie,* she thought.

"Everyone involved with the play is going on a field trip to the Globe Theatre next week," she told him.

"Oh, yes?" he said. "That's the place on the Thames, isn't it?"

"That's right. It's supposed to be an exact replica of the theatre that stood there in Elizabethan times, when Shakespeare's plays were first being performed. Mrs. Wiseman thinks it'll inspire us to perform better if we have a look at the real thing."

"Sounds like fun," her father said. "And speaking of fun, your mum telephoned the owners of that cottage in Tintagel that we went to last summer. We've booked it from Monday week for a fortnight. What do you think?"

"Sounds great," Tania said, carefully hiding her dismay at this suggestion; a family holiday was going to be yet another barrier between her and the search for Titania.

"So Mrs. Wiseman wasn't annoyed with you for

going awol, then?" her father asked.

"No, she just made a few pointed remarks about working with prima donnas and then got on with the rehearsal."

"I suppose you'll need to do some extra sessions to catch up, though?"

"I expect so."

"Does she want you to go in tomorrow?"

Tomorrow was Saturday, the day she and Edric hoped to slip away to Richmond.

Tania looked apologetically at her father. He had given her the perfect opportunity to avoid a direct lie. "There is some stuff that needs doing," she said. "Would you mind driving me over here about ten o'clock in the morning?"

"No problem," he said. "And when you're done, just give me a call and I'll come and pick you up again."

"There's no need. I can find my own way home."

"I don't think so," her father said firmly. "I'll pick you up from the school, okay?"

Tania nodded.

"By the way," her father said, changing the subject in a very obvious way. "What happened to that book? You know, that nice old leather-bound book that we took into the hospital for your birthday, the one sent by your mysterious benefactor."

Tania knew exactly where the book was. It had been put back in its proper place in the Great Library in the Faerie palace—standing on a shelf between the Soul Books of her sister Rathina and of her uncle, the Earl Marshal Cornelius.

"Don't worry," Tania said, gazing out of the car window. "I put it somewhere safe."

IV

It took Tania and Edric an hour on the Underground to get from Camden to Richmond. They came up to ground level in a crowded main street with wide pavements lined with black railings.

It was a relief for Tania to be out of the claustrophobic swelter of the tube train, but even out on the streets, the Saturday crowds hemmed her in as she walked hand in hand with Edric toward the first of the post offices that he had found on the Internet.

It turned out to be a busy main branch with a steady stream of customers coming and going through the double swing doors.

"There must be about fifty people waiting," Tania said gloomily, peering through the doors. "We'll be here all day."

"Don't join the queue," Edric suggested, holding open one of the doors for her. "Go straight up to a counter and ask to speak to the manager."

"If you say so." Tania slid between the racks of greetings cards and stationery and made her way up to the first counter. A woman was being served.

Tania fixed a friendly smile on her face. "Excuse me," she said to the customer. "Could I interrupt for a moment?" The woman gave her a blank look. Tania turned her smile on the clerk behind the glass partition. "Would it be possible to speak with the manager, please?"

"Just a moment." The man slid off his chair and went into a back room. Tania gave the woman at the counter an apologetic look. "Sorry about this," she said.

The clerk came back. He pointed to a closed door at the far end. "She'll meet you there," he said.

"Thanks," Tania said.

She circled the long queue and came to a security door that could be opened only by pressing out a code number on a keypad.

"Fingers crossed," Edric said, joining her.

"I've got *everything* crossed," Tania replied.

After about a minute the door opened and a small, plump Asian woman looked out at them with a questioning smile. "Can I help you?"

"I hope so," Tania said. "I know this is going to sound weird, but I think my mother was here a few days ago. She posted a parcel: a large book. It was going to an address in Camden."

The manager looked puzzled. "Yes?"

"The thing is," Tania continued, "my mum looks

just like me—red hair and green eyes—so I was kind of hoping that one of your staff might remember serving her."

The manager gave her an incredulous look. "Do you have any idea how many customers pass through these doors every week?"

"Quite a few, I should imagine," Tania said with a weak laugh.

"Hundreds," the woman said. "And you want us to remember one in particular? I don't think so. Why don't you just ask your mother about the parcel if there's a problem?"

"I would," Tania said hesitantly, "but Mum's gone . . . gone away . . . and . . . and the parcel never arrived and I'm worried that it might have got lost in the post."

The manager rolled her eyes. "You want a lost parcels form," she said, pointing to a rack of forms. "Fill it in and hand it over at the counter. We'll do what we can." With a brief nod of her head the woman stepped back through the door and closed it with a sharp click.

In silence they made their way back onto the street.

"It was a bit of a long shot, I suppose," Edric said. "And there's still the other branch." He pulled an *A–Z* map out of his pocket. "It's in St. Margaret's Road, on the other side of the river."

"I need something to drink first," Tania said,

pointing across the street to a sandwich bar. "Let's try in there."

The bar had a long narrow interior decorated in bright blue and white tiles. Along one side was a glass-topped counter lined with cakes and filled baguettes, and on the other side were rows of wooden tables. Most of the tables were already occupied, but Tania managed to find an empty one near the back while Edric joined the line.

A minute or two later Edric slid into the chair opposite her, placing a tray on the table. He handed her a tall cup topped with brown foam.

"We can't take too long," he said as she stirred her coffee. "Post offices only stay open till one o'clock on Saturdays, and it's already gone twelve."

As she drank, Tania became aware that a young woman dressed in a black-and-white waitress uniform was staring at her from the end of the counter.

Tania met her gaze. The waitress smiled and walked over to their table.

"I'm sorry," she said. "But I have to ask—has your mother ever been in here?"

"My mother?"

"There was a woman in here a week or so ago and she had exactly the same hair color as you—that really fabulous glowing red." She looked more closely at Tania. "In fact, you look exactly like her! She was very well dressed in a designer business suit and with really classy salon makeup. That's her, isn't it?"

Tania's heart was pounding with sudden exhilaration. "Yes," she said. "I think it probably is."

"I knew it!" said the waitress. "I never forget a face."

"Did you catch her name?" Edric asked, and Tania could hear the excitement welling up in his voice.

"Her *name*?" the waitress echoed, sounding confused. "I'm sorry, I don't know what you mean."

"How did she pay?" Tania prompted. "Did she use a card?"

The waitress frowned. "Cash, I think. I remember her sitting at that table over there. She had a briefcase with her and a large brown envelope—you know, one of those big padded ones. She was writing the address on it." She smiled again. "Sorry, I'd better go and earn my keep. I love your hair, though. I'm totally envious!"

Tania and Edric sat staring at each other.

"It was her," Tania said. "She was in here last week—with the book." She put her hand to her chest. "Edric, she was *here*! We've found her. Now all we have to do is ask around the neighborhood, in shops and restaurants—everywhere. Someone must know who she is and where she lives."

She broke off as her cell phone chimed. She scooped it out of her bag. "Uh-oh. It's home," she said, looking at the lit-up screen. She pressed a button. "Hello?"

"Hello, dear." Her mother's voice. "Your dad and I are going out to do a bit of shopping soon, and as we'll be near the school, we thought we might as well stop off there on the way back. How much longer do you think you're going to be?"

"I'm not sure—a little while yet."

"Not to worry. We'll be there about half one. We can wait if you're not quite finished."

"There's no need," Tania said.

"It's not a bother," her mother said brightly. "It'll save us going home and coming out again. I won't interrupt you any longer. Bye, now."

Tania pressed another button on her phone to bring up the time. 12:14.

She had exactly one hour and sixteen minutes to get back to the school. They could do it—just—but only if they left right now.

"We have to go," she said.

"I know. I heard," said Edric. "I could stay if you like—start asking around."

She frowned. "I'd rather we did it together." She trusted Edric, of course, but part of her couldn't bear for him to find Titania without her. "I'll try and get away again tomorrow."

This delay was frustrating—they were potentially only a few steps away from finding out where Titania lived—but Tania's well-meaning mother had put a halt to their search just when things were looking promising.

Tania knew one thing for sure: She was going to do everything she could to get away tomorrow. She was about to be reunited with her Faerie mother after five long centuries of separation, and there was nothing that would keep her from that.

* * *

They had luck with the tube trains, and it was still only twenty past one when Tania and Edric arrived back in Camden. They stood on the street corner, looking down toward the high wire fence that surrounded the school.

Tania peered up and down the street at the parked cars. "Good, they're not here yet," she said. "But they could turn up at any minute. You'd better make yourself scarce. I'll wait outside the gate for them."

"Call me," Edric said, reluctant to let go of her hand.

"I will. Don't worry. I'll get away somehow tomorrow. I'll tell them I'm going to Camden Market with Jade."

He looked up into the clear blue sky. "It's the first night of the full moon tonight," he said. "In Faerie the full moon in July is called the Traveler's Moon." A wistful tone came into his voice and his fingers tightened on hers. "A long time ago—before the Long Twilight came—on the first night of the Traveler's Moon, everyone from the palace would board ship and sail off to the island of Logris. The celebrations on Logris would go on all night: It was called the Festival of the Traveler's Moon." He looked at her. "I wonder if they've revived the custom now that time is running normally in Faerie again," he said. "I'm sure they have." He sighed. "It's a shame you can't be there. I don't suppose you remember it at all, do you?"

Tania shook her head. The vast majority of her Faerie childhood was lost to her, and even those things that she had been told about sounded like events that had happened to someone else.

"I don't think my mum and dad would be up for my popping into Faerie for an all-night rave," she said with a smile. "I'm on a nine o'clock curfew, remember?"

"True," Edric said. "But it's a pity, all the same. You'd have loved it."

A dark blue car came gliding around the far corner of the street. "That's them," Tania hissed. "Go now. I'll call you."

There was no time for a proper good-bye. Edric let go of her hand and slipped out of sight around the corner.

Tania walked quickly toward the school, hoping that her parents weren't going to ask too many questions about the nonexistent rehearsal.

"I still can't believe that Jack dies!" Tania exclaimed as the end credits of *Titanic* rolled up the TV screen. "He shouldn't die. They should live happily ever after!"

It was late evening and she was sprawled on the couch in the living room with her mum and dad. They had just watched the DVD of one of their all-time favorite movies.

"He has to die for the story to work properly," her mother said. "It's more romantic that way."

Tania frowned. "What's so romantic about the love of your life freezing to death and drowning about ten minutes after you've met him?"

It had been a perfect few hours with her parents, almost like old times. Tania had decided not to spoil it for herself by bringing up the story of going to the market with Jade in the morning. No more lies today.

But while she had been watching the movie, the euphoria of knowing that she and Edric may be within a day or two of finding Titania had worn off. She had found it hard to concentrate on the movie, her troubled thoughts often turning to what would actually happen once they found the lost Queen.

She had promised Oberon that she would return to Faerie once the Queen had been found, but did that mean he would expect her to live there permanently? She couldn't imagine doing that. She loved her mum and dad and couldn't bear the idea of abandoning them. But she couldn't live in both worlds at the same time.

She was Anita Palmer *and* Princess Tania—two people in one body—but what did that really mean?

Let's just concentrate on finding Titania. I'll worry about what happens next when I absolutely have to.

"I think I'll head on up to bed," she said, uncurling from the couch and stretching. "It's been a long day."

She closed her bedroom door behind her, but she didn't switch on the light. She walked over to the window. The night sky was full of stars, paled by the glowing disk of the full moon.

"The Faerie moon is bigger," she murmured. She remembered Edric's words: . . . *on the first night of the*

Traveler's Moon, everyone from the palace would board ship and sail off to the island of Logris.

Could she slip into Faerie? Just to look at the Traveler's Moon for a minute or two.

Mum and Dad would never know. What harm could it do?

She took the simple side step. . . .

And found herself in that small tower room again.

She gave a gasp of delight. The full moon was shining in so brightly through the window that its light threw sharp-edged shadows across the walls. The teeming stars blazed, filling the jet sky with flickering silver.

Tania's head filled with the perfumed Faerie air. The night scent of Faerie was strange and mysterious: a mix of aromas that blended to make a perfect whole. An icy tang of distant snow-capped mountains; the dark, earthy scent of deep forest glades; the wild smell of open moorlands, wind-scoured and rain-swept under racing skies.

Tania leaned out of the window, gazing over the tree-scattered downs. The notched silhouettes of the towers and roofs of the palace stood black and sharp against the rim of the sky, but the palace windows were lit up with a thousand candles, like a river of diamonds strewn across a ribbon of black velvet.

A sound came trilling into her ears, so soft at first that she had to strain to hear it. The gentle jingling of bells.

Something was moving through the trees. It was an open carriage drawn by a single black horse with bridle and trappings hung with crystal bells. A man in a dark green cloak was driving the carriage and in the open back sat a Faerie lord and lady.

"The Earl and Countess of Gaidheal," Tania said, recognizing the two passengers. She had seen them at the ball that had been thrown to celebrate her return to Faerie. The earl had a noble face with dark deep-set eyes and a high forehead with swept-back raven hair. The countess was serenely beautiful, her golden curls cascading to her waist.

Tania darted away from the window and ran down the spiral staircase. She came to an arched wooden door; lifting the latch, she pulled it open. A moment later she was running through the trees after the carriage.

"Hello! Hello, there!"

The earl gave a sharp word of command and the carriage pulled up only a few yards ahead of Tania.

"Princess Tania," the earl said, his eyes wide with surprise. "My lady, how come you to be here in the deeps of night?"

"I was looking at the moon," Tania said.

The countess smiled. "We have come from our manor in the fastness of Esgarth Forest to attend the

Festival of the Traveler's Moon," she said. "Will you ride with us, my lady?"

Tania hesitated. Should she risk it? As long as she was back before dawn, her parents would never know she hadn't been in bed all night. And from what Edric had told her, this festival was worth seeing.

"Yes, please," she said. "That would be great."

The earl held the door of the carriage open for her.

The driver shook the reins and the carriage moved off with a jerk, rolling out of the trees and down the grassy hillside toward the Privy Gardens. It wasn't long before they were on the tree-lined lanes, passing between sculpted hedges, the leafy shapes of animals and birds seeming more than half alive in the charmed moonlight.

The lofty red-brick walls of the Royal Apartments loomed over them, and soon they drew close to a gatehouse with brown stone steps that led to arched double doors.

"I'll get out here, if that's okay," Tania said. "I'd like to go and find my sisters."

"As you desire, my lady," said the earl, calling the carriage to a halt and jumping down. He lifted a hand to help her out.

"Thanks." She stepped onto the yellow path.

"We shall meet anon upon the white strand of Ynis Logris, my lady," said the countess.

"I'm sure we will." Tania felt a flicker of excitement inside her. She was back in Faerie!

She waved as the carriage moved away, then she ran up to the arched doors and pushed them open. The long entrance lobby was lit by scores of candles set in tall, floor-mounted candelabras. The dancing yellow light reflected off the polished red and green floor tiles and glowed warmly on the soaring walls of carved white stone.

Tania ran along the aisle of candlelight, her bare feet hardly making a sound on the cool tiles. She came to the foot of a grand, ornately carved dark-wood staircase. It led to a high gallery lined with paintings. She ran her fingers over the warm banister and began to climb.

Two floors up, she reached the long winding staircase that would take her to the Princesses Gallery. She was barely halfway when she heard the patter of feet coming down. Moments later her sister Zara appeared, clad in a sky blue gown with her long flowing golden hair bouncing on her shoulders as she skipped down the stairs.

"Tania!" she cried in surprise. She came down the rest of the stairs at a run and fell into Tania's arms, her fine-featured face wreathed in smiles. "I did not expect you this night!" She hugged Tania tightly. "It is marvelous indeed that you are here! I feared you would miss the revels."

Tania laughed, hugging Zara back. "I never miss out on revels if I can help it," she said. "But the whole place seems empty—has everyone already gone?"

"Most have," Zara said. "All but one of the ships set

sail from Fortrenn Quay early this morning. The last is departing soon. I came up here for this." She drew a slender wooden flute from the folds of her gown. "The Festival of the Traveling Moon would not be complete without music," she said, and she put the flute to her lips and sent a stream of clear liquid notes into the air.

"I didn't know you could play the flute as well as the spinetta."

"I play all instruments," Zara said, and then her eyes widened and she stared aghast at Tania's clothes.

"By my troth, what garments are these?" she said. "A princess in leggings—and in such a flimsy shred of a shift that a breeze would blow it away? Tania, you cannot be seen in public in such attire. It is . . . it is entirely *improper!*"

"It's fairly normal back in the real—I mean, in the Mortal World," Tania said. "You don't think people will approve, then?"

"Approve?" said Zara. "Nay, I do not! To clad your legs thus, as might a court jester or a serving man? No, we must find you something more suitable. And quickly, too, or the *Cloud Scudder* will be gone without us."

"The *Cloud Scudder?*"

A broad grin spread across Zara's face. "You do not remember, do you?" she said. She linked her arm into Tania's and led her down the stairs. "It shall be a surprise, then, my darling—a most wonderful and exquisite surprise!"

* * *

"Choose quickly, Tania or we shall be late!" Zara chided.

Tania stood in front of her wardrobe in her bedchamber, trying to pick a gown from the dazzling array. Zara was hurrying her along. She had not even allowed her a few moments to look again at the living tapestries that hung from the wood-paneled walls. When Tania had first arrived in Faerie, the tapestries had been simple scenes of faraway places: mountains and wild heaths, seascapes and ice floes under a cold naked sky. But on the day that she had finally accepted her Faerie heritage, all the tapestries had come alive: The wind had started to blow through the trees, the frozen waves had begun to roll and swell, clouds had moved across distant skies, birds had flown, rivers had run, waterfalls tumbled and foamed.

"Give me a chance!" Tania protested, pulling out a lilac gown. It was simple and elegant with purple stitching and a low square neck and long scalloped sleeves. She held it against herself and gave Zara a questioning look.

"Yes, it will suffice," Zara said.

Tania quickly shed her outer clothes and climbed into the gown. Zara stood behind her, tying the laces that drew the bodice tight around her.

She turned Tania around, her hands on Tania's shoulders. "Yes, that is much improved," she said. "Now you are a princess again. But we must run now, swift as the wind!" She clasped Tania's hand and the two of them ran from the room. Tania began to be caught up in Zara's enthusiasm; she laughed as they raced down the corridors, her long skirts rustling as they sped along, her hair streaming.

Zara brought them to a breathless halt at a familiar doorway.

Tania looked at her sister, puzzled. "This is your room," she said. "I thought we were in a hurry to get to the Festival."

"Indeed we are," Zara said, her eyes shining.

"Then what—"

"Open the door!"

Puzzled, Tania turned the handle and pushed the door open.

She already knew what she would see: the walls and ceiling painted to resemble a seascape, the floorboards colored like shingle, the furniture shell-encrusted and draped with navy blue covers. But all alive—a living painting in constant silent movement.

And that was exactly what she did see as she swung the door wide—except that when she had been in this room before, it had been in daylight; now the room was wrapped in the sultry, dark glamour of a Faerie night.

The second thing that struck her as she stepped over the threshold was that she could hear the sound of waves washing over shingle. There had been no sound from the living paintings before. Was this some new enchantment? But before she had the chance to ask, she realized that it was not wooden boards that she felt beneath her feet; it was crunching, yielding shingle. And then she saw that there was no furniture, no walls, no ceiling. The door opened onto a long beach that glimmered under the huge, shining sphere of the Traveler's Moon.

"The King has not opened this gateway since before the Long Twilight," Zara said. "See yonder: The *Cloud Scudder* is in full sail. Shall we board her, or would you stand here forever on the brink of wonders with your mouth agape?"

Ahead of them, the pebbled shore sloped down to the foaming sea. A small rowboat lay close to the beach. A man stood by the boat dressed in a uniform the color of the summer sky, the water swirling around his booted legs.

But the small boat did not hold Tania's attention for long—something far more astonishing took her breath entirely away.

A three-masted galleon lay at anchor on the rolling sea. Its planks and timbers and ropes and masts and spars; its sails and rigging; its decks and prow and the deep, wide curve of its keel all shone silver-white, as though the whole vessel welled with trapped moonlight, casting a shimmering sheen onto the dark waters that lapped its hull.

"Behold the *Cloud Scudder*," Zara whispered, her lips close to Tania's ear. "For five hundred years she has lain becalmed in a cold harbor, but tonight she will fly over the moon to the Island of Logris."

Hand in hand they crunched their way down the shingle. They stepped into the water, the lapping waves sucking the pebbles from under their feet with a sound like distant high-pitched laughter. Foam sizzled on the sea-rounded stones.

The waiting man bowed low and helped them board the small boat. They sat together in the stern as the man pushed the boat clear of the beach and jumped aboard. He fended the little vessel away from the shore with one oar, then sat and began to row with long, powerful strokes.

It wasn't long before they drew up alongside the towering silvery ship, their boat bumping gently against the timbers as the oarsman grasped a rope hanging from the deck. Zara stood up, using the man's shoulder to steady herself. More ropes came snaking down the side of the ship, including a long loop of rope with a small wooden platform at the base.

Zara stepped onto the side of the boat and then onto the wooden platform. She held on to the rope with both hands.

"Haul away!" called the oarsman, and Tania watched as her sister was hoisted up the lofty side of the ship.

A few moments later and Tania craned her neck to see Zara being helped onto the ship. The loop of rope slithered down again. The oarsman nodded toward the wooden platform.

The boat bobbed and shifted under her as Tania stepped up onto the side, holding her skirts with one hand. The oarsman took her arm to steady her as a gulf of water opened between the boat and ship. But a moment later the sea nudged the boat forward again, and she was able to step easily onto the platform.

She clung to the rope with both hands as she felt herself being lifted. She gazed shoreward: Behind the shingle banks, the land rose in grassy dunes, and beyond them gray-brown hills rolled dimly away on the edge of sight. She saw that the ship was anchored in a wide bay with dark curving arms of land stretching out to either side. To the left, a black finger tipped the arc of the bay, capped with a tongue of flame, distant but jewel-bright on the dark horizon.

"Give me your hand, Princess." She was at the level of the deck. A sailor was waiting for her, wearing a cream shirt and sky blue trousers tucked into high leather boots. Tania took his hand and stepped on board the ship.

A familiar voice rang out from the throng of Faerie folk who were gathered on the deck.

"Welcome! Welcome indeed, my daughter! This is a joy unlooked for." King Oberon stepped forward and took her into his arms. He was dressed all in white, with diamonds sewn into the folds of his padded doublet and with a fine filigree of charcoal thread patterning the collar and cuffs. His white crown circled his forehead, holding back his long yellow hair, the crystal band inset with a ring of precious and rare black amber stones.

Tania gazed into his face with its close-cut golden beard and mustache and those deep-set piercing blue eyes. "Hello," she said, embracing him fondly. "It's nice to be back."

"And you have returned in perfect time for the Festival of the Traveler's Moon," the King said. "Come, tell us your news quickly, before we set sail for Logris."

Clasping his hand, Tania looked around at the familiar faces that surrounded her on the deck. Her sister Hopie was there with her husband, Lord Brython, at her side, both of them clad in simple brown. Cordelia was there, too, her red-gold hair shorn about her shoulders and her face a mass of freckles. She held up one arm, a kestrel on her wrist. Sancha was at her side, dressed in her usual sable velvet, her clever brown eyes dancing in her smiling face.

"I've got some good news," Tania said, seeing the light of hope in Oberon's eyes. "We haven't actually *found* Titania yet, but Edric and I have spoken to someone who has met her. Or at least who met someone who looks exactly like her."

"I had not looked for you to find the Queen so swiftly," Oberon said.

"The search isn't over yet," Tania said. "But we'll keep going, I promise. I couldn't have got this far without Edric's help."

"Where is Master Chanticleer?" Sancha asked. "Did he not come with you?"

"Well, no," Tania said. "I didn't really mean to come here myself, but I kind of got carried away."

"And so shall we all, ere the night is much older!" said the King. He gave Tania a final loving look, then turned toward the high quarterdeck at the stern of the ship. "Admiral Belial, all are aboard. Weigh anchor and let us be gone!"

The admiral was standing at the quarterdeck rail, tall and gaunt and wrapped in a navy blue cloak. He raised his hand and the decks sprang alive with sky-blue-clad sailors, swarming down ropes and running across the decks. Wide capstans turned slowly to the rhythm of whistles and tambourines. Voices called from mast to mast.

"Isn't Eden here?" Tania asked, looking around for her eldest sister. Zara also seemed to have disappeared.

"Indeed she is," said Sancha. "She is below decks preparing for the voyage. She will be with us soon."

"Come to the forecastle," Cordelia said. "Eden and our father will be there shortly."

Tania made her way through the gathered courtiers. She saw the Earl and Countess of Gaidheal among them; they smiled and nodded to her as she passed. She climbed the stairway that led to the forecastle and walked forward along the narrowing deck. Sancha and Cordelia joined her as she stood at the rail, gazing out over the prow of the ship.

"How far is Logris?" she asked.

"Oh, many hours by water—but not so far by air," Cordelia said with a mysterious smile. Tania was still wondering what she meant when her sister lifted her arm high into the air.

"Go, Windfarer!" she called. "Lead the way!" The kestrel spread its wings and leaped from her arm. It swooped low from the side of the ship. Tania leaned out, watching as the bird almost skimmed the waves before it flapped its wings and soared upward into the night sky.

"The wind has died down," Tania said, looking up at the hanging sails. "How are we going to get moving?"

"Zara will whistle us up a fine wind," Cordelia said.

At that moment Tania heard the high, clear notes of the flute come wafting toward them. It was a beautiful melody, slow and melancholy at first, a song that might be sung by mariners who had been too long at sea. Tania felt tears prick her eyes as the aching melody drifted over the ship. But then the tune grew livelier, filled with hope and joy—a tune from the hearts of sailors who have seen their home port by the light of a rosy dawn.

A breeze began to stir the great silvery sails. At first it was only the merest trembling of the canvas, a flicking and fidgeting of rope ends and the warmth of moving air on Tania's face. But soon the cheeks of the sails began to fill. The ship creaked and sighed, the sails belling out, the timbers thrumming. Tania's hair blew fitfully across her face until she had to hold it back in her fist, her eyes narrowed against the rising wind.

Zara's tune came to a crescendo, the melody rising until it ended in a piping skirl of music.

The shattered reflection of the moon lay on the sea, the countless stars like pinpoints of white fire dancing around it on the black water. Tania leaned farther over the rail, watching the dark water burst into white foam as the prow ploughed the waves.

"Well met, my beloved sister."

Tania turned and saw Eden standing behind her, her pure white hair flying in the wind. Many of the care lines seemed to have been smoothed away from her sister's face since the last time they had met.

"I think we're close to finding Titania," Tania told her.

"I hope it is so," said Eden. Her voice was calm, but Tania knew that her quest meant more to Eden than any of them, for it was Eden who had sent their mother through the Oriole Glass into the Mortal World.

Oberon mounted the stairs to the forecastle.

"Eden?" he called. "Shall we give the *Cloud Scudder* its wings?"

"Yes, Father." Eden squeezed Tania's arm and walked to where the king was standing.

"What's going on?" Tania asked Sancha. The ship was moving already, its sails full-bellied with Zara's enchanted wind.

Sancha smiled. "You will see."

Oberon and Eden stood side by side in the middle of the deck, their heads high, their deep blue eyes reflecting the moon. Slowly and with perfect symmetry their arms began to rise, their hands palm upward, held open with fingers spread wide.

And as their arms lifted, Tania became aware that they were speaking in chorus, their voices blending together in a slow, mesmerizing chant:

> *Hallowed moon—blesséd moon—belovéd moon*
> *wingéd moon aloft in the crucible of the night*
> *Traveler's Moon, the dreamer's moon—the starlit*
>   *songster of time*
> *sing your songs of years unending—dream your*
>   *dreams of roads unbending*
> *listen, yes, listen now—the star-filled silences*
>   *call across the seas*
> *light our way hence to Ynis Logris—the Island*
>   *of No Hope's Fading*
> *guide our footsteps true—to the Island of All*
>   *Time's Waking*
> *lead us through this pure night to the Island of*
>   *No Love's Parting*
> *to Ynis Logris—the Isle of Our Delight*

Tania was so caught up in the solemn hymning of the two rich voices that it was a minute or two before she was aware that the angle of the deck was changing under her feet. She adjusted her stance, taking hold of the rail as the slope of the deck steepened.

It was as if the ship was rising on the swell of a huge, slow wave, but surely no wave could rise and rise for such a long time. Surely there had to be the crest and the fall into the trough. *Surely?*

The Faerie lords and ladies on the lower deck had

become silent. Mariners hung watchfully from the rigging.

Puzzled, Tania looked over the rail. The ship was rising prow-first from the waves. White water cascaded, foaming and swirling as the great silver hull lifted higher and higher.

Tania gaped, clinging to the rail as the keel drew clear of the sea. Drops of white water fell from the curved timbers as the ship rose into the sky. She heard gasps and exclamations from around her as the horizon fell away. The receding face of the sea looked like beaten black iron as the galleon sailed into the star-filled night.

The prow turned and now the ship was heading toward the round disk of the moon. If it had been huge before, now it was colossal. Moment by moment, its light grew brighter. Frozen with astonishment, Tania hung on the rail as the moon expanded until it seemed to fill the entire sky.

At last she had to throw her arm over her face and close her eyes against the blaze of light as she felt herself washed over by a surge of liquid silver.

A few moments later Sancha's voice sounded close by. "We are there."

Tania opened her eyes. The moon was gone and the chanting had ceased.

Tania gasped. "What happened?"

Sancha pointed back along the ship. The great full moon lay astern now—still immeasurably huge, but less blindingly bright. Eden and the King were standing at the far rail, the King's arm around his daughter's shoulders.

"Zara played up a wind for our sails, and Eden and the King guided our course," Sancha said. "Look you now—Ynis Logris lies below."

The ship was high, high above the waves, the sails straining and the hull creaking gently as it divided the air. Far below, an island of green-clad hills floated in a girdle of white sand on the dark bosom of the sea. Three galleons lay at anchor in a shallow bay on the nearside of the island. Tania could see small boats coming and going as people and provisions were ferried to the shore. Higher up the long sandy beach, bonfires had been lit, and the aromatic scent of woodsmoke came up to her as she leaned over the prow.

The *Cloud Scudder* was dipping now, moving in a long slow curve toward the island.

The ship touched the waves so gently that Tania would have been unaware of it had she not been watching with a fast-beating heart as the sharp keel clove the water and sent up flukes of white foam.

The *Cloud Scudder* settled in the water close to the other three ships. Commands rang out and the anchors were loosened and the sails furled. Boats were already being lowered from the sides.

"What now?" Tania said.

"Now we go ashore," Cordelia said. "The bonfires are lit, the entertainments have been arranged: Let the revelries begin!" As she spoke a small shape came soaring down out of the night sky, and with a series of keening cries, Windfarer came to rest on her wrist.

"Yes, indeed, my friend," Cordelia said to the bird. "You speak true. It has been an age of sorrow since last we set foot upon the dancing sands of Ynis Logris. But tonight all that shall be amended."

Eden came walking across the deck toward Tania. "Come," she said, holding out her hand. "Our boat awaits."

The festivities took up the length and breadth of the white beach. Tania wandered enthralled among the revelers—sometimes with one or two of her sisters, sometimes alone—watching high-born lords and ladies make merry alongside footmen, servants, and stable boys. Kitchen maids danced with earls, a marchioness sang a duet with a gardener, a groom shared a joke with a princess. For one night all the folk of Faerie were equal under the Traveler's Moon.

Tables stood near the bonfires, laden with flagons of ruby and white and crisp yellow cordials, and with dishes and bowls of fruit and sweetmeats—honey-cakes and sweet pies and fire-roasted chestnuts and frosted candies.

Tania met up with Hopie and her husband, Lord Brython, and they walked together along the seashore for a while, listening to the music and the laugher that mingled with the gentle wash of the waves.

"You have not asked about Rathina," Hopie said, pausing, her arm linked into her husband's. "Do you not wish to know her fate?"

Tania looked awkwardly at her sister. "I saw she wasn't here," she said. "Is she okay?"

"Is she ooh-kay . . . ?" Hopie echoed slowly, as if exploring the strange word on her tongue. "No, Tania, I would not say that our sister is *okay*."

Tania vividly remembered the last time she had seen Rathina. It had been in the Hall of Light. Oberon had come to Tania's rescue, thwarting Drake's intention to do her harm after his schemes to gain the power to walk both worlds had failed. But then Rathina had revealed her part in Tania's ordeal and her secret love for Gabriel Drake. Her last words to Tania were burned into her memory. *I hate you. I wish you were dead.* Not a good memory to carry of someone she had thought was her closest friend in all of Faerie.

"Your sister fled the palace two nights ago," said Brython. "She was seen by a stable boy, clad only in her gown with neither cloak nor bag, riding her horse out onto the northern downs in the dark watches of the night."

"Perhaps it is best that she is gone," Hopie said quietly. "Maddalena is a wise beast and she will ensure that her mistress comes to no harm. And it may be that with time and solitude, the madness of her passion for the traitor Drake will abate." She gazed out toward the horizon. "Such is my wish," she said. "But I have little hope that it will end thus. The poor child was fey with the bitter dregs of unrequited love!"

"Fey?"

"Touched by madness," Hopie said. "I fear that even

were the King to use his Arts to find her and bring her back to us, the creature that returned would be but the husk of our sister, and that we would know her not."

Tania turned away, her heart breaking at the thought of her sister alone and friendless, gnawed by love for a man who had used her and who had never cared for her.

Tania spent a while walking alone along the seashore after her conversation with Hopie. The memory of Rathina's betrayal and of her hatred was still raw in her heart and mind.

"No!" she said. "This is meant to be fun!" She turned, intending to go back up the beach to where there were people to distract her, but she saw Zara and Cordelia coming across the sand toward her.

"Well met!" Cordelia called. "But why do you walk here alone?"

"She is playing the part of the sorrowful maid in the ballad," Zara said. "Do you remember Evensong, Tania?" She began to sing.

> *Of an evening in December, when the frost lay*
> *on the ground,*
> *she was walking wild with fever by the bitter*
> *ocean strand*
> *and the wind gnawed at her fingers, and the ice*
> *cracked in her hair,*
> *weeping seagulls swept around her, she did*
> *nought but stand and stare*

Tania smiled. "Did I look that fed up?" she said. "Sorry. I've been talking to Hopie about Rathina. It made me feel bad."

"Indeed, the treachery of our sister throws a darkness over all our hearts," Cordelia said.

"But there is nought to be gained by such long faces," Zara said. "I will not have it, not on such a night as this. See, I shall lighten your spirits." She drew her flute from the confines of her dress. Putting it to her lips, she walked into the shallow waves.

"Where's Windfarer?" Tania asked Cordelia.

"He is away in the hills, hunting up a supper," she replied. "He will return when his belly is full."

Zara came to a halt with the waves eddying around her knees, her gown clinging in wet folds to her legs. The tune she was playing was quite different from anything Tania had heard before. Streams of dancing notes rippled among languorous rolling melodies, descending at times into long, deep, rumbling tones that reverberated in Tania's ears and made her shiver.

"She is playing an ocean song," Cordelia said softly.

A few yards beyond where Zara was standing, the face of the sea began to boil and seethe. Suddenly a host of fish came leaping into the air, shedding water like jewels off their iridescent scales.

A larger shape plunged out of the water: a dolphin, its sleek sides gleaming as it twirled tail over snout before sliding beneath the waves once more. Then more dolphins joined in the wonderful marine ballet, leaping in high curves from the sea, crossing one another's paths, shedding trails of shining water droplets, somersaulting and vanishing again into the water with a flick of their fluked tails.

Closer to the shore, where the water was shallower, a dark, hard-edged shape emerged slowly from the waves. It was a few moments before Tania could tell what it was—but then she recognized the blunt bullet head and the smooth green dome of the shell and the powerful flippers that hauled the huge turtle up into the surf.

Beside her, Cordelia stiffened. "That ancient gentleman is an unusual visitor on these shores and at such a time of year," she murmured. "Maybe he has news for me." She ran to the creature and crouched in front of it, her hand on its head, speaking softly to it as it lay among the lapping waves.

At last Zara brought the fluting to a stop and walked out of the sea, holding her flute in one hand and her wet skirts in the other. The fish and the dolphins vanished under the water and the surface became still again. The huge turtle turned laboriously and crawled back into the foaming sea. Cordelia came walking back to where Tania and Zara were standing, her face thoughtful.

"Is something wrong?" Tania asked.

"I do not know," Cordelia said. "Yonder seafarer told me that he roams often beyond the rocky shores of Dinsel and out into the waters that lie between our Realm and the cruel island of Lyonesse."

"Let us not speak of that place," Zara pleaded. "Not tonight!"

"What's the problem?" Tania asked.

"He told me that he has seen lights in the ruined fortress of the King of Lyonesse," Cordelia said. "Lights where there should be no lights."

"Jack-o'-lanterns and marsh goblins belike," Zara said with a shudder. "It is thousands of years since the King of Lyonesse and his Gray Knights brewed their evil in that haunted place. While our father holds sway in Faerie, we need never fear that deadly peril again." She caught Tania's arm. "I have great thirst after playing such salty songs. Come, let us eat and drink and be merry. The night is yet young and we have much to see and do before morning."

Tania looked at her. "Morning?" she said. "Zara, I can't stay that long. I'll get into big trouble if my parents find out that I'm not in my room."

"Fie!" said Zara. "'Tis no problem. Eden will call down a fire-bearded comet for you when time runs short. You shall ride aloft, skimming the stars all the way back to the Mortal World, and none asleep there now shall ever know of your journeyings."

Persuaded by Zara's confidence, Tania danced and sang and applauded the entertainments and hardy noticed as the huge moon floated away across the Faerie night. It was not until she saw the great white disk dropping below the hills that she realized how much time must have gone by.

She quickly went to find Eden. Her sister was

seated on a rug on the sand. She had several Faerie lords and ladies with her, and they were speaking together in subdued, urgent voices.

Seeing Tania, Eden got up.

"What were you talking about?" Tania asked. "It sounded serious."

"Cordelia told us that lights have been seen in the Fortress of Bale Fole on Lyonesse," Eden said. "We were discussing the possible causes for such a thing. The black fortress of Lyonesse has been deserted for a very long time—it would be grim indeed if some evil came creeping back there."

"But the King of Lyonesse is still a prisoner in the dungeons beneath the Faerie Palace, isn't he?" Tania pictured the dusty, clouded amber globes that lined the corridors where she had gone to free Edric after he had been imprisoned by Drake. Each globe held a prisoner, an enemy of the Realm of Faerie, frozen alive in orange glass.

"Aye, and must be for all eternity," Eden said. "In the Great Wars he came close to being our downfall and it was only the powers of King Oberon and Queen Titania combined that caused his defeat. But when Bale Fole was razed and the Sorcerer King's power overthrown, his Queen, the wicked Lady Lamia, was never found. It was hoped that she had fled, powerless without her Lord. But it might be that she has at last returned and wishes evil upon us." Eden smiled grimly. "But enough of such talk. The lights in Bale Fole most likely portend nothing at all.

So, Tania, do you wish to return to the Mortal World?"

"Yes. Zara said you might be able to help me? Something about calling a comet down for me to ride home on?"

Eden laughed. "Zara magnifies my abilities beyond all reason! But I can be of service, I believe. Come, let you bid farewell to friends and family, then meet me down by the shore. I will have transport for us by then."

The small slender boat had a single spiraling mast like the horn of a swordfish and a broad triangular sail of some strange, translucent coral-colored material. The inside of the hull glowed with a silky, mother-of-pearl sheen, its outer flanks ribbed as though made from seashells. It had only room enough for Tania to sit in the front with her back to the prow, and for Eden to sit at the back with her hand on the rudder.

Tania saw Eden's fierce eyes rise to the masthead. Her lips moved soundlessly. Moments later a wind filled the sail and the sleek vessel skimmed away from the island at a breathtaking speed. The boat moved so smoothly that Tania wondered whether it was actually touching the waves, but the fine spray that filled her eyes and sparkled in her hair suggested otherwise.

Within a few seconds the island dwindled to a bright dot and then fell away below the horizon, and she was alone with her sister on the open sea.

"Can you talk, or do you need to concentrate?"

"Once the spirits are awoken they will perform unbidden," Eden said. "You have some burden on your mind, I think. Something that gives you unease."

Tania nodded. "I had a dream," she admitted. "It was about Drake."

She described what she had seen: the lashing rain and the thunder and lightning, the knife-edged rocks, the beast that was pursuing them, Edric and her hand-in-hand—and then Edric turning into Gabriel Drake.

You will never be free of me! Did you not know? We are bonded for all time!

"The thing is, was he telling the truth?" she asked. "And what was that place?"

"The island of Maw," Eden said, and there was a shudder in her voice. "Ynis Maw lies in desolate seas to the far north of Faerie, beyond even the bleak storm-wracked coasts of Prydein. I know of it only from books and tales. It is called the Island of No Return, sometimes the Island of Good-bye Forever." She looked somber. "But you need have no fear of Drake, sweet sister. There is no coming back from such an exile, not while Oberon wears the crown of Faerie."

"But could Drake . . . could he somehow drag me there with his mind?"

Eden frowned thoughtfully. "You should not fear the powers of the great traitor. He is pinioned on the island and I do not believe he can do more than trouble your dreams—not unless he was able to use someone in the Mortal World to aid him, someone with the power to create a bridge between the worlds. Such people do exist in the Mortal World, I know, but they are very few and it is most unlikely that you will meet such a one." She looked at Tania. "The Ritual of Hand-Fasting has a potency, that I will not deny, but it is nothing that you need fear. What bond there is between you has not the power to draw you to him nor he to you."

She leaned forward and touched her fingertips to Tania's forehead. Tania felt a kind of cool content-ment seep into her mind, like waves or clouds or soft summer rain.

"There, may your sister's touch banish the traitor from your mind as Oberon has banished him from Faerie," Eden murmured. She looked over Tania's shoulder. "And see, our journey will soon be done. We are at the mouth of the river Tamesis. Can you see the lights of the Royal Palace? We will moor at the eastern-most jetty of Fortrenn Quay and take a carriage to Bonwn Tyr, to the brown tower on the grassy downs."

Tania turned her head. They were skimming the waves toward a great dark spread of land cloven by a river estuary. Eden was right: It was the Tamesis, and on the northern bank of the estuary she could see the twinkling lights of the Royal Palace. Soon she would be home.

The horse-drawn carriage came to a halt under the walls of the brown tower. Tania had stopped off at her bedchamber to change back into her ordinary clothes and then Eden had driven her to Bonwn Tyr.

"I wonder what time it is," Tania said.

"The night is entering the fourth quarter," Eden said.

"I was hoping for something a bit more specific than that—like, half past two, or something."

"Ever the mortal part of you rises up to cause confusion in your dear heart," Eden said fondly. "We do not count out the passing moments as mortals do. Remember your Faerie soul, Tania. Let time be not your master."

Tania sighed. "It's a nice idea," she said. "But not very practical right now." She kissed her sister goodbye and stepped from the carriage. "I'll come back again as soon as I can," she promised. "And with any luck, I'll have Titania with me!"

"Fare you well, sweet Tania. May angels of mercy attend your every step both in Faerie and on the dark paths of the Mortal World."

Tania stood at the door, watching as Eden lightly flicked the reins and the horse trotted away through the aspen trees.

She went into the tower and closed the door behind her. With the moon low in the sky, the winding stairway was dark, and she had to be careful not to miss her footing as she made her way to the upper room. She took a final wistful look from the narrow window then turned her back on the Faerie night. She filled her mind with thoughts of her Camden home. She took a deep breath and made once more the side step between the worlds.

There was carpet under her feet, not bare floor-boards. The sound of trees whispering in the breeze had gone. Her bedroom was in deep darkness. She tiptoed to the bed and looked at the red display of her bedside clock: 3:52. No wonder she was feeling so tired.

Moving as quietly as possible, she fumbled her way around, shedding her clothes and putting on her pajamas. She sat on the edge of the bed, debating whether she should risk going to the bathroom to wash her face and clean her teeth.

She ran her tongue over her front teeth. They needed brushing. She got up and padded over to the door. She was just reaching for the handle when it turned by itself and the door opened toward her.

Startled, Tania gasped and jerked her hand away.

The door opened wider and she saw her father's face in the crack.

"Dad! You nearly frightened the life out of me! What is it?"

Her father looked unsmilingly at her. "You're back, then. Would you like to tell me exactly where you've been all night?"

Tania stared at her father in dismay.

"Where have you been, Anita?" he asked again.

"There was a party," she said, and her voice was just a ghost in the tense darkness. "Does Mum know I went out?"

"No."

"Are you going to tell her?"

There was a deadly pause. "No," he said at last, and even in her misery, Tania felt a shred of relief. "I'm too angry with you to talk about this right now," he said. "I can't even begin to tell you how disappointed I am in you."

"I'm sorry," she whispered.

"Go to bed now."

He quietly closed her door. She stood there listening to the soft pad of his feet along the landing. She heard the click of her parents' bedroom door closing.

She walked to the bed and sat on the edge, her elbows on her knees, her face in her hands. Crying would be good now, if only to relieve the tension. But no tears came to wash away her pain.

She hated the lies she had to tell. She hated making her father believe she was behaving badly when all she was doing was trying to make sense of the two halves of her self. She couldn't expect her parents to come to terms with the truth of who she really was, but did that mean that she could *never* be honest with them?

Would she have to lie to them for the rest of her life?

Part Two:

Mortal Lives

"You are a Pisces sheep and your element is metal. Yours is the most feminine of the star signs. You are good-natured and kind-hearted, but you loathe criticism and you are ruled too often by your emotions."

Tania was sitting to one side of the black-clothed table, only half-listening as the fortune-teller made her pitch to Jade. She had only come into this poky little cupboard at the back of the New Age Mystics shop to stop Jade talking about it all day, and her thoughts were very much elsewhere while her friend was being "read."

Her dad had said nothing that morning about what had happened the night before. He had behaved perfectly normally at breakfast, almost as if their brief, wretched conversation had wiped the slate clean. But Tania knew that it was not forgotten—and she knew that she had let him down very badly and that she would not be forgiven so readily a second time. Even thinking about the sight of her father's face in her bedroom doorway made her feel physically sick.

She couldn't bear to call Edric, even though she had promised she would. She knew she couldn't go with him to Richmond, not after last night. One more mouthful of lies would choke her and she didn't want to talk to him yet about what had happened. Feeling like an absolute coward, she had left him a text message.

I can't come today. Sorry. I'll explain on Monday.

Then she switched off her phone, knowing he would call her back.

And then an hour or so later, Jade called her on the house phone. "What's with turning off your cell phone, dummy? I've been calling you all morning."

"Sorry. What's up?"

"I want to do some pre-holiday shopping at the market and I hate shopping on my own, so you're coming with me."

"I can't."

"Of course you can. I'll pick you up about eleven o'clock. It'll be fun. See you."

"Jade? No—listen. . . ."

But the line was dead.

And that had been that. Jade had arrived half an hour late as usual, and the two of them had headed over to the busy open air street market. Her father had said nothing about the outing with Jade, and her mum had been positively enthusiastic about the idea, as if she saw it as a sign that Tania was behaving normally again.

The market was a major tourist trap, and on a hot midsummer Sunday like today the people were swarming everywhere. Tania was happy to join the jostling crowds; at least the bustle would take her mind off her problems for a while. She was looking forward to exploring the colorful stalls and shops with their tempting displays of handmade jewelry and fashion accessories, their designer clothes and arts and crafts and antiques.

But the first place that Jade had wanted to go was the fortune-teller's booth tucked away at the back of a New Age shop. She said it would be a laugh.

The fortune-teller was a small, painfully thin, middle-aged woman with a frizzy mass of dyed black hair and with bloodred lipstick on her thin lips. She had a high, nasal voice that Tania soon found grating; but Jade was obviously having a great time, her eyes wide with excitement as she leaned over the table.

"You're a hopeless romantic and you are motivated by accord," the woman declared, examining Jade's palm. "You can be jealous, defensive, vulnerable, and unbalanced. Your season is summer, your orientation south-southwest, and you are fire negative."

Tania stifled a sneeze. The air in the booth was thick with incense. Beyond the slightly tatty maroon curtain, she could hear two people in the shop debating the merits of tarot cards over rune stones for helping you to decide your pathway through life.

Wouldn't that be great? Tania thought. *To leave all the difficult stuff to a handful of stones. I could live with that.*

"What do you mean exactly by 'unbalanced'?" Jade asked the woman.

"You have a predisposition toward letting your emotions overwhelm you," the woman said. "And this can make you gloomy and negative and introverted. These are tendencies that you must learn to control."

"Gloomy? Me?" Jade said. "No way."

"It is also in your nature to hide these negative traits," the woman said. "You keep them secret. I see many—"

The high, thin voice halted.

"Yes?" Jade asked. "You see many what?"

There was a long pause. Tania looked at the woman. She was staring at Jade's open hand with a puzzled expression on her face.

"What do you see many of?" Jade prompted.

The woman seemed to come out of a trance. She glanced up at Jade. "Many secrets," she said. "But not all the secrets belong to you. Some are secrets that are hidden from you by a friend. You have a friend with a secret. A big secret."

"Really?" Jade's voice was filled with curiosity. "Who is it? What kind of secret?"

The woman lowered her head and closed her eyes. Tania could see her eyeballs moving rapidly under the thin lids.

"It's not clear," the woman said, and now Tania thought she could hear a hint of unease in her voice.

"It's very confused . . . but there's more to this friend than you could possibly imagine."

Tania swallowed. Was this oddball woman talking about *her*?

"No!" the woman said suddenly, leaning back and letting Jade's hand fall. "There's nothing more. I can't see anything else."

Jade frowned down at her hand. "I wanted to know if I'd meet someone on holiday," she said. "Didn't you see any cute guys?"

The woman gave a pointy little smile. "There will be plenty of men like that in your future, my dear," she said. "I don't need the second sight to tell you that."

Jade grinned at Tania. "Your turn!"

"I'd rather not," Tania began, but Jade wouldn't take no for an answer and rather than argue with her and have to spend even more time in this stuffy little room, they swapped places and Tania took the seat opposite the fortune-teller.

"She was born the same year as me, and her birthday is the thirteenth of June," Jade told the woman as she squeezed into the other chair.

"Ah," the woman said. "A Gemini. A woman of two halves, a woman of discontent." She reached across the table and, reluctantly, Tania rested her hand palm upward in the waiting hands.

The woman nodded. "The roses that you pick are never so beautiful as those that are just out of reach," she said. "But you don't blame yourself for not being able to touch them; you blame the roses for being so obstinately beyond your grasp."

"I wouldn't say that," Tania said lightly, determined not to take this seriously and not even sure what the woman was trying to tell her.

The woman looked into her eyes for a moment and Tania felt a cold shiver run down her spine. "No?" the woman said. "Well, maybe not. If you say so." She concentrated on Tania's palm again. "Your element is also metal, but there is something else, something I can't quite make out. You are not at ease with the metal part of your makeup—it gives you pain. It confuses you. The dual element of your nature pulls you in different directions. You are uncertain of who you are and of where you should be."

The woman's eyes flickered closed and her voice lowered to little more than a whisper. "Your image is blurred . . . it comes and goes . . . you take a step and you disappear . . . you take another and you return . . . I don't understand. . . ."

Fairly alarmed by this, Tania tried to pull her hand away. But she found she was unable to move. It was as if every muscle in her body had frozen in position: Her hand resting on the thin woman's palms, her stiff body leaning forward a little over the black table.

Fear began to well up in her. She tried to speak, to cry out, but the words were locked in her throat and she was unable to make a sound. The blood pounded thickly in her temples, making her head ring, and the throbbing of her own blood was the only sound that

Tania could hear in the deadly stifling silence.

The incense-thick air in the booth was so hot and still and heavy that she had to fight for breath. An unpleasant taste came into her mouth: The taste of rusty iron. She couldn't turn her head, but she managed to swivel her eyes toward Jade, hoping her friend would see what was happening and do something to break her free of this terrifying paralysis.

But Jade was sitting on the small chair at the side of the table, picking absently at her nail polish and completely unaware of Tania's predicament.

Then Tania heard a new sound through the thundering in her head. A voice. An echoing voice speaking very softly from far, far away. A man's voice incanting words that she could not quite catch—the same set of phrases over and over—gradually growing louder.

Tania turned her eyes to the woman's bowed head. The woman's bloodred lips were trembling, moving in time to the chanting voice. Her eyes had opened just a thin slit—and the sliver that showed under her heavy lids was silvery and flickered with a deadly light.

As Tania watched in growing terror, the woman's eyes opened wider and a pair of cold, silver eyes stared up at her through the tangle of her black fringe. And at the same moment Tania recognized the voice and finally, with a terrible, chilling clarity, she was able to hear what it was saying.

"You will never be free of me! Did you not know? We are bonded for all time!"

The eyes staring at her from the woman's face were Gabriel Drake's eyes, and the voice coming from her mouth was his voice.

Through the horror that was darkening her mind, Tania recalled Eden's words:

You should not fear the powers of the great traitor . . . I do not believe he can do more than trouble your dreams—not unless he was able to use someone in the Mortal World to aid him—someone with the power to create a bridge between the worlds.

She had been crazy to come here. Tania realized that now. But it had just been for fun, a joke, a piece of nonsense that she had agreed to only to please Jade. She had automatically assumed the fortune-teller would be a fake, a harmless phony playing the part of someone with mystical powers for the amusement of gullible tourists.

But the ridiculous little woman with her bloodred lips and her badly dyed black hair obviously had real psychic powers, and Gabriel Drake was using those powers to reach across the worlds to ensnare Tania.

"Well met, my lady," said Gabriel's silken voice from the woman's red-lipped mouth. "Long have I ached for the touch of your hand in mine." And as he spoke, the woman's thin fingers closed around Tania's hand in an icy grip. "You will come with me, my lady. I will brook no refusal. If I am to be banished, then you will share my torment. I would have you at my side through all the long, slow ages of the world!"

No! Tania's voice howled in her mind. *No! Never!*

"Yes, my lady. Yes!"

The booth suddenly grew pitch-dark and Tania heard a wild wind rushing toward her, whipping her hair, stinging her face with a thousand spiteful points of rain. The chair that she was sitting on and the floor of the booth fell away from under her and she dropped into a black gulf, her plunge halted with a wrenching jolt that filled her arm and shoulder with agony. Her feet kicked uselessly as she hung there suspended from the cold fierce grip of Gabriel Drake's hand.

She was back in her nightmare.

Fangs of shining, rain-scoured rock reared around her. Storm clouds rolled and seethed, black and yellow, their swollen undersides lit by forked lightning. In the deep darkness beneath her Tania heard claws scraping on rock and the heavy, rasping breath of something huge and dreadful.

"The monster approaches swiftly," Gabriel called down to her. "Can you not hear its breath? It will eat you alive, my lady. Only I can save you." His free hand was pale in the darkness as he reached down toward her. "Take my other hand, my lady, so that I can pull you up—else you will surely die."

Tania twisted her head and stared into the black abyss. Red eyes shone like fire beneath her. She could hear the chomping of jaws. A great, clawed arm reached up.

"Take my hand or die!" Gabriel shouted. "There is no other choice!"

But a gentle, soft voice sounded in her head, as frail and bright as a glimpse of blue sky through the thunderclouds. "There *is* another choice, Tania," the woman's voice said. "Remember, once on a time you had wings! Trust in yourself and you shall be winged again."

Hope ignited in Tania—and a fierce need to fight back, to break Gabriel's power over her. She would not let him control her like this, she would not let him drag her into this nightmare world. She would *not*!

She cried out in pain as twin knives slashed at her shoulder blades. But the pain only lasted for a split second, and then she felt the sudden awakening of sinews and muscles that expanded from her back, spreading and growing like opening fingers, like unfurling leaves, like strange new limbs.

She wrenched her hand free from Gabriel's grip. She heard him shouting as she fell, but the whirling wind drowned out his words. She spun in the air, feeling the power surging through her newborn wings. The monster roared beneath her, its eyes blazing like furnaces, its claws reaching up for her.

But she wasn't afraid anymore. Her wings cupped the air, sending her soaring upward in a long, smooth curve.

She flew high into the rain-filled sky, her body tingling with delight as her wings curled and spread, lifting her above the black crags and chasms of Ynis Maw. The taste of iron was gone from her mouth. She stretched her arms above her head, her hands together palm to palm like a diver. She twisted in the air, her wings beating fast, and with a single deep breath, she plunged upward into the heart of the storm.

A dense blanket of sodden darkness closed around her and for a few uneasy moments she was afraid that the storm would swallow her whole as she fought to beat her wings in the drenching, airless wet belly of the cloud.

But then, with a suddenness that took her breath away, she burst into bright daylight.

She climbed into the vast blue sky, her wings beating freely, her heart leaping with an almost unbearable joy. This was what it felt like to be truly alive! Laughing aloud, she folded her arms around herself and went spiraling, higher and higher, until she felt that she could reach up and touch the face of the sky.

Then, with another peal of laughter, she wheeled around and hung poised for a moment in the upper air, feeling the wind of her wings stirring her hair. She glanced over her shoulder at the gossamer-thin film of her wings as they stroked the air and held her aloft.

Between her feet the island of Ynis Maw was hidden beneath a boiling mass of dark cloud. Behind her, and to her left and right, the gray-green sea stretched on forever, but in front of her a dark peninsula lifted out of the troubled water, white foam breaking on its craggy cliffs.

"Now what?" Tania said aloud to herself, trying to think through the euphoria of the moment. "What happens next?"

Her mouth was suddenly flooded again by that horrible taste of iron.

"You awake from the dream, my lady," said a smooth, chilling voice. "And you return to the nightmare."

Cold fingers closed around her hand. The blue sky was snuffed out like a candle. Darkness roared all around her again, and her hand was caught in an icy grip. Her wings were gone and Gabriel's voice was crawling like poison in her mind. "Did you think it would be so easy to be free of me, my lady?"

But Tania refused to be beaten, not when she had known what it was like to break away from him and fly. With a huge effort she jerked her hand free. Gabriel let out a shout of anger that dwindled away to nothing as the dark of Ynis Maw bled away and was replaced by the incense-scented gloom of the fortune-teller's booth.

Too startled to react, Tania stared across the table at the woman. The fortune-teller's face was ashen, her brown eyes staring in shock at Tania as if she had been awoken from a deep sleep by a slap across the face.

"Is that it?" came Jade's peevish voice. "She comes and goes and you don't understand it? What about meeting tall, dark, handsome boys? What about going on long journeys? What about fame and fortune and all that?"

Tania looked at her friend, trying to unscramble her brain. Clearly Jade had no idea of what had been going on between Tania and the fortune-teller.

The woman spoke, and her voice was weak and subdued and full of confusion. "That's all there is. I can't see any more," she said.

"What *did* you see?" Tania asked, looking into the woman's face and trying to read from her troubled eyes how much she knew of what had happened between them.

"Nothing," the woman said. "I didn't see anything. I went blank for a few moments, that was all. You should go now."

"I think maybe we should," Tania said, realizing with relief that the fortune-teller had no idea of how Gabriel Drake had used her.

"But—" Jade began.

"Go now, please," the woman said, standing up suddenly and pulling the curtain aside. "The reading is over." Jade and Tania were almost pushed out of the little booth. The curtain swirled shut again behind them.

"What a weirdo!" Jade said, loud enough to be heard.

"Come on," Tania said. "Let's get out of here."

She fought to act normally, not to give Jade any indication of what had just happened. She was not even sure herself what had been real and what had taken place in her mind.

Had Gabriel Drake really managed to drag her out

of this world? Or had it all been an illusion—a terrifyingly real illusion—a psychic battle fought between them in the dark places of her mind?

Either way, she had one shred of comfort: She had fought free of him. She had escaped from Ynis Maw and from the numbing power of his dreadful eyes. But what if that stupid visit to the fortune-teller's booth had allowed him to get a lock on her?

She had only just escaped this time. Would she have the strength to get free from him the next time he came for her, either in her dreams or in the waking world? And if she wasn't strong enough to break away from him, what would happen to her? Would she simply vanish from the Mortal World and find herself trapped with him on Ynis Maw? It was a terrifying prospect—and all too possible. After all, it had been Gabriel who had pulled her into Faerie in the first place, that time using the power of the amber necklace. But now they were bound together by the Hand-Fasting Ritual, and that was a far more potent connection between them—and one that could not be severed.

Jade's voice snapped into her thoughts. "I'd like to have known what she meant about my having a friend with a secret," she said as they came into the narrow stall-lined street.

"I shouldn't think she meant anything at all," Tania replied.

"Really?" Jade raised an amused eyebrow. "Well, I think *you're* the friend with the big secret," she continued, nudging up against Tania. Her eyes flickered with mischief. "A big secret, eh? Something to do with . . . oh . . . let me think . . . with *Evan*?"

"Give it up, Jade," Tania said, relieved that her friend was preoccupied with her own reading. "There's no big secret. You wanted to do some shopping, so let's shop!" She pointed to a nearby stall. "Look, scarves. I could do with a new scarf. Coming?" And she pushed her way through the crowds, not even stopping to see if Jade was following.

It was an hour or so later. Tania and Jade were sitting at a round wrought-iron table, eating vegetable tortilla wraps. They were in a small paved area alongside the Stable Market, a block of old brick buildings that housed arts and crafts, antique furniture, fabrics and paintings, and prints and electronics.

Calypso music was being piped from somewhere nearby. The sun was high in the clear sky and Tania was feeling a little too hot, a little bit grubby, and footsore and bruised from sixty minutes of fighting her way up and down the market. She had largely recovered from her ordeal in the fortune-teller's booth, but the image of Gabriel Drake's face would seep into her mind every now and then and send a chill of fear through her body.

Jade was wearing a new pair of sunglasses with round blue lenses. As she sucked her Diet Coke through a straw, she peered at Tania over the silver frames.

"So," she said, "do you want to tell me why you're

wearing that cheap-looking chunk of stone on your wrist instead of the fabulous bracelet that I bought you for your birthday?"

Tania glanced down at the black amber jewel on its lilac ribbon. "I was worried that yours might get damaged or stolen in all these crowds," she said, improvising quickly. "It's too nice to wear just any old time."

"Fair enough," Jade said. "But that doesn't explain why you're wearing that skanky thing."

"Edric gave it to me."

"Cedric?" Jade squawked. "Who the heck is Cedric?"

"I meant Evan," Tania stammered, feeling a rush of blood to her cheeks. *Stupid mistake!* "Evan gave it to me."

Jade eyed her. "So why say Cedric?"

"I didn't say Cedric—I said *Edric*," Tania responded, trying to sound less flustered than she felt. "Edric is his real name, but he doesn't use it much."

"I don't blame him!" Jade spluttered with laughter. "Your boyfriend's real name is Cedric? How lame is that?"

"Edric!" Tania insisted with a frown. "It's a kind of family name. Don't go around school telling everyone he's called Cedric, or I'll have to kill you."

"Whatever," Jade said with a dismissive flick of her fingers. She leaned across the table. "Show me that thing," she said, reaching for the black amber bracelet. "Is the stone worth anything?"

Tania pulled her arm back. "It doesn't matter what

it's worth," she said defensively. "Evan gave it to me—that's what matters."

"Oh, please!" Jade said. "Show it to me. What's so special about it? Come on, take it off and let me have a proper look."

"No," Tania said. "I promised I'd wear it all the time." She kept her arm out of Jade's reach. It would be just like her in one of her playful moods to snatch the thing off her wrist and that was a risk Tania definitely didn't want to take, not while she was sitting on a metal chair at a metal table.

Jade gave up and slumped back in her chair. "Fine, crazy girl," she said. "Keep your little secrets. I hope you and Cedric will be really happy together."

"Edric!" Tania said.

Jade grinned at her. "You think Edric sounds *better*?" she said. Then Tania noticed her eye-line shift as if something behind Tania had caught her attention.

"Well, well," Jade said. "Here comes Cedric now."

Tania turned. She was right. Edric was making his way toward them. That was odd—how did he know where to find her?

"Hello, Cedric," Jade said. "How's it going?"

"What?"

Tania quickly got up so that she was between Edric and Jade. Her friend was in mischief-hyperdrive right now and not to be trusted.

Edric looked at her, and behind his fixed smile she could tell that he wasn't entirely happy. "Can we speak for a minute?"

"Yes, sure," Tania said, knowing he meant out of earshot of Jade. She gave Jade an unconcerned smile. "I'll just be a second," she said.

"Fine by me," Jade said. "Off you go, then, *Tanyaah*—have your little chat with Cedric."

Tania led Edric away from the table.

"Why is she calling me that?"

"Don't ask." Tania sighed. "I made a mistake and used your real name. She misheard, and she thinks it's hilarious. How did you know where to find me?"

"Your phone was switched off so I called Jade's house to see if she knew where you were. I didn't call your home line in case your parents answered. Jade's mum told me you'd come here."

"I'm really sorry about the text," Tania said. "And about switching off the phone. But I couldn't explain everything to you right then."

"Did you enjoy yourself at the Festival last night?" he asked, taking her by surprise.

"Yes—but how did you know I'd been?"

"The scent of Faerie is all over you," he said. "I can smell it on your skin and in your hair." He smiled properly at her. "I'm glad you went. I hoped you would."

"I didn't really mean to go. It just kind of happened." She looked into his eyes. "I told them about finding someone who had seen Titania. They were really pleased. I wish you could have come with me."

"Me, too, but it would have been too tricky to do it

without your parents finding out."

Tania gave him a haunted look. "My dad did find out," she said.

His face became uneasy. "How?"

"He doesn't know *where* I went," she said, "but he must have checked on me while I was gone." She caught hold of Edric's hand, needing the comfort of physical contact. "I told him I'd been to a party. He didn't yell at me or anything, but I could tell he was really hurt. The only good news is that he hasn't told my mum. I don't think she'd be as calm about it as he was."

"I'm sorry," Edric said, squeezing her hand. "It's my fault. I shouldn't have told you about the Festival." He frowned, his voice lowering. "I just wanted you to experience more things in Faerie, to get to know the place better."

"That's okay, I understand," she said. She looked into his eyes. "Something else has happened. Something worse." She glanced around, making sure there was no one nearby to overhear.

"I went with Jade to have my fortune told," Tania explained. "I didn't really want to but she kept going on about it. I thought it would just be a waste of time but . . . but something happened." Falteringly, she told him everything that had happened in the fortune-teller's booth. "I didn't even remember what Eden had told me till it was too late," she finished. "The woman must have been a real medium or something, and Drake used her to get to me."

Edric's face went pale. "Are you out of your mind?" he said. "How could you do something that dangerous?"

Tania winced. She had been expecting sympathy and concern from him, not a lecture. "It was a mistake," she said, pulling her hand out of his. "But it was all right in the end. I managed to get away from him."

"*This* time you did," he said, his voice full of reproach. "Eden told you that Drake could use mortals to get to you, but you still thought it was a good idea to go and have your fortune told?"

"It was only meant to be a bit of fun," Tania said defensively.

"Fun?" he snapped back. "The King of Faerie has lost his wife; your sisters have lost their mother. We should be searching for the Queen but instead of that, you're out here having fun with that idiot friend of yours? How could you be that stupid?"

"I couldn't come to Richmond with you today after my dad found I'd gone out last night," she reminded him coldly. "And I don't like being told I'm stupid, Edric. I'm doing my best. You have no idea how hard this is for me."

"And is it easy for me?" he asked. "Trapped in this benighted world, knowing that I can get back home only with your help. Knowing that you've spent your whole life among these people, that you're surrounded here by all the things you grew up with. Watching you grow more comfortable here all the time, afraid that . . . that . . ." His voice trailed off.

"Afraid of what?" Tania asked, her throat tight with anger.

"Afraid that the quest for the Queen will grow less and less important to you the more time you spend here," he burst out. "Afraid that you'll choose to stay here with your Mortal parents and your Mortal friends—afraid that the Faerie part of you will be lost."

She studied him without speaking. Didn't he trust her to keep her promise to Oberon that she would find Titania? Did he think she would forget all about it?

When she finally spoke, her voice was thick with hurt. "I have no intention of abandoning the search for Titania," she said. "And as for the other thing . . . If you don't understand how much my mum and dad mean to me, then you don't know me at all." She began to tremble. "I have enough problems to deal with right now without you making me feel even worse."

"As do I," Edric said, a hint of Faerie formality coming into his voice. "The difference between us, Tania, is that my loyalties are clear." Tania's head spun as she felt a horrible gulf yawn between them. "Where do you want to be?" he asked. "In this cursed place, or in Faerie? You're going to have to make the choice one day. Let me know when you decide."

He turned and walked quickly away, soon becoming lost in the crowds.

Tania stared after him, feeling quite numb. It was

as if the sky had come crashing down on her and she had been left standing in the smoking rubble of her life.

"Hey!" It was Jade. "Trouble in paradise?"

Tania closed her eyes, fitting the shrapnel of her brain back together again, preparing herself for her best friend's inquisitiveness. She took a deep breath and walked back to the table. She sat down and scooped up her paper cup of Coke. The melting ice rattled as she sucked at the straw.

Jade was watching her intently. "If that was a sample of what being in love is like, count me out!" she said.

"What do you mean?"

"Look at you," Jade replied. "All grim-faced and angry. I'll tell you what you need, girlfriend! You need some fun. Listen, dump Cedric and play the field for a while. Get a life!"

"I have a life," Tania said tersely.

A life? She had *two* lives—that was the problem.

"Oh, really?" Jade persisted. "I've seen you when you think no one is watching. You look like you've got the weight of the whole world on your shoulders. That can't be right. Look, it's the summer holidays in a few days. Get rid of Evan, have some laughs, go wild. Act like you're sixteen for once."

Tania looked at her without speaking, desperately wishing things were that simple.

"You've got very weird lately, you know," Jade said, and her voice was uncharacteristically serious. "What really happened to you while you were missing? Come on, I want the truth."

"The truth?" Tania said levelly. "Okay. The truth is I went into another world and found out that I'm a Faerie princess."

Jade gave a snort of laughter. "Good one! And Evan is a prince, I suppose?"

"No, not exactly. But he lives in the Royal Palace."

Jade gave a curt sweep of her hand. "Fine!" she said. "Forget I asked."

Tania smiled tiredly. "You see?" she said. "I tell you the truth and you don't believe me."

VII

School. Monday. Late afternoon. The assembly hall.
"Okay, that went well on the whole. But I want you to keep working on those lines, and think about the meaning of the words. A few of you are still spouting Shakespeare's immortal verse like you're reading the cafeteria lunch menu. Technical rehearsal tomorrow; next rehearsal for the performers is Wednesday after school. No excuses, please. We're coming up to the line now, people, so keep your energy levels up. Okay, off you go. Evan and Anita, I'd like a quick word with the two of you, please."

Tania wasn't surprised that Mrs. Wiseman wanted to speak to them. Their performances had not been good.

The swing doors flapped shut on the last of the others. Edric and Tania stood slightly too obviously apart, not looking at each other, their body language awkward and wrong.

Mrs. Wiseman was sitting on a chair by the wall, making notes in her play script.

After a few moments of Tania conspicuously not looking at Edric and being very aware that Edric was avoiding looking at her, Mrs. Wiseman lifted her head and gazed from one to the other. "Would you like to tell me what that was all about?" She tapped the script. "I don't remember anything in the stage notes for Act Three, Scene Five, that says Romeo and Juliet can't even stand to look at each other. Quite the opposite, in fact. They're supposed to be madly in love by then. So what went wrong this afternoon?"

Neither of them spoke.

Mrs. Wiseman sighed. "Look, if the two of you have some personal issues to sort out, then go off somewhere else and do it. Fast."

"I'm sorry," Edric said. "You're right. I was—"

"We won't let it happen again," Tania interrupted. "Don't worry about it."

Mrs. Wiseman's eyes widened in mock surprise. "Worry? Me? With the performance only four days away and half the costumes still to be finished and the scenery not done and my two leading actors doing love scenes as if they're at the wrong end of a bad marriage? Why should I worry? Everything will be fine; we'll make history. It'll be the first production of *Romeo and Juliet* where the two lovers have a fistfight in the final scene."

"We get the point," Tania said testily.

"I'm glad to hear it." Mrs. Wiseman dropped her

eyes to her script again, giving a dismissive wave of her hand. "Wednesday, three thirty. And *try* to act like you're fond of each other."

Tania walked to the door. She was intensely aware of Edric walking a couple of paces behind her. She felt it the way a stalked animal knows when danger is near; it made her face burn and her stomach harden into a painful knot. It made her clumsy, fumbling at the door handle, wanting more than anything in the world to be out of there, away from Edric—anywhere but right here and right now.

She couldn't understand where all her anger was coming from. It made her want to lash out, and it made her want to curl up in a ball and wallow in the pain.

How could Edric not understand how difficult this was for her, torn between this world and the demands of her Faerie heritage?

Neither of them spoke as they walked down the corridor.

If only he'd say something; take back what he had said, apologize for doubting her. She ignored the small voice in her head: *You should speak first.*

No! Never! He hurt me. He has to make the first move.

She came into the entrance lobby with its colorful murals and crowded bulletin boards. Beyond the glass doors she could see the teachers' parking lot, almost empty now, and beyond that, the main gates. Her dad's car was parked at the curb. She knew Edric would go out of one of the side exits to avoid him. But there was still time to put this right.

She stopped in the middle of the lobby, not turning, but waiting for him to catch up with her. Giving him the opportunity to speak.

A chasm of absolute silence yawned behind her. At last she couldn't stand it anymore. She spun on her heel.

He was gone.

Okay, be like that. I don't care. She shoved her way through the doors and ran across the parking lot, unshed tears burning behind her eyes.

I don't care!

For long stretches over the next twenty-four hours, Tania kept her phone switched off so Edric couldn't contact her. Then she would relent and turn it on, hoping desperately for messages from him. There were never any. Her moods swung from misery and despair to a kind of crazy euphoria. Good riddance to him and to everything to do with him. She was better off without all that stuff. She owed them *nothing*. Hadn't she already done enough? She'd brought back the sunshine into Faerie—she'd ended the Long Twilight, or whatever they called it. What more did they expect from her? Let someone else find Titania.

On top of that, she longed to feel safe from Gabriel Drake. She was haunted by thoughts of him; her head filled with vivid memories of his silky, evil voice and of his deadly shining eyes. And a new thought came to her in her moments of desolation: If she turned her back on Faerie—on Oberon and Edric and her sisters and on the quest for Titania—then maybe she'd finally be rid of Gabriel as well. Free of him and of Faerie and of everything that was causing her all this torment and pain.

But then there were the times when she longed to be in Edric's arms, to tell him how frightened and confused she was, to have him say something that would make everything right again.

She managed to avoid seeing Edric all day at school on Tuesday. It was a relief, but it was agonizing as well. These emotional swings were almost becoming a normal part of her now; it was hard for her to remember when she last felt complete and content within her own skin.

School was over, and she and Jade were heading for the exit with a bunch of other people when suddenly Edric appeared around a corner ahead. Tania felt herself tensing up. She avoided eye contact as they approached each other. Some people barged past and Edric bumped against her. She didn't glance at him, didn't even acknowledge him.

"Hmmm," Jade said. "That was interesting."

"What was?"

"Oh, nothing. So, no rehearsals with lover boy today?"

"Tomorrow," Tania said, tight-lipped.

Jade peered into her face as they walked along the corridor. "Getting on okay, are you—you and Cedric?"

"Fine and dandy," Tania said in a flat voice, using one of her father's expressions. *Fine and dandy*.

"Well, that's good, then. Is that why you're so cheerful, little Miss Sunshine and Lollipops?"

"I'm perfectly okay, thanks," Tania said.

"I don't think so," Jade said. "In fact, I think it's time for Nurse Jade to prescribe a cure." She linked her arm with Tania's. "And I've had a brilliant idea. You're coming with Mum and Dad and me to Florida."

"Good plan, Jade," Tania said, deadpan. "Are you going to check me in with the luggage, or were you planning on squeezing me into your backpack and stuffing me in the overhead bin?"

"Okay, that was very sarcastic," Jade said, "but you've been under a big emotional strain recently, so I forgive you." She squeezed Tania's arm. "Now listen to how this is going to work. Dan called from uni last night. He's finally made up his mind to go with his pals on some kind of spiritual trek across India. I think he wants to sit in the lotus position on a mountaintop and play finger-cymbals or something equally bizarre. The point is, we now have a spare ticket for the flight and a spare bed in the apartment, all booked and paid for. My folks said it would be totally cool for you to come with us." She looked at Tania. "What do you say? Is that the answer to all your prayers or what? Am I the best pal you've ever had in the entire world ever? Answer the last question first."

Tania had come to a stunned halt in the middle of the corridor. "Florida?" she said, gasping.

"Yes. You'll get away from all your problems and have some top-of-the-range fun with a flat-out party girl." Jade peered at her and then frowned. "Oh, come on, you don't need to take a vote on it!" she said. "This is a once-in-a-lifetime offer."

"I'll have to ask my mum and dad," Tania said dazedly. "They're expecting me to go to Cornwall with them."

"Hmmm." Jade tapped her lips with an extended finger. "Let me see. Cornwall with your folks or Florida with me? Which sounds like more fun?"

Tania had to laugh. "I'll talk to them this evening," she said.

"Do that," said Jade. "But don't kid yourself, girl. You *are* coming to Florida with me, and that's final."

"Are you sure you're okay with this?" Tania asked, looking from her mother to her father and back again. They had accepted the idea of her going to Florida with the Andersons so easily that it had taken her by surprise.

"If that's what you'd like to do, then we're fine with it," her mother said. She raised a finger. "In principle, that is," she added. "We'll need to have a chat with Tony and Miranda and iron out all the details, but I think you'd be completely barmy not to take them up on their offer."

They were in the kitchen with their used dinner plates in front of them. Tania had left it till after the meal before she had launched the idea, in case it went down badly.

"I'll give Miranda a ring right now," Mrs. Palmer said, getting up. "I know Jade told you they don't expect you to pay for the trip, but we're certainly going to give them something for the flight and for your keep." She raised her eyebrows. "Dan has decided he wants to be an Indian mystic, has he?"

"Something like that," Tania said.

"Strange boy," she said as she headed for the living room. "Still, Tony and Miranda must be pleased he's finally settled on a career path."

Tania looked at her father. "*Are* you okay with this?" she asked quietly.

He took a long breath. "Not entirely," he said. "But I'm not going to stop you." His face became stern. "But remember, we're trusting you to behave responsibly. You can't go wild just because you're on the other side of the Atlantic."

Tania lowered her head. "I won't."

"See that you don't."

A tense silence descended. Tania got up and began to clear the table.

A couple of minutes later her mother came back into the kitchen. "Well, Miranda seems perfectly happy," she said. She looked at Tania. "You realize we're heading off to Cornwall on Monday, don't you? That means a night here on your own." She smiled. "Are you sure you can be trusted to behave yourself and not throw a wild party the moment we leave the house?"

Tania glanced uneasily at her father. His face was concerned, but he didn't say anything.

"I promise to behave myself," Tania said. "And it's only half a night, anyway. Jade's parents are coming over to pick me up at four in the morning."

She shooed her parents out of the kitchen and filled the dishwasher. She felt as if a big load had been lifted off her. Next Tuesday she'd be getting on a plane and flying away from all her troubles for two sun-soaked weeks of fun and chaos with Jade. It was exactly what she wanted: a chance to clear her brain, to forget all about Queen Titania and Faerie and everything that went with it. The chance to get far away from the fear that Gabriel Drake was going to reach across the worlds and drag her to her doom.

But it would also be two weeks without Edric.

She slammed the dishwasher closed and set the program. She leaned over the worktop, her hands spread on the surface, her head down. Two weeks without Edric.

I won't miss him. I won't even think about him.

She ran upstairs to call Jade. Her friend would have plenty to say—plenty of plans to make—and with Jade's voice buzzing in her head, she wouldn't have any room to think about Edric.

She threw herself across the bed and grabbed up

her canvas shoulder bag, foraging around in it for her phone.

Her fingers made contact with something unexpected, something small and rounded and silky.

Puzzled, she sat up, pulling the bag into her lap and opening the flap.

"Oh!" She lifted the thing out. It was a white rose on a long thornless stem. "Beautiful," she murmured, holding the curled satiny petals to her nose and sniffing. Her eyes widened. The rose smelled of Faerie.

"Edric!"

He must have slipped it into her bag when he had bumped against her in the corridor.

She heard the double *bleep* of an incoming text. Rolling the rose across her lips and breathing in the enchanting scent, she reached into the bag for her phone.

It was a message from Edric. A single word. SORRY.

Tania let out a sigh, her heart melting as she gazed at the screen of her phone, all the anger and hurt and resentfulness draining out of her.

"You idiot!" she murmured under her breath, not sure whether she was referring to herself or to Edric.

Her fingers played over the keypad.

SO AM I. SPEAK TOMORROW.

She pressed SEND and rolled onto her back, still holding the rose to her lips.

Sometimes it only took a little thing to make life perfect.

Sometimes all it took was a white rose from Faerie and a one-word text message.

It was lunchtime the following day. Tania and Edric were sitting together on a bench in a quiet part of the school grounds.

"How about we promise never to fight again?" Tania said as the two of them dipped plastic forks into a prepacked tub of tuna and sweet corn salad.

"Fine with me," Edric said.

"That's a deal, then." She looked at him. "You do know I never intended to stop looking for Titania, don't you?"

"Of course I do," he said. "I don't know why I was so mad at you about that. I guess it was because I got so freaked out when you told me about the fortune-teller; the rest kind of went on from there."

"Do you think I gave Gabriel an opening?" she asked quietly. "I've been frightened to death every time I've gone to sleep since it happened, but I haven't dreamed about him again."

"I think you opened the door to him just a crack," Edric said. "But you beat him in the end; you slammed it right in his face. That's a good thing."

"I escaped by the skin of my teeth, you mean," Tania said with a wry smile. "Next time I might not be so lucky."

"Then we need to make sure there isn't a next time," Edric said. "We're in this together. We'll keep you safe from Drake, and we'll find the Queen."

She smiled and rested her head on his shoulder. "And you really don't mind that I'm going to Florida for a fortnight?"

He shook his head. "It'll do you good to get away for a while."

"We'll start searching for Titania again the moment I get back. We'll have her address and telephone number within a week."

"Is that a promise?"

"You bet it is," she said, lifting another forkful to her mouth. For some reason that casually spoken sentence flashed in her head like a neon sign. *We'll have her address and telephone number within a week.*

Suddenly a thought struck her and she sat bolt upright, staring into the distance. "There's something we've totally forgotten," she said breathlessly. "Titania sent me the Soul Book, didn't she?"

"Yes, I think we can assume she did."

"So she knows my address."

Edric's eyes widened. "So why hasn't she just knocked on your front door and asked to see you?"

"Exactly!" Tania said. "She's been keeping track of me for the past five hundred years, she sends me my Soul Book as a sixteenth-birthday present, and then? Nothing! How weird is that?"

"There has to be a reason," Edric said. "While you were in hospital, did anyone call at your house? Anyone your parents didn't know?"

Tania shrugged. "They never mentioned it."

"Did you ask them?"

"Well, no. . . ."

"Perhaps you should."

Tania looked at him. "Yes. Perhaps I should."

They had a full dress-rehearsal run-through of the play after school that day. Everyone was twitchy. The nurse forgot her lines. Mercutio tripped over his sword, and part of the scenery fell over onto one of the actors.

Apart from that—and apart from the fact that Tania was anxious for the rehearsal to be over so she could go home and ask her parents the vital question—everything went fine.

She phoned home to let her dad know he didn't need to pick her up; the mother of the boy playing Tybalt had offered her a lift to her door.

She dumped her bag in the hall and went through into the living room. Her parents were watching the news on television.

"How was the dress rehearsal?" her father asked.

"So-so," Tania said. "Mrs. Wiseman practically had a coronary when a piece of the trellis nearly flattened Peter Cray, but apart from that it was okay."

She perched on the arm of the couch. "I was wondering," she said. "Did anyone come to the house asking about me when . . . when I wasn't here?"

Her mother raised her eyebrows. "You mean apart from the police and friends and neighbors?" she said. "No, not that I can remember."

"There was that odd thing with the posh car,"

Tania's father said, his attention still mostly on the news.

"What odd thing?" Tania asked, keeping her voice calm despite her excitement. "What posh car?"

Her father tore his eyes away from the screen. "It was a black Lexus with tinted windows," he told her. "It came here the night after your birthday. Your mother was upstairs, lying down. Betty Howe had popped in from next door. She answered the door, actually. I had a quick look out of the window, just to see who it was. The chap who rang the bell looked like some kind of chauffeur—you know, gray uniform, peaked cap. He had a few words with Betty then went back to the car. There was someone in the back, because he tapped on the window and someone from inside opened it."

"Did you see who was inside?" Tania said.

"Not really; it was too far away."

"Do you know what they wanted?" Tania asked.

"Betty said the driver asked if you were here. 'Is Miss Anita Palmer at home?' he said, very formal, apparently. Betty told him that you'd gone missing the day before and no one knew where you were. And that was that."

"And the car never came back?" Tania asked.

"Not as far as I know," her father replied. "Do you know who it was, then?"

Tania shook her head. "Not a clue."

"So why the sudden interest?"

"No reason," Tania said, bounding off the couch. "I'm starving."

"Cannelloni in the fridge," her mother called after her as she headed for the kitchen. "Two minutes in the microwave will be enough."

"Thanks," Tania called back as she scooped up her bag and ran into the kitchen. But she wasn't thinking of food. Someone in a really expensive car—someone with a *chauffeur*—had called on her the day after her sixteenth birthday.

The waitress in Richmond had said that the woman with the red hair and green eyes was wearing a designer business suit. Was the owner of the Lexus the same person who had ordered an espresso and filled in the address on a big manila envelope while she drank it?

Was the Queen of the Faeries a successful businessperson in present-day London?

VIII

After lunch on Thursday Tania, Edric, and the other students involved with the play met with Mrs. Wiseman by the front gates of the school and, after a quick head count, set off to the Underground station for the field trip to the Globe Theatre. Half an hour and one change of trains later they came out of Mansion House station and set off across Southwark Bridge to the south bank of the Thames.

Despite living her entire life in London, Tania had never previously visited the Globe Theatre, and she was looking forward to exploring the modern reconstruction of William Shakespeare's famous sixteenth-century "Wooden O."

Walking across the bridge with Edric at her side, she gazed down into the murky waters of the Thames. She was struck by how different it looked from the clear blue waters of the Tamesis. The Faerie river followed the same curves and loops as the Thames, except that in the Mortal World the river wound through the noisy, dirty heart of London while in Faerie the vast Royal Palace stretched along its northern bank, with a great green forest to the south.

Tania was very impressed by her first sight of the Globe Theatre. It was a tall, circular building, oak-built and reed-thatched and with lime-washed walls that gleamed white in the sunlight. It stood in the middle of a complex of other smaller buildings: shops, cafés, and restaurants, an education center, and a brick-built indoor theatre for winter and bad weather.

"This way, everyone, keep up," Mrs. Wiseman called, taking them along a riverside walkway to the exhibition center. The Globe Exhibition spread over two floors, with large-screen televisions that ran continuous videos and displays that explained the roles of actors and musicians both in Elizabethan times and in modern day.

Once they had toured the center and the theatre itself Mrs. Wiseman allowed them to split up and explore on their own.

"Let's go and look in the theatre again," Edric suggested to Tania.

She nodded and the two of them made their way around to the entry foyer. They pushed through the heavy glass doors and took the stairway that led up to cafés and a wide piazza. There was a matinee performance of *A Midsummer Night's Dream* later in the afternoon, and the piazza was busy with people enjoy-

ing the sunshine while they waited for the announce-
ment to take their seats.

"It's nice to be on our own at last," Tania said as
they climbed one of the external stair towers that led
to the upper seating levels. "This is an amazing place."
They entered the theatre in the Middle Gallery and
then moved down through the rings of padded seats
to stand at the wooden balustrade.

From here they could look down into the round
open-air auditorium. Two sturdy pillars rose from
either side of the rectangular stage, holding up a flat
roof that was topped with a thatched gable. All the
woodwork of the stage had been painted to look like
marble and stonework, the carved oak picked out in
dark grays and browns and forest greens and deep,
russet reds. Above the stage was a long balcony for
musicians and actors—a balcony from which Tania
imagined Juliet might lean when she heard Romeo's
voice on the night of their first romantic meeting.

But Tania couldn't think too much about the
school play; she had other things on her mind.

"It must have been Titania in the Lexus," she said
to Edric. "Do you know how expensive those cars
are?" She shook her head. "I don't honestly know
what I expected Titania to be like when we found her.
I never really gave it much thought. But I suppose I
imagined her living in an old house like Miss
Haversham in *Great Expectations*, all alone and a bit
crazy maybe and wearing royal clothes that had got
all moth-eaten and ragged over the years. I never

imagined her cruising around London in a chauffeur-driven luxury car."

Edric smiled at her, leaning with one elbow on the balustrade. "She's a Queen, Tania," he said. "The daughter of an ancient Faerie House. She's not going to be sitting around in a tatty cardigan, drinking tea out of a cracked cup and watching daytime television."

"I suppose not." Tania stood upright. She looked at her watch. "We'd better make our way to the front to meet up with the others." She put her hand on his arm. "I know we were going to hold off the search till I got back from Florida, but I can't. Not now."

He looked inquiringly at her. "So?"

"I'll get away on Saturday," she said. "I'll tell Mum and Dad I'm going shopping for holiday stuff. As long as I buy something in Richmond while we're there, it won't be a lie."

"And this time we'll keep our eyes open for a black Lexus," Edric said.

They made their way to the back of the gallery and started down the stairs that led out to the piazza.

Halfway down Tania paused, intending to ask Edric whether they had theatres like this in Faerie. But as she turned her head everything began to spin in front of her eyes. The staircase twisted and tipped and everything around her blurred and streamed like watercolor images being washed away by rain. She groped blindly for the banister, her feet stumbling on the shifting treads.

She was vaguely aware of Edric's face: a blob of pale color, his mouth a dark circle opening and closing soundlessly. Then her legs gave way underneath her and she sat down heavily on the stairs, the dense air clogging her ears, ringing in her head.

She closed her eyes, gasping for breath, but her throat felt tight and constricted and the air was thin and painful in her lungs. She coughed—a cough from deep down in her chest, a cough that hurt her throat and made her head throb.

"Mistress Ann! Mistress Ann! How you do misbehave, child!"

It was a warm voice, a woman's voice, filled with urgency and concern. A hand took Tania's wrist and she was pulled to her feet.

She opened her eyes. Her surroundings were similar, but strangely different. The woodwork of the stair tower seemed older and the stair treads were more worn, as if from many years of use.

A plump woman stood on the stairs below her, a woman she had never seen before. And yet . . .

The woman was dressed in a floor-length red frock, her face as round and rosy as an apple, her hair gathered up under a white pleated cap.

Tania gazed dizzily at her. The woman was huge; even standing three treads below her on the stairs, she was Tania's height as she pulled her to her feet.

Dazed, Tania blinked and stared around her. More giant people were moving up the stairs, and all were dressed in Elizabethan clothes.

"You are a caution and no mistake." A plump finger wagged in her face. "Come now, your father did tell you most specifically that you were not to wander and get under foot." And so saying, the huge woman started to tow Tania down the stairs.

And that was when Tania realized that she was no longer in her own body. She had shrunk, dwindled away to almost nothing, her arms and legs stick-thin under her child's dress.

The world had not grown huge around her; she was *smaller*, and she knew somehow that she was also much younger. But how much younger? It was hard to tell. Ten years old, maybe?

The woman drew her out of the way of the constant tide of people.

Tania coughed again, a pain burning in her narrow chest.

"Hearken to you now!" the woman said anxiously. "There's your punishment for gadding about the place, and you only a few hours up and about after three days a-bed with the ague, child." The woman's voice was full of affectionate concern. "I told your father it was a mistake to bring you here, but the master will not hearken to the likes of me when his mind is made up." A large warm hand was applied to Tania's forehead. "I can feel the fever in you still, Mistress Ann, truly I can. Will ye sit here quietly for a moment?"

Tania stared at the woman, her vision blurred, her head throbbing. "Who are you?" she murmured.

"Bless me, the child is wandering in her head," the woman said. "Do you not know your own Bess, child? Your loving Bess, who has taken such pains over you since first your mother gave me charge of you to cosset you and care for you and fret over you all the waking hours of your life?"

Tania smiled. "Bess," she said softly, and there was strange comfort in the name, although she had no idea why. "Bess."

"That's it, my poppet," said the woman. "It's your Bess here, and I'd as soon take you straight back to your bed, but the master was most insistent that you be allowed to see him on the stage, and he'll take it ill if I disobey him." Bess crouched down, her hands heavy on Tania's shoulders. "I shall take you to the side of the stage," she said in a conspiratorial voice. "You may watch your father for a few moments, but then I will take you back to your bed and call a physick to tend you, and let the sky fall on me for my temerity if I have acted wrongly and done anything to cause you harm."

Bess got laboriously to her feet again, puffing hard. Tania took her hand, feeling the weighty love of the big woman as they walked together along the curved wooden corridor.

She did feel weak. She could easily believe that she had been ill, that she was still unwell. The pain was like a fire burning in her chest; every now and then it would flare and burn into her throat and she would be wracked by fits of coughing.

She allowed Bess to lead her onward until they came to a narrow place surrounded by costumed men who were all looking in the same direction. Beyond an entrance of angled wooden slats Tania saw the stage and the auditorium, the vertical galleries filled with people, the circular standing area teeming with a silent throng.

Her eyes were drawn upward. The ceiling of the stage was extraordinary: midnight blue panels were ribbed with gold and painted with suns and stars and moons and all the signs of the zodiac. But then her attention was taken by a tall, handsome man who stood alone, center-stage, dressed in ermine and velvet and with a crown upon his head.

"Father!" she heard herself whisper. "That's my father. . . ."

The man began to speak, his voice rolling confidently over the rapt audience. "Now is the winter of our discontent/Made glorious summer by this sun of York . . ."

Bess brought her mouth close to Tania's ear.

"There he is now," she whispered. "Richard Burbage himself, your great thespian father. Does he not look magnificent in his robes and with the crown upon his head?" An arm circled her shoulders. "I tell you, my poppet, your father is the finest actor ever to perform before the Queen."

Tania gazed into the big round face. "Do you mean Titania?"

"Bless you no, child," said Bess with a throaty

chuckle. "I mean Her Grace the good Queen Elizabeth, may God preserve her."

"Oh." Tania was beginning to feel as if things were
drifting away from her. "That's a pity. I thought
you meant Titania . . . only I've been looking for
Titania . . . and I thought . . . maybe . . ."

"Tania?" The voice was a blur of unfocused sound
that boomed in her ears like distant thunder. "Tania?
Are you okay?"

"Edric?" Tania had the bizarre sensation of
expanding inside her own body like a butterfly straining at its cocoon, like she was about to burst right out
of her own skin. She let out a yelp of pain and then a
gasp as the unpleasant feeling fell away from her.

She opened her eyes and found herself sitting on
the wooden stairs in the Globe Theatre with Edric
kneeling in front of her.

"What happened?" Tania asked.

"You tell me," said Edric, helping her to her feet.
"Are you okay now? Can you stand up on your own?"

"Yes. I'm fine."

"Did you faint?"

Tania looked at him. "No, I didn't faint," she said.
"Let's get out of here."

Tania and Edric were sitting in the piazza outside the
theatre. Tania had just finished telling him, as clearly
as she could, what had happened to her.

"Well?" she said. "What do you make of it?"

"I think you just had a flashback to one of your

previous mortal lives," Edric said quietly. "You were in Elizabethan times, you said?"

Tania nodded. "The woman called Bess mentioned Queen Elizabeth," she said. "But I felt so ill, Edric. And I was so thin. Bess said I'd been ill for three days. She only let me out of bed because my father wanted me to see him on stage." She gripped Edric's hand. "I've got the most horrible feeling about her," she said. "I don't think she got better. I think she died, Edric. I think I *died*."

Edric took her hands. "You already knew you'd lived a lot of mortal lives before now," he said soothingly.

"Yes, I did," Tania said. "But there's a big difference between being told about it and actually finding myself inside the skin of one of my previous selves." She gave a shudder. "How many times have I lived and died, Edric? How many people have I been?"

IX

"A glooming peace this morning with it brings;
The sun, for sorrow, will not show his head:
Go hence, to have more talk of these sad things:
Some shall be pardon'd, and some punished:
For never was a story of more woe
Than this of Juliet and her Romeo."

Tania was on stage, lying across Edric with her eyes closed. The play had reached its tragic climax and both of them were dead, Romeo by drinking poison, Juliet by a self-inflicted stab wound. She listened to the moment of absolute silence that followed the Prince's closing speech, and then couldn't help but grin widely as she heard the applause come rolling over the stage from the packed hall.

She opened one eye and saw the red velvet curtains sweep across the front of the stage, blocking out the view of the audience but allowing the applause and the cheering to come welling through.

There was a mad scramble to clear the stage. Mrs. Wiseman was in the wings, urging them off. "Brilliant!" she was saying, her face split by a gigantic smile. "You were all absolutely brilliant!"

The next few minutes passed in a whirl for Tania. She was aware of standing crowded together with the other performers in the wing of the stage, her hand tightly holding Edric's hand, her heart pounding, the blood singing like angels in her ears. In front of her people peeled off, running onto the stage to take their bows.

There was a push in her back and she and Edric ran into the open space in the middle of the stage. The entire audience was on its feet, cheering and clapping and whistling. Tania and Edric bowed low.

They stood up and the rest of the cast moved forward to stand level with them, linking hands to take another bow. The curtain swept closed in front of them.

The stage lights dimmed. Gradually the applause died down to a few final whistles and shouts, and then there was the noise of people getting up to leave, the voices an excited hubbub of noise beyond the curtain.

"That was wonderful," Mrs. Wiseman said. "I'm so proud of you! You've all worked really hard."

Then there was the rush to get through the constricted space of the wings, down the back stairs, and along to the basement storeroom where they could get changed. A makeshift screen had been set up to separate the boys from the girls. Still trembling with excitement, Tania stepped out of her gown and climbed into her ordinary clothes.

There were refreshments set up on a table. She didn't feel in the least bit hungry, but she had a long swig of orange juice. She saw Edric at the other end of the room, chatting to some of the other cast members.

He spotted her watching him. He grinned and waved, and mouthed, "I'll be with you in a second." She nodded, blissfully happy.

The principal came to congratulate everyone. Mrs. Wiseman was buzzing around, thanking everyone all over again.

"Are you coming for a pizza with the rest of us?" Tania was asked.

"Yes. Of course I am," she said. "Just give me a minute." She needed to find her parents first. They had been watching her from the far end of the third row. She had caught sight of them very early on, but from then on she had deliberately avoided looking toward that part of the audience and did her best to forget they were there at all. For her, parents and performing didn't mix; they made her feel too self-conscious.

She edged her way through the milling people and came out into the corridor like a cork coming out of a bottle. More people were out there—students with their parents, guests, teachers, school governors, all chatting excitedly about the performance.

"You were marvelous, Anita!"

"Thanks, Mrs. Taylor."

She saw her parents making their way along the corridor.

"A star is born!" called her father, opening his arms as she ran forward.

"Did you enjoy it?" she asked, gathered in a hug by both parents.

"It was stunning, truly it was," said her mother.

Tania beamed. "The others are heading off for a pizza. I said I'd go with them."

Her parents didn't respond and Tania's smile faded as she looked into their faces.

"Is there a problem?"

"Will Evan be going with you?" her mother asked.

Tania gave a surprised laugh. "I should think so," she said. "They're hardly going to forget Romeo. He's not really dead, you know. He was just acting."

"Then we'd rather you came home with us," her mother said, ignoring her joke.

Tania stared at her. *Miss the after-play celebrations?* They had to be kidding.

"We think it's for the best," her father added. "You know why."

Tania frowned. "Listen, I know you don't want me seeing Evan, but this isn't a *date*. There'll be about fifteen of us there. It's not like we're going to sneak off around the back for a quick snog."

"You're still under curfew," said her mother, and there was a sharp tone in her voice. "You agreed to our terms, home by nine at the latest." She glanced at her watch. "It's nearly ten now."

"I don't believe this," Tania hissed. "You'd actually stop me going out to celebrate with the others because of a stupid curfew?"

She saw the eye-line of her mother and father shift. They were both looking at something over her shoulder—and from their stony expressions, she could guess who they were looking at.

She turned. Edric was heading along the crowded corridor toward them.

Tania walked to meet him, stopping him in his tracks. "This isn't a good time," she warned.

He glanced at her parents. "Trouble?" he asked. "I thought I'd come and say hello."

She shook her head. "Not now. They don't want me to go to the pizza parlor with the rest of you."

"That's not fair."

"I know, but there's nothing I can do about it," Tania said. "Remember, you and I are going to Richmond tomorrow. I don't want to have a big row with my parents now. It's not worth it."

Edric hesitated.

"Please!" she said, pressing her hand against his chest. "Just go. Tell the others I've got a headache."

Edric shot a final bleak glance at her parents before pushing his way back along the corridor. Tania took a deep breath then turned and walked back to where her mother and father were waiting.

"Okay," she said, her voice cold and clipped. "You win. Let's get out of here."

She stalked ahead of them along the corridor. She managed to fake a smile and a pleasant response for the few people she met on the way to the car.

She climbed into the back, sitting very stiff and tense as her mother and father got in.

Her mother turned to look at her. "I'm very sorry if we've upset you," she said. "But you agreed that you would stop seeing that boy outside school."

"Yes," Tania said sharply. "I did. So?"

"Oh, please," her mother said. "I saw how you were with him just then. At least you'll have no reason to see him for the next few weeks now that the term is over. And perhaps when you come back from Florida, your head will have cleared a bit."

"What's that supposed to mean?" Tania said.

"It means you're obviously not over him yet," said her mother. "You need to make a clean break."

"Hey, let's not start an argument," said her father. "We've just had an amazing evening. Let's not ruin it."

"It's not me who's ruining it," Tania said.

The rest of the journey passed in a simmering, resentful silence. Tania just wanted to get home and get away from her parents before she said some things she would regret.

They were almost home when her mother broke the silence.

"I will not apologize for preventing you from seeing that boy," she said.

"Why are you being like this?" It irritated Tania that her voice sounded so shrill.

"I'm being like this because you obviously have a crush on him, Anita," said her mother. "And until you get it out of your system, it's our duty as your parents to stop you from doing any more stupid and dangerous things because of him."

"Don't call me Anita. My name's Tania."

"Then listen to me, *Tania*. The bottom line is you're still a child, and as long as you live under our roof, you will obey our rules."

Mr. Palmer pulled into the curb and stopped the car. Incandescent with rage, Tania threw the car door open. "I am not a child!" she screamed, struggling out of the car and standing on the pavement, glaring in at her mother. "For heaven's sake, don't you know who I am?"

Her mother opened her door and stepped out of the car. "You know," she said, and her voice was horribly calm and quiet, "there are times when I really don't."

Tania stormed into her bedroom and slammed the door. Panting and shaking with rage, she walked toward the window. Halfway, she made a small side step.

She stood there, silent and still and moon-bathed in the upper room of Bonwn Tyr. She felt exhausted by anger, twisted and wrenched and warped by it.

For heaven's sake, don't you know who I am?

In her rage, she had come close to blurting out the truth: *You can't treat me like this. I am a princess of Faerie!*

She looked over her shoulder, imagining her parents coming up to her room, opening the door, finding . . . nothing.

"I don't care," she said aloud. "Let them!"

She turned and ran down the spiral stair. She crossed the stone floor and opened the door. Shreds of white cloud scudded across the starry sky. The moon was shining down between the branches of the aspen trees, so big and full that it stopped her in her tracks. She reached up with both arms, curling her fingers so that it looked as if she was holding the moon between her hands.

She stepped out of the grove of trees. The palace glowed with lights: Amber and orange and red and warm yellow. A nightingale piped from somewhere nearby. Another answered from farther off, its high clear voice rippling through the crystal air.

Feeling like a sailor cast onto a serene green island in the aftermath of a shipwreck, Tania began to walk down toward the palace. She had not gone far when she noticed a small dark shape moving up the hill toward her. She paused, peering down the long moonlit slope.

It was an animal. A horse, maybe? No, not a horse. She could see wide branching antlers growing up from its head.

A stag!

Delighted and intrigued, she sat on the grass and waited as it came closer. Now she could hear the steady thud of its hooves on the turf. Now she could see the rough brown fur and the black cloven fore-hooves rising and falling. She could see the muscles bunching under the skin. She could see the huge dark eyes and the steady nod of the head.

The magnificent creature came to a halt in front of her. It lowered its head and snorted, moonlight reflecting silver in its wise eyes.

"Hello there," Tania said, reaching out carefully to stroke the velvet soft muzzle.

The stag snorted again and nudged her hand with its head, one forehoof striking the ground impatiently.

Tania got to her feet. The animal walked a slow, stately circle around her and then waited, facing the palace.

"You want me to ride you?" Tania guessed.

A nod of the heavy head. A snort.

"I don't even know if I can get onto your back." She was wearing jeans, but the stag seemed dauntingly tall, although it was clearly waiting for her to climb on.

"Okay," she said. "I hope I don't hurt you." She threw her arms over the broad back, then flexed her knees and sprang. She wasn't quite sure how she managed it, but somehow she found herself with her feet clear of the ground, sprawled across the creature's bony back. She wriggled and squirmed and managed to get one leg over the stag. Then it was just a case of evening up her posture and using her hands to lift herself into a sitting position.

Tania sat astride the stag, her feet dangling, the

spine making a somewhat uncomfortable ridge underneath her. She had her palms spread out flat on the animal's shoulders. The antlers rose up like many-fingered hands in front of her eyes. With a final snort, as if of approval, the creature began to trot back down the hill the way it had come.

Tania was not comfortable. She didn't even feel particularly safe, perched up there on that broad, lumpy back while the trotting animal jounced her up and down like a rag doll. But she didn't fall off, and all the time, the palace was drawing nearer.

The thud of hooves on grass changed to the crunching of gravel as the stag made its way through the gardens. They approached the gatehouse and Tania saw a slender figure standing at the head of the steps that led to the arched doors.

"Cordelia!" she shouted. Of course. Who else could have sent a stag to come and fetch her?

Cordelia waved and ran down the steps.

The stag halted, pushing its muzzle into Cordelia's shoulder as she lifted her hands to fondle its head. "Well met by moonlight, Tania," Cordelia said with a grave smile. "And thank you, my lord, for playing the beast of burden."

Tania slid off the stag's back. The ride had been an extraordinary experience, but she felt glad to have her feet back on solid ground.

Tania rested her hand on the stag's thick, muscular neck. "Thank you," she said. "What's his name?"

Cordelia's eyes were filled with moonlight.

"Animals do not like their true names to be spoken aloud," she said.

"Oh. Okay." Tania patted the stag's neck again. "Well, tell him thanks very much from me."

Cordelia brought her lips close to the stag's ear and spoke in a low voice. Tania couldn't make out the words, but the sound was like the wind in trees, the soft pad of hooves on pine needles, the swoop of an owl's wings.

The stag bowed its head to Cordelia then turned and trotted away.

"You sent him to fetch me, didn't you?" Tania asked, following her sister up the steps. "How did you know I was here?"

"Eden sensed that you were in Faerie, and that you were in distress," Cordelia said. She looked at Tania. "Your sisters await. Come, take heart's-ease and leave behind you all the troubles of the Mortal World." She paused before going through the doors. "There is something in the air this night," she said, and Tania saw that her eyes were uneasy.

"What kind of thing?"

Cordelia shook her head. "I know not. But it is portentous. All the animals sense it: An oppression in the air, as of a thunderstorm approaching, but there are no dark clouds and the wind is set fair in the southeast." Her eyes narrowed. "And perhaps there lies the threat . . . perhaps." She looked at Tania. "But enough of such talk. The night is fine. Come, you are expected."

Cordelia threw open the door to the long gallery. "Behold, she is here!"

"Hi, everyone," Tania said, stepping into the room with its thick patterned carpets and its colorful wall hangings and comfortable chairs and couches.

All her sisters were there—all save for Rathina, of course.

Hopie and Sancha were together on a long couch, reading from a large book that hung open as it floated in the air in front of them. At a gesture from Sancha the book closed itself and drifted off to rest on a nearby table. Eden was standing at a window, staring out into the night, her hands folded behind her back, her face grave. Zara was at her spinetta—the small pianolike instrument that stood on the dais at the far end of the room—and the tinkling sound of the plucked strings chimed brightly in the air.

Eden walked briskly to greet Tania. She rested her hands on Tania's shoulders. "I felt your distress, precious sister," she said. "What is it that you fear?"

Tania looked at her in surprise as the other sisters gathered around her.

"I'm sorry, I don't know what you mean," she began hesitantly. "I was upset because I had a row with my parents. That must be what you sensed." She looked into Eden's eyes. "Unless you're talking about Gabriel. . . ."

"What of the great traitor?" Eden asked. "Has he

sent more dreams to trouble you?"

"No, not exactly," Tania said. "Remember you told me that there might be people in the Mortal World he could use to attack me? Well, the thing is, I met one of them. And you were right: He pulled me through onto Ynis Maw. At least I think he did, but it might have been only in my mind. Either way, it was really scary." She shuddered at the memory. "I got free of him, but only just."

"That was well done!" said Eden. "But he is a greater danger to you than I had feared. You must be ever vigilant, Tania. Do not let him come upon you unawares." She frowned. "But Drake is not our only enemy. Do you feel the other portents?"

"What other portents?"

"Oh, 'tis nothing!" Zara said lightly, coming up behind Tania. "Eden has been envisioning monstrous events all day, but see?" She spread her arms and smiled. "We are still here and all is well." She wagged a slim finger at Eden. "You dwell too much on dark thoughts, White Malkin! You will worry yourself to a whittled stick!"

"The animals sense something, too," Cordelia said. "As though a thunderstorm were brewing."

"Then 'tis best we wear wide-brimmed hats or the rain shall beat upon our bare heads and give us all the brain-ache!" Zara said.

Cordelia shook her head. "Neither hat nor gabardine coat shall protect us from this storm."

"I feel nothing," Hopie said, looking from

Cordelia to Eden. "Whence comes the peril, do you think?"

"Remember the words spoken to Cordelia by the sea turtle," said Sancha. "There have been lights seen in the old Fortress of Bale Fole. Lyonesse is waking from its long dark sleep. I fear the Lady Lamia has returned. I fear our peril comes on the southeast wind."

"'Tis not possible," Hopie said. "The King of Lyonesse lies trapped in amber in the dungeons beneath our feet. Without his sorcery Queen Lamia can do us no harm."

"That is so," Eden agreed. "But it is not on the wind that I sense the peril. It lies closer to hand." She frowned. "I reach for it and reach for it, but my fingers close on nothing."

"Because there is nothing there to grasp," Zara said. "Come, what manner of welcome is this for our dear sister? I shall play a merry air and we shall speak no more of impending doom!"

She began to sing:

> *There is no way of ending*
> *no thought of descending*
> *this dream will continue forever*
> *for there is always the sun in the sky*
>
> *We dance in the evening*
> *to firelight gleaming*

this dream will continue forever
for there is always the moon in the sky

Though leaves are still falling
and echoes are calling
this dream will continue forever
for there are always the stars in the sky.

Sancha slipped her hand under Tania's arm and drew her to sit on a couch. The other sisters gathered around, Hopie to one side, Cordelia to the other, and Sancha on a padded stool at her feet. Eden stood behind the couch, glancing every now and then out of the window as if she expected to see something sinister riding across the night sky.

"You spoke of a disagreement with your mortal parents," Sancha said to Tania. "Speak to us of your troubles, and by sharing, so diminish them."

"My mum and dad won't let me see Edric," Tania admitted. "They blame him for my disappearing—when I was here before, I mean." She looked into Sancha's intelligent eyes, comforted by the presence of her sisters. "I haven't told them the truth about what happened but I'm beginning to think I should."

Hopie patted her knee. "I shall mix you a draught of myrtle and pennyroyal," she said. "It will balance your humors and it will be an aid to clear thought." She stood up and walked to a dark-wood cabinet lined with drawers.

Zara joined them, taking Hopie's place beside Tania.

"Should I tell them the truth?" Tania asked.

"Why would you do so?" said Sancha. "To ease your heart, or to give ease to theirs?"

Tania frowned. She hadn't thought about that. "To make things easier for me, I suppose," she said at last. "At the moment they just think I'm some idiot girl with a crush on a boy at school. And so long as they think that, they're going to assume I'll get over it if they can keep me apart from Edric. But if I tell them the truth?" She shook her head. "That will change everything forever. There's no going back once they know that stuff—even if they believe me in the first place."

Hopie stooped over her, holding out a brown pottery cup. "It will cause them pain, this knowledge?" she asked as Tania took the cup from her.

"What, that I'm actually a princess of Faerie with a whole other family? I should think so," Tania said.

"Drink," Hopie urged. "The potency of the infusion fades swiftly."

Tania looked into the cup. The liquid was swirling as if stirred by an invisible spoon. It was a deep, deep blue and smelled like cold, clear mountain air. She brought the cup to her lips. It felt as though she was drinking the night sky. Starlight seemed to flow down her throat, neither warm nor cold, sweet nor bitter, but as the vapors filled her head, she felt a quiet calm sweep through her.

"Can you keep them ignorant of the truth forever?" Sancha asked.

"I can try," Tania said, handing back the cup to Hopie. "I don't have the faintest idea how I'd even start to try and explain. 'Hey, Mum, Dad, guess what? I have a second life in a parallel world—and that includes a totally different mum and dad and a big bunch of sisters. What do you think of that?'"

"So once your quest for our mother is done and you come to live with us here, will you just depart without a word of explanation?" Cordelia asked.

Tania was dumbfounded for a moment. It had never occurred to her that her sisters took it for granted that she'd want to live permanently in Faerie. "I haven't really thought about it properly," she said. "I don't know what I'm going to do."

"'Twould be unfair to leave them so," Zara said. "'Twere best to tell them the truth before you depart, however hard that may be for you to tell and for them to hear."

Sancha reached out and took Tania's hands. "I think you maybe do not see fully into our dear sister's heart, Zara," she said gently. "It is not the telling of her mortal parents that confounds her, it is the choice she must make."

Tania felt Eden's long slender hands rest on her shoulders. "Sancha sees more clearly than others in this," Eden murmured, leaning over and touching her lips for a moment against the top of Tania's head. "Our sweet sister has not returned to us as that same girl who disappeared all those centuries ago. Her spirit has dwelt in over sixty human forms since that day."

Tania tilted her head to look into her sister's face. "That many?"

"Aye, the human called Anita Palmer is the sixty-third reincarnation of your Faerie Spirit," Eden said. "Threads and remnants of those past lives lie still within you—I sense them—and each new human form has left its imprint on your soul."

"What does that mean exactly?"

"It means, my love, that you are now half Faerie and half human," Eden said. "And in that dilemma lies the agony of your choice."

Zara grasped Tania's arm with both hands. "No! No!" she cried. "Tania is our sister; she belongs with us." She stared up at Eden and there was a wild, frightened look in her eyes. "You cannot think she would wish to remain in the Mortal World?"

"That would be a grievous choice," Sancha said. "There is an age-old rhyme, a foretelling by the blind poet Draco Sinister of Talebolion:

> *When Faerie soul in mortal lies*
> *it burns too bright, and swift the mortal dies*
> *but if it dwells for sixteen years*
> *the choice is there to make—for joy or tears*
> *If Faerie turns to Faerie true*
> *then Faerie soul is born anew*

If Faerie lives 'neath mortal sky
then Faerie soul shall fade and die."

A heavy silence followed Sancha's words. Tania looked around at her sisters, seeing fear and anxiety and sympathy in their faces.

"So I have to choose?" she said. "I have to make up my mind whether I want to be here or in the Mortal World?"

"If I have interpreted the text correctly, then that is so," Sancha said.

"But my gift is the ability to move from one world to the other," Tania pointed out. "What kind of sense does that make if I have to choose between them?"

"You may travel from world to world," Eden said. "But you can have only one home, and it must be the choice of your heart."

"How quickly do I have to decide?"

"That I do not know," Sancha admitted.

"But it could be soon, could it not?" Cordelia said. "The perils of the Mortal World are legion, and if Tania dies there, she will not be reborn this time. Is that the true meaning behind the old rhyme?"

Sancha nodded.

"Fear not, sweetheart," Eden said, leaning close over Tania again. "Anita Palmer has a strong spirit in her body, else that mortal life would already be done. Confusion reigns in your soul for now but mayhap time will show you your true path."

"Or maybe it won't," Tania said bleakly.

"Would you really choose to live in the Mortal World?" Zara asked, her eyes wide.

Tania looked at her in silence for a few moments. "I love my mum and dad," she said.

Zara cocked her head. "But they will die, Tania, they are but mortals. What then?"

"I hadn't really thought that far ahead."

"But—"

"Peace, Zara," said Hopie. "You would grind away the very mountains with your endless questions."

"Yes," Tania said, sitting up and forcing herself to smile at her sisters. "Let's not talk about me anymore. It's wearing me out." She looked up at Eden. "Is there any news of Rathina?"

"Silence surrounds her as a cloak of mist," Eden said. "I can neither see her nor feel her presence anywhere in the Realm."

"Our father frets over her," Cordelia said. "I have asked the animals for news, I have sent birds to scour the land, but they have seen nothing."

"The last news we have of her was when she took Maddalena and headed north as though the unicorns of Caer Liel were at her heels," Hopie added. "But I for one have no wish to see her again. The King pities her but I do not. The evils she performed, the great harm she would have done to Tania, they were not the result of a broken mind. They were the acts of a cruel and heartless child!"

"No, Hopie," Eden said. "Do not meet dark deeds

with dark thoughts. I, too, pity the poor child. Mayhap had her gift revealed itself, then her feet may have been set on a true course."

"That is true enough," added Sancha. "She spoke little of it, but I know that she brooded betimes over the fact that her gift never manifested itself."

"She was but seventeen when the Great Twilight fell," Hopie said. "My gift of healing did not come to me in a moment upon the dawn of my sixteenth year. Instead it grew as grows a tree or a garden, by slow degrees and nurtured always by diligence and effort. Rathina expected her gift to fall out of the sky into her lap."

"Like mine did, you mean?" Tania said.

"Your gift was prophesied," Eden said. "You are the seventh daughter spoken of old. As Hopie says, it was different for us. Our gifts grew slowly. Rathina's gift would have shown itself, had she given it time and patience."

"Patience was never among her virtues," Zara said. She glanced at Hopie. "And yet I pity her also, so lorn and forsaken out there in the wildlands."

Tania looked at Eden. "But if you can't sense her, does that means she's not in Faerie anymore? Where could she have gone?"

"I know not," Eden said. "What ship would bear her over the sea to another land? How would we not hear tell of it?" She shook her head. "She is veiled from me and I can do nothing to help her. She must return or not, in her own time and in her own way."

Tania looked at her watch. It showed one minute to ten, the hands frozen at the exact time that she had stepped out of her bedroom. "I have to get back," she said. She looked at Cordelia. "I don't suppose you have another stag on standby?"

"We will find a smoother ride to take you back to the Brown Tower," Sancha said.

It was heart-wrenching for Tania to have to say good-bye so soon to her sisters and to leave Faerie after so short a time, but she felt an urgent need to get back home.

Home? She still thought of the Mortal World as home.

And yet when she was here, didn't she also think of this as home?

How would she ever be able to choose between her two worlds—between her two selves?

Sancha flicked the reins and the pony cart came to a jingling halt among the aspen trees.

"Thanks for the ride," Tania said. "I loved the stag but it's a bit rough on the backside." She climbed down.

"Your troubles swarm around your head like angry wasps, I know," Sancha said. "But remember this, Tania: Even in the Mortal World, you are Princess Tania of the Royal House of Faerie." Her dark eyes flashed. "Behave accordingly!"

Tania smiled at her. "I'll try," she promised.

"Farewell, beloved sister," Sancha called as she

touched the reins and set the pony trotting. "May angels of mercy defend you till we meet again."

"Thanks," Tania called, waving as the cart jogged off through the trees.

Her bedroom was dark and quiet. She listened for a moment, standing in the middle of the room where her side step had delivered her. She could faintly hear the sound of the television from downstairs. She glanced at the digital display on her bedside clock. It was a quarter past eleven. She had been in Faerie for a little over an hour.

She opened her bedroom door, feeling curiously calm. She adjusted her wristwatch as she descended the stairs, spinning the hands to make up the time that had been lost in her other home.

Sancha's parting words rang in her ears.

You are Princess Tania of the Royal House of Faerie. Behave accordingly!

Sancha was right. Tania couldn't pout and yell and stamp about the place and then expect to be treated like an adult. If she was going to make things right with her parents, then she would need to "behave accordingly." And that meant sitting down with them and discussing their problems coolly and without anger.

She opened the living room door.

Her parents were in their usual places: Dad in his armchair, Mum on the couch with her legs curled under her. Their faces turned to her as she walked into the room. There was a kind of wary anticipation in their eyes.

"Can we talk, please?" Tania asked.

"Of course," said her mother. Her father reached for the remote and muted the television.

Tania took a deep breath. "I'm sorry for the way I behaved earlier," she said. "I know you're only thinking of me, and I do understand your concerns about—about Evan. I really do. And I know I've done things recently that mean I have to earn your trust again. I'm determined to show you that I can be trusted, and I'll try my utmost never to hurt you again. But there's something you really need to understand. Evan means a lot to me, and he isn't to blame for anything I've done."

"I don't think—" her mother began.

"Mary! Let her finish," her father said.

"I don't want to be separated from Evan over the holidays," Tania said. "I'd like you to change your minds about our seeing each other. He cares about me, and you're punishing him for something he didn't do. Let me start earning back your trust. Trust me to be with Evan—and trust him to be with me." There was an odd silence once she had finished. She gave a weak smile and spread her hands. "That's it," she said. "I'm done."

Her mother looked piercingly at her. "He means that much to you?"

"Yes, he does."

"First love is always very intense," her mother said.

"But it rarely lasts. You realize that?"

Tania nodded. She wanted to tell her parents that the love between her and Edric was special—unbreakable—but she didn't. In millions of homes all over the world she knew that millions of teenagers were telling millions of parents that their love was special—and millions of times they were wrong. How could she prove to her parents that the bond between her and Edric really was exceptional, without telling them how and why?

"If we're going to treat you as an adult, then you must act like one," her mother continued. "You're still under curfew, and we want you to do other things as well as seeing Evan. Balance your life out; don't spend all your time with him. See other people. Do other things."

"And work hard at your summer assignments for school," added her father.

"I'll do all those things," Tania promised. "I'll do everything you want. Does that mean I can see him?"

"I suppose it does," her mother said. "But not today! The curfew stands."

"Thank you! Thank you so much!" Tania bounded up the stairs, eager to phone Edric with the good news. No more having to sneak around behind her parents' backs. No more having to lie about where she would be, who she was with.

She ran into her room.

It was like running into an exploding bomb.

A wall of burning, pitch-black force smashed into

her—as powerful as a gigantic punching fist—lifting her off her feet and sending her flying backward through the air.

She gasped, the breath knocked out of her as she came crashing to the carpet. The blackness surged over her like an avalanche, crushing her into the floor, blinding her, clogging her ears and nose and mouth, sending out tendrils of amber light to fry her eyes and sear her mind.

And then she had the sensation of falling—falling—falling through darkness into a bottomless black pit.

And then . . . nothing.

X

Tania woke up feeling strangely clear-headed. She wondered why she was lying flat on her back on her bedroom carpet. The door was open and although the room was unlit, a wedge of light was streaming in from the landing. She sat up and blinked around her. What was she doing on the floor? And what was that horrible taste in her mouth?

It was like . . . like rusty iron. *Yuck!*

She got up. Her watch showed eleven twenty-five. It had been a quarter past eleven when she had stepped back from Faerie. She had gone down to speak with her parents, and then she had come running up here to call Edric with the good news.

And then she had woken up on the floor. . . .

Strange. She must have fainted.

She made a face. The taste of iron was still in her mouth. She switched the light on and closed her door.

She found a pack of mints in the front pouch of her shoulder bag. Sucking one, she took out her phone and went over to the window. She gazed out at the dull gray-blue of the cloudy night sky as she speed-dialed Edric's number.

By the time she heard his voice the mint had completely overpowered the taste of iron in her mouth.

It was the following morning.

The rain flailed down the long curve of George Street, bouncing high off the pavements, gathering in dancing and spitting puddles, swirling in the gargling gutters. It ricocheted off cars and vans and umbrellas, sending pedestrians running for cover in shop doorways.

Tania wasn't bothered by the downpour. She and Edric ran hand-in-hand down the pavement, kicking up curved fins of rainwater as they went.

"Rain all you like!" she shouted. "Nothing's going to upset me today!"

"*You cataracts and hurricanoes, spout!*" Edric howled into the sky, "*Till you have drench'd our steeples, drown'd the cocks . . . That make ingrateful man!*"

"What's that a quote from?" Tania asked.

"King Lear, Act Three, Scene Two. A stormy heath."

"Is there any Shakespeare you *don't* know?"

Edric grinned at her. "Not much. Didn't I mention? Shakespeare had Faerie blood in him."

"Truly?"

He nodded. "Truly!"

"Wow!"

They came to the dogleg where George Street met Hill Street. The post office was on the corner. The sandwich bar was only a little farther down the road, just by the roundabout that led to Richmond Bridge.

The rain eased as they walked along. The dark clouds slid away, making way for a lighter layer that had an almost pearly sheen to it.

"The rain looks like harp strings," Tania said, gazing toward the white, stone-built bridge. "Millions of harp strings strung between the earth and the sky. Do you have weather like this in Faerie? It's always been blue skies and sunshine when I've been there."

"We have all kinds of weather. We have storms like you wouldn't believe, with thunder and lightning and rain that falls so heavily that the river can rise two or three feet in one day. And in the winter there are winds from the north that can freeze the sap in an oak tree, and snow that lies across the land like a deep white ocean. And on some nights in the depths of midwinter the cold is so intense that you can hear a sound—a whisper—that is like the stars frosting over." He smiled. "On nights like that the best place to be is in a warm room in front of a blazing fire of yew logs."

Tania gazed at him. Would she ever sit with him on a winter's night and watch the yew flames crackle and dance?

He gave a wry smile. "But for now it is a rainy summer's day in Richmond, and we have to decide where to look first."

"We're pretty sure that it was Titania in that chauffeur-driven Lexus," she said. "So I suppose we could start off by looking for a black Lexus."

"Or for the kind of firm that would pay its people enough for them to have a chauffeur-driven Lexus," Edric added.

"I still can't get over the idea of Titania being some high-powered business person," she said. "What do you think she does for a living?"

"It could be just about anything," Edric said. "Remember, she's had a long time to pick up money-spinning skills."

It was obvious they needed to get off the main shopping streets, to find roads where shops gave way to offices and business centers. Even though it was Saturday, so there wouldn't be any office workers about, Tania thought they might find something to give them a clue—though she stopped short of hoping to find a plaque on a door reading "Titania, Queen of Faerie."

After about fifteen minutes of fruitlessly tramping the back streets, Tania was just going to suggest a rethink when they passed a side street that made her pause. She stopped and looked at the name. Spenser Road. She stared down the street, not sure what it was that had made her stop.

The rain had eased to a fine drizzle and the sky was the color of porcelain, the clouds so thin in places that the pale sun could occasionally be seen, its misty disk soft and blurred like a tablet dissolving in water.

"What is it?" Edric asked.

"I'm not sure," Tania said. On the right-hand side of the street she saw a low, red-brick wall surmounted by black railings. She led Edric to a high-arched wrought-iron gateway. Above the gateway words were picked out in wrought-iron letters: THE SPENSER ROAD FORUM. Beyond she saw a wide sunken courtyard of rain-washed gray stones. There were raised red-brick flower beds, and on three sides of the courtyard stood modern-looking office blocks of red brick with large windows that reflected the sky.

Tania lifted the latch on the iron gate and pushed it open. They walked down stone steps into the courtyard.

"No Lexus," Edric said, looking around. "Nowhere for cars to park at all."

Tania frowned. "I was so sure that this was the right place."

But Edric wasn't looking at her. He was staring at a large freestanding sign that showed the names of the companies that had offices in the courtyard complex.

He pointed at the third name down. "See that one?"

THE PLEIADES LEGAL GROUP.

"Does that mean something to you?" Tania asked.

Edric began to laugh softly.

"Edric!" Tania said, tugging at his hand. "Tell me!"

"I take it you've never been interested in astronomy," he said.

"Not especially," Tania replied. "Why?"

"The Pleiades is a star-cluster that's visible in the Northern Hemisphere," Edric explained. "It lies between the constellations of Taurus and Aries."

"Yes?" Tania was becoming impatient now. "And?"

"And it's also known as the *Seven Sisters*," Edric said.

A thrill like a buzz of electricity tingled through Tania's body. Seven sisters—and Titania had seven daughters.

"It can't be a coincidence," she said breathlessly, her fingers gripping Edric's hand. "Which way?"

Edric pointed across the courtyard. "They're in unit five, over there."

Water splashed underfoot as they ran to the steel-and-glass door.

They stepped side-by-side into a lofty reception area. There was a high-fronted curved desk in front of them and a seating area to one side. On the wall behind the desk, a huge tapestry hung behind glass.

Tania stopped in her tracks, staring up at the tapestry. It looked extremely old and its colors were faded, but the image was still perfectly clear. It depicted a vast tree with wide-spreading branches filled with a sea of green leaves, and in hollow spaces among the leaves, as though they were perching there and peering out, were the faces of a whole host of animals.

There were lion and tiger and monkey faces in the tree, but there were also bears and horses and elephants and gazelles, otters and dogs and cats, goats and pigs and crocodiles. And among this collection of familiar animals Tania saw the heads of far more fantastic beasts: unicorns and griffins and basilisks—and at the very top of the tree, a dragon with open jaws and a long, curling forked tongue.

Faerie beasts!

She was still standing there when a blond head appeared over the high edge of the desk. "Hello there. Welcome to the Pleiades Legal Group. How may I help you?"

Tania and Edric approached the desk.

The receptionist was sitting at a lower desk behind the high front. She was smartly dressed, with fashionable rimless glasses and shining blond hair.

"I know this is going to sound stupid," Tania said, leaning over the counter. "But is there a woman working here who looks like me?"

"Soaking wet, you mean?" asked the receptionist brightly, then she smiled. "No, sorry, I was just kidding."

"Her hair is a really vivid red when it isn't wet," Edric said. "Long flaming red curls."

The receptionist looked closely into Tania's face. "Oh!" she said, her eyes widening. "Yes! I didn't . . . well . . . with the wet . . . But yes, if your hair wasn't wet, you'd look a lot like Ms. Mariner." The eyes grew even wider. "It's quite amazing, actually."

"Who is Ms. Mariner?" Edric asked.

"She's our managing director."

Tania was vaguely aware of someone descending a flight of stairs that angled down behind the reception area. "Carol?" a man called. "Are these my twelve o'clock?"

"No, Mr. Mervyn," the receptionist replied. "They're asking about Ms. Mariner."

There was a brisk rap of shoes and a middle-aged man in a blue suit appeared beside the reception desk. He studied Tania and Edric, his gaze lingering first on their wet hair and then down to the slowly spreading pool of water that was gathering at their feet.

"I'm George Mervyn," he said. "Senior partner, corporate law. Can I be of assistance?"

"My name is Tania Palmer. It's really important that I speak to Ms. Mariner, please."

"I'm afraid Lilith Mariner isn't in the office today," Mr. Mervyn said.

"When will she be back?" Edric asked.

"Not for several days. She's on business in Beijing. Could I inquire as to the purpose of your visit?"

"It's a personal matter," Tania said. "It's very important that I make contact with her. Do you have a phone number I could use?"

Mr. Mervyn raised an eyebrow. "I'm afraid it's not our policy to hand out telephone numbers to people," he said. "If you'd care to leave your details with Carol here—your names and a contact telephone number— then I'm sure she'll arrange for them to be passed to Ms. Mariner when she returns."

"Please, listen to me," Tania said. "You don't have to give us her number, but just call her and tell her that Tania Palmer needs to speak to her. She *will* understand, and she will want to speak to me, trust me. She will."

"Ms. Mariner is an extremely busy person," Mr. Mervyn said. "I would need some very compelling reason to disturb her."

"I'm her daughter," Tania blurted out.

Mr Mervyn's eyes narrowed and his jawline hardened. "That is absolute nonsense," he said, and now his voice was ice cold. "How old are you? Seventeen? Eighteen? I've worked with Lilith Mariner for twenty years and it is quite impossible for her to have a teenaged daughter! Now then, whatever your intentions are, I recommend you leave these premises immediately."

"I'm not *lying* to you! I—" Tania's words were cut off short as Edric's hand came down on her arm. He pulled her away from the reception desk and towed her across to the doors.

A moment later she found herself standing in the drizzling rain seething with frustration.

"Did he think I was just making it up?" Tania exploded.

"Yes, I think he probably did," Edric said. "Let's find somewhere to sit down out of the rain and cool off." He released her arm. "Come on. I saw an internet café on the way here. We'll go there and decide what to do next."

They were seated at a window table in the internet café. Edric had logged on and was busy tapping at the keyboard. Tania sat perched on the high stool, her elbows on the table and a frothing mug of cappuccino warming her cold hands.

"Lilith Mariner is Titania," she said. "She has to be."

"Yes, I think so," Edric agreed, looking intently at the computer screen. "The name would make sense. Oberon is known as the Sun King and Titania was the Moon Queen, and Lilith is a name that is often given to the moon. There's a children's rhyme: 'By Lilith's sombre light, I wandered through the night, till came the blessed sun, another day begun.' I don't remember the rest of it, but the point is that Lilith was the moon."

"And Mariner?"

"The Queen always loved the sea," Edric said. "Sailor—seafarer—mariner. I can see why she might choose a name like that." He tapped the keyboard. "Aha!"

"What?"

"Take a look at this. I've found the Pleiades Legal Group's website."

Tania leaned close. The home page was dark blue with seven white stars. As Edric ran the cursor over the stars, words came and went.

ABOUT US. SITE MAP. FAQS. NEWS. LEGAL DIVISIONS. MANAGEMENT STRUCTURE. POLICY AND SUPPORT.

Edric clicked on MANAGEMENT STRUCTURE.

A new page came up.

"Oh . . . my . . . lord . . ." Tania whispered.

The page showed photo portraits of four people. A large one at the top of the page, and three smaller pictures beneath, one of which was of George Mervyn.

But it was the top picture that held Tania's breathless attention.

The heart-shaped face that looked out at her was of a woman who could have been in her midthirties, a beautiful woman with no lines or wrinkles or other signs of aging on her flawless white skin, and no hint of gray in the flaming red curls that tumbled onto the shoulders of her dark green jacket. Tania saw the familiar high, slanted cheekbones and the full-lipped mouth. And there, gazing serenely out at her, were those smoky green, gold-flecked eyes—the same eyes that Tania saw every day when she looked into the mirror.

Her eyes slid to a block of writing underneath the picture.

> *Lilith Mariner, L.L.B., L.L.M., Q.C.*
> *Since Lilith Mariner became the MD of the Pleiades Legal Group, the company has grown from strength to strength. Her deep and abiding concern that the very best legal representation should be available for all, and her exceptional command of international law, has made her one of the most sought-after professionals in the whole of Europe. She is also widely known and*

respected for her pro bono work, of which the
Pleiades Legal Group is justly proud.

"What's pro bono?" Tania asked.

"I think it means she'll represent people for nothing if they can't afford the fees," Edric said.

Tania reached out and touched Titania's face with trembling fingertips. "We've found her," she said dazedly. "We've really found her."

"Yes, we have."

"We have to let everyone know," Tania said. "We have to go into Faerie right now—we have to tell them all! Edric, they'll be so happy! Can you imagine their faces when we tell them? Can you *imagine*?"

XI

Despite her burning desire to pass on the wonderful news about Titania to her Faerie family, Tania wasn't about to walk between the worlds in the middle of a busy street. Even in the persistent drizzle there were still plenty of people about, and it was a few minutes before she and Edric managed to find a secluded spot.

They came to it by following a narrow alley that led them to the riverside. There was a paved slipway alongside a tall white public house. The river was flowing slowly, its gray-blue surface stippled with rain, its farther side darkened by the reflections of the trees that lined the far bank. To their left, about two hundred yards away, they could see the pale, multiarched span of Richmond Bridge, busy with traffic.

They walked arm-in-arm toward the bridge, following the riverside walkway under the bridge and coming to an area bordered by sloping lawns and overhung with trees. On a sunny day Tania felt sure that this place would be packed with people, but in the fine penetrating rain the only people they encountered were a few hooded cyclists and the occasional hardy jogger.

They paused under a spreading green oak tree. Here the rain gathered itself into huge drops that fell heavily from the branches. They waited until a solitary cyclist passed and dwindled into the distance.

Tania took hold of Edric's hand.

She closed her eyes and pictured Faerie in her mind.

She walked forward, aware of Edric keeping pace with her.

She took the side step . . .

. . . and opened her eyes to find that nothing had changed. They were still in the Mortal World.

Edric was standing beside her, still holding her hand.

"That was weird," she said. "I'll try again."

She closed her eyes, summoning up a very firm vision of the Faerie Palace. Gripping Edric's hand, she took one pace forward and one to the side.

This time it hurt.

The air about her stung like electricity and a taste of rusty iron came into her mouth. Gasping from the shock, she opened her eyes.

"What happened?" Edric asked, his voice concerned.

"I don't know," she said. "It's not working for some reason."

"Okay," Edric said, drawing his hand out of hers. "Try again without me. Perhaps I'm the problem."

Tania frowned. "You can't be."

"Just try it."

She took a deep breath and filled her mind with Faerie images for the third time. Wincing a little in anticipation of another blast of sizzling air, she sidestepped.

There was no electricity this time and the taste of iron was gone from her mouth. But something wasn't quite right.

She opened her eyes. The distant sound of traffic on Richmond Bridge had stopped abruptly—and Edric was gone from her side.

The sky was slate gray and the rain fell steadily around her, making the swollen river jump and sputter. A wind whipped the puddles of standing water on the path. The branches of the oak tree rustled and creaked above her.

Tania let out a gurgling laugh and ran, stamping through the puddles, her arms swinging, her booted feet rising and falling like pistons as she kicked up fountains of spray.

"Gracie!" called a shrill, pinched voice. "Gracie! You come back here this instant or I shall give you such a smack!"

Tania turned, her arms outstretched, the water dripping off her bonnet. "No!" she shouted to the thin-faced young woman who stood under the tree. "Shan't!"

"You'll catch your death of cold and your mama will be so angry, Gracie."

Tania laughed again, opening her arms and spinning around, stamping and cavorting in the rain, openly defying her new nanny. Nasty Nanny Perks with her silly pointy nose and her eeky-squeaky voice and her skinny little body.

"Come out of the rain or you'll get no supper!"

"Don't care!"

Nanny Perks stamped her foot. "You are the naughtiest little child that ever there was!"

Was she going to cry now? It would be such fun if she did. It would serve her right for thinking she could take the place of Nanny Bobbins. Lovely, soft Nanny Bobbins with her big bolster arms and her baking smell and her lap like a Chesterfield sofa. Nanny Bobbins who looked just like those magazine pictures of Queen Victoria when she was a young woman. Poor Queen Victoria. She had died last year. Everyone had been so sad. Papa had worn a black armband for ages and ages.

Nanny Perks pulled her coat tight around her scrawny body and came marching out from under the tree with her face all screwed up and angry.

Tania turned and ran toward the river's edge. She pranced along the brink of the swollen river, lifting her legs high like the riding horses in Richmond Park.

"Gracie! I shan't tell you again!"

"Good!"

Her foot came down on a loose stone. It fell away under her, turning her ankle and making her cry out as a searing pain shot up her leg.

She stumbled, her arms flailing. The sky wheeled. The rain fell sideways. She screwed her eyes tight as the river rose up to smack her and to pull her under in a dark, chilling embrace.

"*Gracie!*"

"Tania?"

With a gasp Tania opened her eyes. She was back on the path and Edric had his arms around her. Her legs felt weak; her whole body seemed to be falling away from her like a thing made of water. If Edric hadn't been holding her, she would have crumpled to the ground.

She panted, clinging onto him, her forehead on his shoulder.

"What happened?" he asked.

"Drowned . . ." Tania gasped. "The poor thing. . . ."

"You're all right now," he said. "I've got you."

"It happened again," she said. "Like at the theatre. But it was a different girl this time." She looked around. "It was here, and things were almost the same. It couldn't have been all that many years ago, but *when*? Oh, wait. . . . Queen Victoria had just died. That means I must have gone back to the start of the twentieth century." She pointed toward the river. "She was there—acting up, you know? Being naughty. And she fell into the water." She screwed up her eyes. "Is this going to keep happening to me now? Am I going to keep reliving scraps of all my past lives?" Her voice shuddered. "And my deaths?"

"I don't know," Edric said. "I don't understand why this is happening. Maybe Eden will be able to explain it, or maybe the King will be able to stop it."

"But I can't *reach* them!" she said. "I can't get into Faerie. My gift doesn't work anymore."

"Perhaps this is a bad place to try," Edric said with a reassuring smile. "It might be like those places where you can't get a proper signal on your cell phone. You're just not getting a good signal here, that's all."

She looked at him, wanting to believe him. "You think?"

He nodded. "We should try somewhere else. Listen, let's go back to the station. We can get an over-ground train to Hampton Court. You're bound to be able to get through there."

"Yes, I'm sure you're right," she said. "Come on." She glanced uneasily at the spot where Gracie had fallen into the river. "I want to get away from here."

The day was beginning to brighten up, and to the west the sky was showing blue under the ragged trailing hem of the departing clouds. Tania and Edric stood side by side on a lawn that sloped down to the river. The tall red-brick Tudor towers and walls of Hampton Court Palace reared up behind them, with their white stone windows and their ornate decorations and gap-toothed battlements.

It had taken them three-quarters of an hour and two changes of train to get here, and so far as Tania could see, it had been a complete waste of time. Faerie was still barred to her. She had tried six times: three times with Edric, three times without. All she had got for her effort was a foul taste in her mouth and a fierce stinging sensation that swarmed all over her body like a painful rash.

She stared moodily into the river, aware of Edric watching her in strained silence.

He didn't know what to say. Neither did she.

At last she spoke, her voice hardly audible over the swirl and swish of the moving water. "Why can't I get through? That's my gift, isn't it? The ability to walk between the worlds. So what's gone wrong?" She looked at Edric in sudden alarm. "Eden and Sancha told me that one day I'd have to choose where I wanted to be: Here or in Faerie. And if I chose to be *here* then the Faerie part of me would die. What if that's already happened? What if I can't ever get back?"

When she had first gone to Faerie she had been told how there were certain places in the Realm where the skin that divided the two worlds was at its thinnest, places where the membrane that separated them was as fine as a dragonfly's wing. Hampton Court was one of those places: If even a shred of Tania's Faerie self remained, then she should have been able to step into Faerie here.

And yet she couldn't.

Edric took her hand. "You still have Faerie alive inside you," he said. "I can feel it. There has to be some other reason."

"Something strange happened last night," Tania said. "After I'd spoken with my parents, I went upstairs to call you. The next thing I remember is waking up on the floor in my bedroom." She stared at him as the full memory came back to her. "I had a taste of iron in my mouth when I woke up. The same taste that I'm getting now." Her eyes widened. "The same taste I had in the fortune-teller's booth. Do you think Gabriel Drake has something to do with this? Is he stopping me from getting into Faerie?"

"I don't know," Edric said. "Does he have that much power over you?"

Tania swallowed hard. "Perhaps he has," she said. "Perhaps this is just the first stage of something bad he's planning to do to me." She gave Edric a haunted look. "First he makes sure I can't escape into Faerie, then he comes for me."

"He can't harm you if you fight him," Edric said gently. "You proved that in the fortune-teller's booth. You got free of him."

"Yes," Tania said breathlessly. "But only just."

"Listen, you're exhausted," Edric said. "Let's go home. You shouldn't wear yourself out trying to get through anymore, not for a while, anyway. And it might not be Drake at all. It might be some kind of mental block you've got because we're so close to finding the Queen. And even if it is Drake, you're going to be a long way from here soon. You just have to be strong for a couple more days, then he won't know where you are."

Tania wasn't comforted by this. "And what about when I come back?"

"When you come back, we'll find the Queen and she'll know what to do."

Tania felt a surge of desperate love for him. She put her hands on his cheeks, staring into his face. "Promise?"

Edric smiled. "Promise."

"But what if I can never get back?" she asked. "You'll be trapped here as well. You won't ever be able to get home."

He gave a half-smile. "Home is where the heart is," he said quietly. "And my heart is with you."

They stepped into each other's arms and for a long time they stood there by the flowing river, clinging to each other while the clouds crumbled apart above their heads and long raking beams of sunlight shone down on them.

XII

Tania lay on her bed, her eyes closed, her arms thrown up over her face. The taste of iron in her mouth was so bad that it was almost making her retch, and her skin was still stinging from her last attempt to break through into Faerie.

It was early Sunday afternoon. Outside her window lay a bright, rain-washed day of scudding clouds and warm summer breezes—not that Tania got any pleasure from it as she lay stiff and tense on her bed and tried to smother the panic that was growing inside her. She dreaded that she would never get into Faerie again, that Gabriel Drake had somehow stolen her gift from her, and that this was just a prelude to an attack on her. The only shred of relief was that he had not come to her in her dreams. She had slept badly last night but the few moments of sleep she had managed to snatch had been blessedly free of nightmares.

She had done what Edric had suggested: She had made no more attempts to enter Faerie on Saturday. She hadn't even succumbed to the urge to test herself as soon as she got up this morning. She had waited and waited with growing impatience and anxiety.

And then she had gone for it—with only a mouthful of rusty nails and a crawling skin to show for her effort.

She could hear muffled bumping and banging noises coming from along the landing, the sounds of her mother yanking suitcases down from the top of wardrobes and opening them on the floor ready to be packed.

She heard footsteps along the hallway and the soft creak of her door being opened.

"I'm fine," she said without uncovering her eyes. "It's just a headache, that's all."

"Did you try again?" It was Edric's voice.

Tania sat up. "Oh, sorry. I thought you were Mum."

Smiling, he came in and sat next to her on the bed. She took his hand, her dark mood clearing a little just to have him near.

"Did you try again?"

She nodded. "There was nothing! I still can't do it." She looked at him. "How did you get in?"

"Your dad was outside with his head under the hood of the car," Edric said. "He said it was okay for me to come up here. Mind you, he didn't exactly look overjoyed to see me."

"Think yourself lucky," Tania said. "A couple of days ago he'd have chased you off with a tire iron."

"There is that," Edric said. "But listen, I've been thinking. You mustn't get yourself into a state about this thing. Even if Drake has put some kind of spell on you, the Queen will know how to break it; I'm sure she will. All we have to do is sit tight till she comes back from China. She'll know how to get your gift back for you."

"But if she knew how to get into Faerie, she wouldn't still *be* here."

"She may not know how to get *herself* back," Edric persisted. "But you already have the gift. You've just lost it temporarily, or you've had it stolen. She'll know how to help you find it again."

"But—"

"That guy from the law firm said Lilith Mariner would be back within a couple of weeks," he said. "And you're about to go away for two weeks. She'll be in London by the time you get back."

Tania looked dubiously at him.

"You trust me, don't you?" he said.

"With my life," she said softly.

"Then stop worrying, or you'll get wrinkles."

She laughed. "Excuse me! I'm sixteen and I'm an immortal Faerie princess, so don't bother threatening me with wrinkles, thank you very much." She stood up, feeling a new hope rising inside her. "Okay," she said, going to her window and throwing it open. "Let's get some fresh air in here. And then . . ." She turned around and looked at him. "Since you're here, you can get my suitcase off the top of the wardrobe and then you can help me to pack."

He looked at her in surprise. "You're not leaving till Tuesday," he said. "You don't need to start packing yet, surely?"

She arched an eyebrow. "Edric," she said, "for a boy who's been around for five hundred years, you don't know much about girls, do you?"

"Drive carefully!" Tania shouted, waving as the car headed off down the road. Her father tooted the horn and her mother's arm appeared out of the passenger window, waving back. Tania stayed there until the car rounded the corner and was gone.

She looked at her watch. It was four o'clock on Monday afternoon. Her mother had told her she should go to bed early that night—eight o'clock at the latest—otherwise she'd be good for nothing in the morning.

"That's all well and good, Mother dearest," she said aloud as she went back into the house. "But sleeping is the last thing I want to do right now." In fact, she wasn't planning on going to bed at all. She had slept fitfully last night, unable to rest for thoughts of Gabriel Drake, and now she was beyond the point of tiredness, wide-awake in a strange, unnatural, and light-headed way.

She went up to her room. Her suitcase was still open on her bed, ready for last-minute toiletries to be squeezed in before the lid came down and the zipper was dragged shut. She smiled, remembering Edric's disbelieving face as he had been introduced to the stark realities of helping a teenaged girl pack for a two-week holiday.

"Poor Edric," she said fondly. "He'll learn."

She picked up her phone and began to text him. HI THERE, GORGEOUS. I'M MISSING YOU ALREA

A shaft of pain seared into her head as if a bolt of lightning had pierced her skull. She screamed with agony, staggering, dropping the phone, her hands coming up to her pounding head.

The room shook around her, the floor shuddering under her feet, the furniture rattling and vibrating. She heard a ghastly howl above her that was like the fabric of the universe being torn open.

It was Drake! It had to be. He had stripped her of her gift—and now, when she was truly alone for the first time, he was coming for her.

She fell to the floor as the brain-shredding noise echoed and re-echoed in her ears. And now there was a hissing and a roaring like a firestorm, and as she stared up with terrified eyes, she saw the ceiling glow a fierce, fiery red; then it began to swirl, faster and faster, gathering speed like a blazing wheel, spitting out sparks and flecks of darkness.

There was a loud crack, like a mountain splitting open, and Tania saw three figures come tumbling out of the wheel of fire: Three figures in long dresses, three figures that plunged through the ringing air and came crashing to the floor.

A split second later a white crystal sword came plummeting point down in their wake, narrowly missing the sprawling figures and coming to a thrumming halt, hilt uppermost, its point embedded in the carpet.

And then with a rush and a hiss the furious circle of flame was gone and Tania was left, stunned and breathless, staring at the three girls who lay stretched out on the floor in front of her.

Cordelia.

Sancha.

Zara.

Sancha was the first to scramble to her feet. "Eden!" she screamed, staring up at the ceiling. *"Eden!"* She turned her frantic, tear-stained face to Tania. "They have caught Eden!" she cried. "They will kill her! They will *kill* her!"

Part Three:

Sisters in Exile

XIII

Tania wondered if she had fainted and fallen into some kind of weird nightmare.

Zara lay in a crumpled heap on the carpet, face-down, groaning. Cordelia pulled herself into a sitting position and gently turned Zara over, resting her head in her lap.

Sancha stared at the ceiling with a look of absolute horror. "Eden has sealed the portal behind us," she said. "*They* cannot follow, but neither can she."

Tania staggered to her feet. Even in her shock she saw that the clothes her three sisters were wearing were stained and crumpled, and that their hair was wild and their faces smeared with grime.

She also noticed that Sancha was holding a bundle of white silk under one arm and that there was another cloth bundle lying on the carpet near to where the white crystal sword had stabbed into the floor—a tied bundle that was tube-shaped and about a yard long.

"Who can't follow?" she asked. "What's happened? How did you get here?"

Sancha gave her a grave, bleak-eyed look. "It is Rathina," she said. "She has betrayed us all." She bit her lip, her eyes glancing fearfully around. "This place may not be safe. We should not remain here." She looked down at Zara. "Is she hurt?"

"Nay," Cordelia said, smoothing Zara's golden hair off her face. "Bruises, nothing more." She looked up at Sancha. "Would that Hopie were here to ease her pain."

"Please!" Tania's voice was shrill in her ears. "I don't understand. Tell me what's happening!"

Sancha took an awkward step toward Tania and put her hand on her shoulder. "It is ill to meet you so, Tania," she said. "We have a grievous tale to tell."

"Had we but known," said Cordelia, shaking her head, "mayhap we could have prevented it."

"Water, please," Zara whispered. "My lips are dry and there is so foul a taste in my mouth that I can hardly bear it."

"Come with me," Tania said. "We'll go to the kitchen. And then you can tell me exactly what's happened."

"Call for a servant," Sancha said. "Zara will need aid if she is to walk far."

"I don't have servants," Tania said, helping Cordelia get Zara to her feet. "I'm on my own here but the kitchen isn't far away." Keeping in step with Cordelia, she supported Zara as they walked to the door.

"This is your bedchamber?" Sancha asked, her voice filled with amazement as she stared around the room. "There are so many curious devices here." She turned to the desk and reached toward the computer. "What is this thing?"

"Don't touch it!" Tania shouted, startling her sister. "It's made of metal."

With a look of alarm Sancha drew back her hand sharply.

"Be really careful, all of you," Tania said. "Please don't touch anything without asking me first. There's metal everywhere."

Cordelia gave her a look of distaste. "You surround yourself with *Isenmort*?" she asked. "How do you abide it?" She glanced around the room with narrowed, wary eyes. "Your chamber is unlovely, Tania. It has too many sharp edges and it is ugly and unnatural. I do not like it." She frowned. "And what is that foul taste in my mouth? Is the air so corrupted in this world that it tastes like wormwood on the tongue?"

"No, that's not normal," Tania said. "I thought Drake was causing it somehow."

"Drake?" said Sancha. "Nay, sister, 'tis far worse a foe. But I would have water to wash the taint from my mouth ere I speak of it."

"We'll go downstairs," Tania said, looking uneasily at her sister. *A worse foe than Gabriel Drake? Was that possible?*

Sancha stooped and picked up the long bundle. She followed Tania as she and Cordelia helped Zara out of the room and down the stairs. Tania was aware of Sancha and Cordelia's eyes moving rapidly and warily around as they took in their new surroundings.

"'Tis all so small and bleak," Cordelia muttered as they came down into the hall and headed for the kitchen. "Do you have no longing for space and beauty in this world?"

Tania didn't reply. She felt strangely embarrassed by her home. The princesses were used to richly decorated and ornamented rooms, and to wide corridors and polished oak stairways hung with tapestries and paintings, to high ceilings of carved plaster and to windows that shone with colored glass. To them this ordinary Camden house must seem drained of all life and color.

"Be really careful in here," Tania said as they entered the kitchen. "This room is full of metal things. Sit at the table and I'll get you something to drink."

Sancha laid the two lumpy bundles in the middle of the pine table and the three sisters sat down. Zara lifted her head, blinking. She was less pale now, and looked as if she was beginning to recover.

"My head swims," she said softly. "Was Eden successful? Is this the Mortal World?"

"Alas, but it is," Cordelia said grimly.

"You're in my home, Zara," Tania said as she took a carton of milk from the fridge and put four glasses on the table. She sat down, pouring milk into the four glasses and handing them around.

"Your home?" Zara said, looking around. "Oh! I had often wondered what it would be like . . . but . . ." Her voice faltered. "It is so strange . . . like a dream."

"Or a nightmare," Cordelia muttered. "I would almost rather we had stayed in Faerie and carried the fight to the Sorcerer King."

"We would have been killed," Sancha said quietly. "And who would have benefited from our sacrifice?"

Cordelia didn't reply.

They all drank thirstily, and for a few moments no one seemed willing or able to speak. As they sat there together, Tania noticed that Cordelia was constantly looking out of the window, gazing at the trees and bushes in the garden with a haunted, longing expression on her face.

Sancha was looking thoughtfully around the room, taking in the things that surrounded them: The fridge and the stove and the microwave and the coffeemaker, the rows of gleaming knives and kitchen utensils that hung on the wall above the work surface. The chrome sink and the shining metal taps.

"This is a strange and curious world," she murmured under her breath. "It discomforts me greatly, but I would know more of it."

"This liquid has the look of milk," Zara said, staring into her empty glass. "But it tastes like no milk I have ever known. What beast does it come from?"

"From cows," Tania said. "Something is done to it so it lasts longer, that's probably why it tastes different."

She looked at her sisters. It was so bizarre to have them sitting there at her kitchen table that she had to keep telling herself that this was really happening.

"There are cows in the Mortal World?" Cordelia said. "Strange. I had not imagined it would be so. They must be sad beasts, indeed."

Tania had no idea what to say in response to that. "Tell me how you got here," she asked, looking from sister to sister. "If Drake didn't do it, then who did?"

"It was Rathina," Zara said breathlessly.

Tania caught her breath. *Rathina?*

"It is small wonder that Eden could sense no trace of our errant sister," Cordelia said. "Eden was seeking afar for her, yet all the while Rathina was beneath our very feet."

"She was in the palace, you mean?" Tania said.

"Indeed she was," said Sancha. "Eden understood too late the wicked deed that Rathina intended. She sensed the brewing of evil in time to save us but too late to prevent Rathina's treachery from rising up and striking at the very heart of Faerie."

"The Palace has fallen to our bitterest enemy," Cordelia said, her face drawn with misery. "The King of Lyonesse has been freed!"

Tania gasped in disbelief. "But he was trapped in amber in the dungeons! You mean Rathina set him free?"

"Aye," Sancha said grimly. "Our own sister loosed this peril on the world once more and brought the darkness upon us."

"All is not yet lost," Zara said. She looked at Tania with her bright blue eyes. "Our hope rests with you, Tania—our last hope."

"You have to tell me exactly what happened," Tania said. "How could Rathina do such a terrible thing? And how did she free the King of Lyonesse? I thought there was nothing in Faerie that could destroy an amber prison."

"It was not with a thing of Faerie that she did the deed," Sancha said. "It was with a thing brought into our realm from the Mortal World. It was with a sword of Isenmort. A sword that lay in the dungeons—the sword that you brought into Faerie, Tania, the sword that you used to free Edric Chanticleer."

Tania stared at her in dismay. When Gabriel Drake had realized that Edric was betraying him, he had encased his servant in a globe of impenetrable amber. Tania had gone into the Mortal World to seek something made of Isenmort—of metal—to break him free. She had sidestepped into modern-day Hampton Court Palace and snatched a sword from a display suit of armor.

Tania had taken the sword back into Faerie through the Oriole Glass. Then Eden had led her to the dungeons and she had searched the myriad tunnels until she had found Edric. The touch of the sword to the amber sphere had destroyed it, but Edric had been weak—she had needed both hands free to help him get away—and she had left the sword lying there on the ground.

"It's my fault!" Tania whispered. "The King of Lyonesse is free because of me."

"No," Cordelia said sharply. "Rathina did the foul deed. None other shares her blame."

"The first I knew was when Eden woke me in the deeps of night," Sancha said. "'Come,' she said to me. 'Be swift and silent. We must wake the others. Dark deeds are afoot this night. Rathina has returned.' 'How do you know?' I asked her. She touched a finger to her forehead. 'I see it in my mind,' she said. 'Alas that I could do nothing to prevent it, but at least we may escape the wrath that is coming.' And so we fled from bedchamber to bedchamber until all sisters were roused." Sancha licked her lips, her eyes hollow. "Rathina's flight from the palace was pretense," she went on. "She allowed the stable boy to see her riding away so that all should think she had departed."

"Had Eden thought to cast her net of seeking to the stones 'neath our feet, Rathina would have been found," Cordelia said. "But she was sending her mind out over the far hills and saw her not."

"Rathina lay hidden from us until the night that you came to the gallery," Sancha said, looking at Tania. "For it was only a short time after I bade you farewell at Bonwn Tyr and returned to my chamber that I was awoken by Eden." She reached out to the round bundle and began to unwrap it. "And this will tell the tale of how Rathina survived the touch of Isenmort and was able to wield the sword that freed the Sorcerer King." She opened the silken cloth to reveal the white crystal crown that had belonged to Queen Titania. The only other time that Tania had seen the exquisite, finely worked crown had been in Titania's melancholy apartments in the Royal Palace.

"Do you see?" Sancha said, pointing to the crown's circlet ringed with inset stones of black amber. "One of the jewels has been prized loose."

Sure enough, Tania saw that one of the black stones was missing from its setting.

"Rathina took it to protect herself from the bite of the Isenmort blade," Cordelia said. "Then she went down to the dungeons and searched until she found the King of Lyonesse."

"And then she set him free," Zara added.

"But why would she do something like that?" Tania asked.

"Of the workings of her mind we can but guess," Sancha said. "But it seems most likely to me that she believed the King of Lyonesse would be able to find Gabriel Drake and bring him back from exile. Lyonesse is a mighty sorcerer; he has great power in him. Rathina must have hoped he would grant her a reward for freeing him, and that the reward should be the return of the man she loves, the traitor Drake."

A coldness pierced Tania's heart. So Drake *did* have a part in all this. "Did he agree to bring Gabriel back?"

"That we do not know," Cordelia said. "But Lyonesse has no honor or gratitude in him. He would not feel bound to reward Rathina for her service to him. Like as not he would have killed her on the spot."

"No," Zara said softly. "I do not believe that she is dead."

"Alive or dead, Rathina's actions have brought ruin and desolation to Faerie," Sancha said. "'What has our sister done?' I asked Eden when we were safely hidden. 'She has freed the Sorcerer King of Lyonesse,' Eden told us. 'Lyonesse has burst out of the dungeons and he has taken Oberon in his sleep and he has cast him into an amber prison. And he has put an incantation upon the sword of Isenmort to form it into bands of adamant wound all about the amber prison so that even Oberon cannot break free.'"

"Oberon is a prisoner?" Tania gasped.

"He is," Cordelia said. "And once Lyonesse had done that wicked thing, he returned to the dungeons and set free his knights. Many of the pale horsemen of Lyonesse were imprisoned over the long centuries of war. I know not how many: One hundred, two, perhaps? They are cruel and evil to the rotted core of their hearts. It is in them to see the Tamesis run red with blood ere they are done with their sport."

"They're *killing* people?"

"Some few who faced them were slain," Cordelia said. "But most fled the palace. Hopie was among those who escaped. She and Lord Brython rode west to Caer Kymry in Talebolion to summon aid, drawing away the attention of the knights from we who remained."

"In the confusion Eden led us to the Queen's Apartments to take the crown," Sancha said. "She did not want the black amber to fall into the hands of Lyonesse. He had already taken possession of Oberon's crown, but at least the Queen's crown was denied him." She reached out a shaking hand and touched the black jewels. "And so we have protection against the perils of this barbarous world," she murmured. "At least until the Gray Knights of Lyonesse come."

"Can they get through?" Tania asked. "You said that Eden had closed the way behind you."

"That is so," Sancha said. "But it will not take Lyonesse long to learn the secrets of the Oriole Glass and use it to send the Gray Knights through into this world."

"Then let humankind beware!" said Cordelia. "There are thirteen black stones in Oberon's crown, so thirteen can be sent through the Glass. And when that happens the Gray Knights of Lyonesse will cut such a swathe through this world that men will speak of it for generations to come."

"Nay, I think not," Sancha said. "More likely they will act with stealth, keeping out of mortal sight until they have found us and put us to the sword. That will be their purpose, to see us all dead. For three days we were kept safe from the knights while Eden worked on an enchantment powerful enough to open a portal into the Mortal World. She had to counter the iron-clad sorcery that Lyonesse had thrown over the land to prevent you from returning and bringing the Queen with you."

"That's why I haven't been able to get into Faerie," Tania said. "I've been trying and trying, but I just couldn't do it. I thought Gabriel had done something to me. I thought he was coming for me." Another thought struck her. "I passed out for a few minutes on Friday night. That must have been when Rathina broke the amber prison."

"Indeed it could be so," Sancha said. "Such sorceries would reverberate twixt the worlds and I doubt not that you felt it."

"Eden led us to the brown tower," Zara said. "But Gray Knights pursued us. We entered with their swords at our very backs. We fled to the roof and Eden had us throw down the trapdoor and hold it shut while she spoke her incantations." Her eyes became circular with remembered fear. "The knights beat at the door and we could not hold them back. But the incantation was complete even as they broke in on us. The floor beneath our feet became a rushing coil of red flame. 'Jump! Jump for your lives!' Eden called to us. There was fear in me such as I have never known, but Eden would brook no delay. She thrust us into the fire, but she did not follow." She brought her hands up to cover her face. "I fear that she was slain!"

Cordelia reached out a comforting hand to rest on Zara's shoulder. "Eden may yet still live," she said. "She has great powers; not easily would she fall to the swords of Lyonesse."

"Indeed," Sancha said. "I feel in my heart that Eden lives still, but the way into the Mortal World is surely barred to her. We are alone and cannot call on her powers to help us." She looked at Tania. "Eden sent us here with a great purpose. We are to aid you in your search for the Queen, for only if we find her and discover the means to take her back into Faerie can our world be saved from falling for all time under the tyranny of Lyonesse. It is only Queen Titania who can free Oberon now—and without Oberon all is surely lost! If Faerie falls then it will not be long ere the dark armies of Lyonesse will pour into this world and enslave all of humankind. For that is Lyonesse's great desire, to become the tyrant of both Faerie and the Mortal World!"

XIV

Despite what Sancha had said Tania felt a crushing weight of responsibility for the evils unfolding in Faerie. It was her carelessness that had given Rathina the weapon she needed to free the King of Lyonesse and set all this in motion.

She had prided herself on being Faerie's savior, the one who brought back light and joy. Now, not only was she responsible for the unleashing of death and terror in Faerie, but if Sancha was right, that horror would soon be stalking the streets of London.

"The Gray Knights will have told the Sorcerer King what occurred at Bonwn Tyr," Sancha said. "He knows that the Mortal World is but a mirror of Faerie. Even if Eden managed to seal utterly the portal that she opened for us, Lyonesse still has the use of the Oriole Glass. It will not take him long to judge where in this world we emerged and then he will send his knights through to kill us before we can find our mother." Her hands were interlocked on the table, the knuckles white. "There can be no delay. Two worlds depend upon us!"

Tania stared at her. "But I don't know what to do."

Sancha's expression hardened. "You have not the luxury of indecision, Tania," she said. "We do not know this world. You must be our guide." Her voice snapped like a whip. "Be strong, Tania! Where is the Queen?"

"In China, about ten thousand miles away."

"So far?" Cordelia said breathlessly. "How may we reach her in time?"

"We can't," Tania said. "But she's coming back here soon. I just don't know exactly when." A sudden need filled her. "I have to call Edric. He has to know about this." Her eyes widened. "And Jade, what am I going to say to Jade? I'm supposed to be flying to Florida in ten hours' time."

"Flying?" Zara said. "I thought the Mystic Arts were gone from this world. How do you fly? Mortals have no wings."

"We use airplanes," Tania said. "There isn't time to explain it now." She stood up. "I'm going to call Edric. We need him here."

"Call him?" Sancha looked puzzled. "How will he hear?"

"We have machines for speaking to each other over long distances," Tania said. "Mine is upstairs. I won't be long. Be careful not to touch anything. If you're hungry, I'll make you something to eat soon."

She ran upstairs to her bedroom. Her hands were shaking so much that she could hardly press the keypad on her phone. She decided to call the Andersons first.

Jade's mother picked up.

"Mrs. Anderson? It's Tania—Anita Palmer."

"Oh, hello, dear. Just a moment and I'll fetch Jade."

"No, listen. I'm very sorry about this. I know how kind you've been in agreeing to me coming on holiday with you, but I can't . . . I can't come."

There was a moment of silence. "Is there a problem? Has something happened?"

"No, nothing bad," Tania said.

"You can't just ring up to cancel at the last moment," Mrs. Anderson said sharply. "What are you playing at, Anita?"

"I'm really sorry," Tania said. "The thing is, I've realized that I need to be with my parents right now. You know, after everything that happened. I thought it would be okay to go away, but I *have* to be with them." That was certainly no lie—she was desperate to be with her Faerie mother and father, more desperate than she could possibly say. "You do understand, don't you?"

"Well, yes I do, Anita, but haven't they gone already?"

"Yes, but I'm going to follow by train. I've checked out the times and everything. It'll be fine. I have to leave right away, though."

"I suppose we might be able to sell the flight ticket

back to the airline," Mrs. Anderson said, the tone of her voice revealing her annoyance. "You really should have thought this through sooner, Anita. Jade will be very disappointed."

"I know. Please tell her I'm really sorry that I've let her down like this."

"I will." There was a pause. "Are you *sure* you know what you're doing?" Mrs. Anderson asked. "Cornwall is a long way to travel on your own."

"Don't worry," Tania said. "It's a straight run on the train, and I'll pick up a taxi at the other end that'll take me right to the cottage. I'll let you know the minute I get there."

"Well, okay then, if you're sure."

"I am. Thanks for understanding. Tell Jade I'll see her soon. Bye."

Tania pressed to break the line. That was one problem solved, for the time being at least, and it was pointless worrying about what would happen when her parents found out she hadn't gone to Florida.

She was shaking worse than ever now. Taking a deep, shuddering breath, she pressed Edric's number. She needed him to be here with her.

A couple of minutes after finishing her call to Edric she received a text message from Jade: I DON'T BELIEVE YOU!!!

She'd texted back: SORRY. I HAD NO CHOICE.

The return text was a single angry word: WHAT-EVER!!!

She didn't respond.

While they were still waiting for Edric to arrive, Tania used a knife to prize three of the black amber jewels from Titania's crown so that each of the princesses could have a protective stone on them.

Once her sisters were safe from the threat of metal Tania took Sancha and Zara on a tour of the house. Cordelia didn't accompany them, preferring to sit on the threshold of the open back door and gaze out into the garden with her fingers knotted in her lap. Being in the Mortal World seemed to weigh heavily on her spirit, more heavily than it did with the others.

Despite the fact that they were still obviously badly shocked from what had happened, Zara and Sancha were curious about the house, asking questions, wanting to know whether all the rooms were for Tania's private use. She explained that her parents lived here with her, but that they had gone away on holiday.

Sancha wanted to know the use and purpose of everything she was shown. Zara wandered the rooms like a puzzled child, running her hands over the furniture, exploring their different textures and contours.

"And what purpose does this gray box serve?" Sancha asked, peering at the television set in the corner of the living room.

"I'll show you." Tania picked up the remote and the television screen burst into life. Some kind of talk show was under way. Sancha's eyes grew wide. She reached to touch the screen.

"'Tis cool, like glass," she said breathlessly. She looked at Tania. "These people are not within the box, are they? We are seeing them from afar. Zara, come look: It is like our mother's gift."

Zara gazed at the television, her eyes filled with wonder. "'Tis like a puppet show!"

"What did you mean about it being like our mother's gift?" Tania asked Sancha.

"The Queen has the gift to see into faraway places by looking into the face of still, pure water," Sancha replied. "But tell me, do all mortals have such devices? Can you use it to seek out the lair of an enemy and to spy upon his actions? That would be most useful to us in our present plight."

"It doesn't work like that," Tania said. "I can't choose what to look at—well, I *can*, but not in the way you mean." The thought of trying to explain modern technology to her sisters made Tania's head spin. "It works with a thing called electricity," she said. "It's complicated."

"I do not understand this play!" Zara said. "The actors speak too rapidly and give no time for their fellows to say their lines." She called out to the television set. "Speak more slowly, I beg you!"

"They can't hear you," Tania said. "And it's not a play, Zara. It's real . . . sort of."

Sancha frowned. "You say it is not a play, and yet you cannot join in as they converse," she said. "So what is its purpose?"

"It's supposed to be entertaining," Tania said. She

sighed. "But mostly it isn't." She pressed the remote and the screen went blank. "Shall we see how Cordelia is doing?"

They went back to the kitchen. Cordelia was still seated cross-legged on the threshold of the garden door. There was a robin perched on the edge of her hand and she was smiling as she listened to the *chirr chirr chirr* of its call.

As they entered the bird took off in a flurry of brown wings and sped in a dipping and rising flight down the garden.

"Sorry," Tania said. "Did we frighten it?"

"A little, perhaps," Cordelia said, getting up. "She speaks well of your mortal father, Tania. She says he talks to her in the garden and digs up worms for her to eat. She is happy here." She smiled. "I am glad that it is so. It eases my heart somewhat to know it."

Tania smiled back. "So maybe the Mortal World isn't quite as horrible as you thought."

Cordelia looked at her. "I would know far more of it ere I believe that," she said gravely.

Edric arrived about half an hour later. Tania had only told him the bare facts over the phone, and it was harrowing to see the horror that grew in his face as Sancha retold the tale of the Sorcerer King's liberation.

They were gathered in the living room now, huddled together like the shell-shocked victims of some terrible disaster. Edric was restless, hardly able to sit still for a minute, constantly getting up and pacing the room. "Are we safe here?" he demanded. "How long will it take for the Gray Knights to track us down?"

"At least a few hours, surely?" Tania said. "Even if the King can work out exactly where this house is in relation to Bonwn Tyr, London isn't like Faerie. They'd have to search the whole area street by street."

"How do you mean, street by street?" Cordelia asked. "Is this dwelling in a town in the Mortal World? In Faerie 'tis but a lone tower on the heath."

Tania opened her mouth to explain, then thought better of it. She went over to a sideboard and took out an *A–Z* map of London. She flicked through the pages to find Camden. She handed the open book to Cordelia; Zara and Sancha drew close to see.

Tania pointed to a spot on the page of crisscrossed roads and streets and avenues and terraces. "That's us," she said. "The rest of the book is all London."

"Sun, moon, and stars," said Sancha, turning the pages. "And do many people dwell in this great confusion?"

"About seven million of them," Tania said. "Give or take."

Cordelia looked appalled. "How do they not lose their sanity to be crushed together in such numbers?"

Tania gave a weak smile. "Plenty of them do," she said. "The point is that we're surrounded by other houses here. The knights won't find us that easily."

"Nevertheless, they *will* find us," Sancha said. "And when they do we shall be in the very greatest peril."

Cordelia grimaced. "As will they!" she said. "Not without hewn limbs and severed heads will they take this life of mine." She picked up the long bundle from the seat beside her and laid it on her lap. "We have not come into this world unarmed." She untied the roll of cloth and opened it. Inside lay three slender swords of pure white crystal.

"Three swords against thirteen?" Zara said. "I like not those odds." She picked up one of the swords and stood up. Tania watched as she spread her footing, one arm curved back, her sword arm thrust forward, her eyes narrowed. "But they will feel my sting ere the final darkness falls!"

"We have four swords," Sancha said. "Eden's blade also passed through the portal before it closed." She looked at Tania. "Four swords and four princesses."

"I don't know how to use a sword," Tania said. "Edric should have the fourth one."

"No," Edric said. "You must have Princess Eden's sword. When the Gray Knights come they'll try to kill you first. Without you the rest of us are stranded here. You have to be able to defend yourself."

She frowned. "I just told you, I don't know how to use it."

"That is not true," Sancha said. "Say rather, you do not *remember* how to use a sword. The skill will come back to you; have no fear."

"Sancha is right," Cordelia said. "You were ever a dazzling swordswoman. Of all of us only Rathina could match you."

Zara lunged across the floor, her blade weaving a sparkling web in the candlelight as she thrust and parried. "The death blow!" she shouted. "And then there were only twelve!"

"We cannot afford to meet them in battle," Sancha said. "Edric speaks true: The death of Tania will be the ruin of us all. Our only hope is to stay hidden until we meet with the Queen."

"Fie!" Cordelia spat. "It burns my heart to run from such carrion! We should make our stand here." Her eyes gleamed. "Or better yet we should take the fight to them. What is thirteen? They will fall like wheat before the scythe!"

"Thirteen is but the vanguard," Sancha said. "Once Lyonesse learns the secret of Tasha Dhul his armies will number in the thousands."

"What's Tasha Dhul?" Tania asked. As with many things in Faerie the name rang faint bells in her head, although she had no idea what it meant.

"It is the hidden mine," Sancha said. "It holds the greatest secret of Faerie. Only there in all our world can black amber be found. For years beyond count the Sorcerer King has lusted to find the mine, and many thousands of Faeries have perished in the wars he waged to conquer us. But the secret is still lost to him, for only King Oberon and Queen Titania know the location of Tasha Dhul and they will never render up the secret, though Faerie be laid waste before their eyes."

Tania understood the importance of black amber;

it was the only shield the people of Faerie had against the deadly effects of metal.

"If the Sorcerer King finds the mine," Sancha continued, "which surely he will once his armies have swept over our land, then he will make jewels of black amber enough to protect an army of tens of thousands." She looked solemnly at Tania. "Then he will send his knights teeming into this world and Isenmort will be no defense against them."

Tania shivered. "How do we stop them?"

"We must find the Queen," Sancha said. "Only she can help to free our father, through the bond that is between them, the unyielding bond of Hand-Fasting."

"Like the bond between me and Gabriel, you mean?" Tania said quietly.

"Like it, but far greater," Sancha replied with sympathy in her eyes. "It is strengthened by many other rites of marriage that you and the traitor did not perform. If we can bring the Queen to our father, I believe that the power that flows between them will suffice to sunder the bonds of Isenmort and break the amber prison and set him free."

"And then the Sorcerer King shall take to his heels," Cordelia said fiercely. "With Oberon at our head, the armies of Faerie will sweep the filth of Lyonesse into the sea."

"Meanwhile we must run from them and we must hide," Sancha said. She looked at Tania. "Know you of a refuge where we can await the return of the Queen?"

Tania tried to think. Where could the five of them hide out for a day or a week or maybe even longer?

"Yes!" she said. "Yes, I do." She looked at Edric. "We can go to Jade's place. It'll be empty for the next two weeks. We've got spare keys for their house."

"Good idea," Edric said. He looked at the three sisters sitting side by side on the couch. "I think you're going to need some different clothes, though. We shouldn't draw attention to ourselves if we can help it, not if the Gray Knights are looking for you."

"I'll sort something out for them," Tania said. "There's only one problem with this plan. The Andersons won't be leaving their house till early tomorrow, not until about four o'clock in the morning."

"That means spending the night here," Edric said. He was thoughtful for a moment. "I think we should risk it," he decided. "Like Tania said, it'll take the Gray Knights a while to track us down and it would be crazy for us to wander the streets all night. But you should all sleep fully clothed in case we need to get out in a hurry."

"We can sleep in my room," Tania said. "We can drag my parents' mattress in there, too. There'll be plenty of room for all of us."

"I'll sleep down here," Edric said, nodding to the couch. "That way I'll be able to give the alarm if anything happens. And I'll keep the keys to Jade's house in my pocket in case we have to get out in a hurry."

Talk of the coming night drew Tania's attention to the fact that the sunlight was waning and that the growing dark of the evening was gradually filling the room with soft, deep shadows. She got up and flicked on the light.

She was startled by the cries and gasps of her sisters as the dim room was filled with electric light. It was such an ordinary thing to do that she hadn't even considered how the princesses would react.

Cordelia sprang to her feet. "'Tis the goblin light of Lyonesse!" she cried, snatching up a sword. "To arms! We are discovered!"

"No! No!" Tania shouted. "It's okay. It's nothing to be afraid of." She switched the light off. "See? It's perfectly safe. I did it." She flicked the switch a third time and the room was full of light again.

Sancha squinted up at the shining bulb, her fingers shielding her eyes. "Sunlight in a bottle!" she said, gasping. "I have seen Eden accomplish such a thing but not without great effort and preparation."

Zara was bent over, her face in her hands. "It is not sunlight!" she muttered. "It is goblin light indeed, too hard and bright for nature. Put it out, Tania, I beg you. It hurts my eyes."

Tania switched it off.

"Maybe candles would be better," Edric suggested. He looked at Tania. "Have you got any?"

Tania went and fetched scented candles, lighting a dozen or more of them and setting them in saucers all around the room. The remainder of the evening was spent bathed in the warm, flickering glow of the aromatic candle flames. They talked some more, and then, as the conversation faded in the deepening night, Zara sang songs to them: Songs of happier times, songs of beauty and of joy, songs to take their minds off what might lie ahead.

Tania was comforted by the sound of Zara's voice as she sat in the circle of yellow candlelight, curled up on the couch with her head resting drowsily on Edric's shoulder. But even at her calmest moments, a darkness lurked in the back of her mind, a constant reminder of the uncertain and dangerous future that was rushing headlong toward them.

Tania was in a world of dark swirling flames. They boiled all around her, spewing thick plumes of oily black smoke that coiled and rolled high into the sky. She ran distractedly this way and that, her hands up to protect her face, her skin sizzling, searching frantically for a way out.

"This way!" A voice called through the wall of leaping flames. "Come to me!"

"Edric?"

"Come to me!" The flames parted to reveal a narrow opening, a way to escape. There was the silhouette of a man at the far end of the corridor of fire, beckoning to her.

She ran toward the man, flinching as the tongues of red flame licked at her. The black shape of the man seemed to recede as she ran forward. "Wait for me!"

His voice drifted to her on the hot dry air. "Come, my lady!"

The flames flared for a moment and finally she saw his face—and it was the leering, silver-eyed face of Gabriel Drake.

"No!"

He lurched forward and his arms came around her, his impetus throwing her to the ground, his weight heavy and oppressive on top of her.

She woke up struggling with the duvet.

Zara was lying in the bed beside her. Tania became still, listening to the soft, steady nighttime breathing of her sister.

She lay like that for a few minutes, scared to close her eyes. Would she never be free of the fear of Gabriel Drake? And now there was also the possibility that the King of Lyonesse may have liberated the evil Faerie lord from his exile on Ynis Maw. How much easier would it be for Drake to ensnare her now that he was no longer a prisoner?

Anger swallowed her fear. It also completely woke her up. She turned her head and looked at the bed-side clock: 1:13.

Three hours till the alarm went off and they could head over to Jade's house. Three hours! Too long to lie there wide-awake.

She slid out of bed and tiptoed to the door. Sancha and Cordelia were huddled under her parents' duvet on the mattress on the floor. They both seemed to be fast asleep; Cordelia was snoring lightly.

Even in the darkness Tania could see the opened drawers and spilled clothes that were the result of trying to find something that the three princesses were willing to wear. Picking clothes to fit them was no problem; even though they weren't all exactly the same size as Tania, the differences weren't especially troublesome. But finding clothes that Zara was prepared to try on had been a different matter altogether.

She refused to consider skirts or dresses that showed any part of her legs and she totally rejected any kind of trousers or jeans, despite the fact that Cordelia had quickly picked a pair of brown cords and a loose-fitting caramel-colored blouse. Sancha had chosen an ankle-length skirt of black satin patterned with huge red roses, and a white cotton blouse to go over it. They had also found an empty backpack, into which they had put the crown, hidden once more in its white silk wrappings.

Half an hour later Zara had finally settled on a full-length, dark blue, cheesecloth gypsy skirt and a loose-fitting top with a high neck and long sleeves.

Once Tania had helped the princesses into their clothes—they found the zippers particularly puzzling at first—she sent a quick text message to Jade: TELL YOUR FOLKS I'VE ARRIVED SAFELY AND EVERYTHING'S OKAY. MUM AND DAD SEND THEIR LOVE. T.

Then they had all gone to bed.

The last thing Tania remembered before she had drifted off was Zara's voice close in her ear. "Why do you have those red numbers by your bed? What is their purpose?" She meant the clock display.

"To tell me the time," Tania had replied sleepily.

"Ah, yes. Eden told us how mortals are held in thrall to time," Zara had said. "It is foolishness, Tania. You are of Faerie. Smell the air to tell the time, watch the moon's passage across the night, take note of the sun's position in the day. That is all the time you need to know!"

"Okay," Tania had said, yawning widely. "If you say so."

And so to sleep. For a little while at least, until Gabriel had turned up to darken her dreams and shock her awake again.

She carefully opened her bedroom door and slipped into the corridor. Her eyes were used to the dark, and she had no trouble negotiating her way down the stairs. The living room door was open. She paused in the doorway, gazing at the huddled shape of Edric curled up under a blanket on the couch.

She had a strong urge to go in there, to sit on the carpet by his head and just enjoy the nearness of him, to watch him while he slept. But she didn't want to risk disturbing him.

She padded into the kitchen. Her clothes felt a bit odd from being slept in but it had been a wise decision not to get undressed, just in case.

She opened the fridge door and the blue light poured out across the floor. She lifted out a carton of milk and took a long swig. It was cool and refreshing.

She walked over to the door that led to the garden. The fridge door swung closed behind her and the light went out.

She felt the need for some fresh air after several hours in a room made stuffy by four sleepers. She turned the key in the lock and opened the door. Cool air wafted over her. She took another long swallow from the milk carton and stepped outside. The paving stones were chilly under her bare feet.

The night was starless and the clouds glowed darkly from the sleepless lights of the city. She paused at the brink of the patio, suddenly aware of an odd smell. She sniffed. It made her think of thunderstorms although she could not have said why. She shivered, intending to go back into the house.

Then a wind came out of nowhere, a cold, biting wind that whipped her hair about her face and clamped her clothes fiercely onto the contours of her body. She stepped back, the freezing air stinging her eyes. She tasted iron in her mouth and heard a noise over the serpentine hiss of the wind.

Neighing. A wild, fierce neighing that seemed to fill the air all around her.

A moment later she heard the clatter of hooves. The carton fell from her hands, bouncing on the stones, spraying milk.

In an explosion of noise and movement a horse and rider leaped the fence at the bottom of her garden and came thudding down into the flowerbed.

The horse was gray and shone like moonlight but

the animal's eyes were red and filled with madness. The hooves stamped down the flowers and plants, the head lifting, another terrifying neigh coming from the gaping mouth.

It kicked and snorted as the rider tugged on the reins. Then it moved forward up the garden, a sickly white glow all around it as its black hooves trod the lawn.

Tania's horror-struck eyes were drawn to the figure on the horse's back. He was wearing a heavy black cloak that cracked in the eddying wind.

As he approached, his silver eyes were fixed on Tania and his pale, handsome face was twisted by a smile of malevolent triumph. She stared up at him, unable to move, as if her body had been turned to stone. The air froze in her lungs and all hope died in her pounding heart.

The rider drew a white sword and pointed it toward her.

"Well met, my lady," said Gabriel Drake as the huge horse bore down on Tania. "Well met indeed, my beauteous bride!"

Tania stared stupefied as the great horse drew steadily nearer to her, the silver-gray eyes of Gabriel Drake transfixing her like a butterfly on a pin. She couldn't move a finger, she couldn't blink, she couldn't even give voice to the scream of fear that swelled in her throat and threatened to choke her.

The night wheeled around her, and at the pivot of the racing madness were those two deadly, exultant eyes and that terrible smile.

Then, when the ghastly horse was only a couple of yards away from her and Tania felt sure she would be trampled under those massive hammering hooves, Gabriel pulled back on the reins and the horse came to a halt, gray mist billowing from its nostrils, red madness flickering in its eyes.

Gabriel threw back his head and let out a ringing shout of command in a harsh, brittle language.

She heard from a distance a howling chorus of response from voices that sounded only half human. Moments later the night was torn apart from end to end as a host of gray horsemen came plunging over the garden fence like a wave of poisoned water.

There were six of them in all. Six Gray Knights on six gray horses, and the red light in the eyes of the men echoed the wild ruby that burned in the eyes of the horses. The knights of Lyonesse were skeletal thin, their faces ash pale, their gaunt features frozen in lunatic smiles, long white hair like cobwebs over their shoulders. Each wore a thin headband and at the center of each forehead lay a jewel as black as a hole in the night. Their narrow bodies and limbs were wrapped in gray material that shimmered dully like fish scales, and across their shoulders stretched billowing cloaks of gray leather that gave off an unhealthy worm-skin shine.

"You will never be free of me, my lady," Gabriel whispered, his eyes boring into her. "Did you not know? We are bonded for all time!"

Then he laughed and drew back and the horse reared on its hind legs, neighing wildly, huge and dreadful as a mountain, the hooves beating the air above her head.

Tania saw her death in those hooves but she could do nothing to prevent it.

But then something caught her around the waist and she was dragged backward across the patio and into the kitchen. A hand reached out past her head and flung the door closed—and the moment that she lost sight of Gabriel, all her senses came back to her and her body came alive and her brain unfroze.

"Get out through the front." Edric's voice was frantic in her ear. "I'll get the princesses."

"No! I'll come with you; we have to stay together."

They ran through the kitchen and into the hall. Behind them she could hear a pounding like hammers on the garden door. The smash of glass.

They raced up the stairs.

Cordelia stood at the head of the stairs, the bundle of swords in her arms, her eyes gleaming. "So they are come!" she called down. "Do we stand and fight?"

"No!" Edric shouted. "Where are the others?"

"They are here," Cordelia said. A moment later Sancha and Zara appeared behind her, Sancha pulling on the backpack that contained the queen's crown.

Tania and Edric ran back down the stairs with the three princesses on their heels. As they scrambled into the hall there came the sound of splintering wood and shattering glass from the kitchen.

Tania glanced over her shoulder. Through the kitchen doorway she saw one of the Gray Knights forcing his way in through the shards of the back door. The macabre smile was still on his face and a crystal sword jutted from his bony fist. His burning red eyes locked onto hers and his narrow jaws opened in a shout that was like the clashing of knives.

Edric reached the front door and wrenched it open.

Cordelia was suddenly at Tania's side, shouting loudly, calling out strange high-pitched words that sounded as if they were in the language of something not human.

A second knight shouldered his way into the kitchen and the two of them began to stalk forward, their glistening cloaks skimming the ground, their faces grinning, their eyes aflame.

Tania became aware of a strident, trilling noise that grew rapidly behind her. She heard Edric give a surprised cry and a second later she was almost knocked off her feet as a whole flock of small dark birds came spiraling along the hallway, giving shrill voice as they funneled through the kitchen doorway like a dark rushing cloud. Now she understood the purpose of Cordelia's cries. She had been calling the birds to her.

The birds wheeled around the two knights, blotting them out with wing and feather, harrying them, pecking and clawing at them.

"The starlings will give them pause!" Cordelia shouted to Tania, grabbing her wrist. "We must go!"

Tania saw the crystal sword blades cutting through the birds like lightning in a black whirlwind. Torn and twisted bodies began to fall, littering the floor, but still the birds kept up their attack.

Cordelia pulled her along the hallway and out into the night. Sancha was running down the front steps to the pavement; Zara was already in the road. Edric was on the threshold waiting for Tania and Cordelia. They sprang past him and he brought the door crashing closed at their backs.

"Where to?" he panted.

"Jade's house," Tania said, gasping. "It's too early but we can hide till they go."

"Yes."

Tania plunged down the steps with Edric on her right and Cordelia on her left, and even in her fear and panic she knew that Cordelia was weeping as she ran, weeping for the birds that were giving their lives so that they could escape.

They came tumbling onto the pavement. The night was still and quiet, the streets empty.

"This way!" said Edric, pointing to the left.

"Where is Zara?" Sancha panted.

Tania saw a flash of movement under a streetlight, a glimpse of a blue skirt between parked cars on the far side of the road, heading to the right.

"Zara!" she shouted.

"She's going the wrong way," Edric said. "Tania, lead the others to safety. I'll get her."

"No!" Tania said. "I will!" She didn't give him the chance to argue as she sprinted across the road in pursuit of her fleeing sister.

"Meet us there!" Edric called after her.

Zara was twenty or thirty yards ahead of her, running like the wind, her golden hair streaming out behind her.

Tania was about to call out to her when she heard the clatter of hooves on tarmac behind her. She darted a quick look over her shoulder. Two mounted knights were in the street in front of her house; she could see them staring around, the horses twisting and turning, shedding their misty gray light.

Tania ducked down, crouching low behind parked cars as she ran along. Zara had disappeared around the long curve of the street.

Tania kept low until she, too, was beyond the bend, then she straightened up and redoubled her efforts to catch up with her sister. She didn't dare call out to Zara in case the knights heard her. The pavement was hard and painful under her bare feet; there had been no time to put on shoes.

As Tania ran determinedly after her Zara came to a side road. She bounded across but her foot must have caught on the far curb, because suddenly she was sprawling on the pavement. It gave Tania the chance to catch up with her.

"Zara, stop!"

Zara's panic-stricken face turned to her, her blue eyes circled with white. "Tania!"

"We have to . . . get off the . . . street." Tania panted. She pointed to a narrow sunken front yard behind black railings. Stone steps led to the door of a basement flat. "Down there!"

The two sisters dived in through the open gate and came to a halt at the foot of the steps, their backs to the high wall. It was a while before either of them had breath enough to speak.

"Sancha?" Zara gasped at last, her eyes filled

with fear. "Cordelia?"

"Safe, I think," Tania said. "Edric's with them. You went the wrong way!"

Zara put her hands up to her face. "I saw them," she said. "I looked out of the window and saw them in the garden and I was so frightened, Tania. I have only heard the Gray Knights of Lyonesse spoken of in tales of horror from times long ago. I had never seen them before. Their faces!" she said. "Did you see their faces?"

Tania nodded; she wouldn't quickly forget those haggard faces with their red eyes and their fixed grins. "Gabriel was there," she said. "I think he was leading them."

"Then the question of whether Rathina got her reward from the Sorcerer King is answered," Zara said. "The great traitor has been brought back from exile and has been made captain of the Gray Knights. These are ill tidings!"

"Tell me about it."

"Do we go back?" Zara's voice was calmer now.

"I don't think so," Tania said, picturing the neighborhood in her mind. Trying to work out a safe route to the Andersons' house.

"Did Sancha take the crown with her?" Zara asked.

"Yes, and Cordelia has the swords. We're to meet them at my friend's house. I haven't got my watch on but it's probably close to two. Which means there are still a couple of hours before Jade and her parents leave and we can get into their house."

"Do we remain here until then?"

"I'm not sure that's such a great idea," Tania said. "The knights are going to be looking for us and we're not far enough away from my house yet. But I have an idea. There's safety in numbers, and there's an old saying: The best place to hide is in plain sight."

Tania looked appraisingly at her sister, raising a hand to lift an errant lock of hair off her face, brushing some flecks of dirt from the front of her blouse. "You'll do just fine," she said with a grim smile.

"Explain, please," Zara said.

Tania crept back up the steps, reaching down to grasp Zara's hand. "Let's put it this way," she said. "Have you ever been to a nightclub?"

"Your age, ladies?" The doorman stood across the entrance to the nightclub, his massive shoulders straining the seams of his suit, his shaved head gleaming from the blue neon sign that hung above the door. STRANGEWAYS: BOOGIE TILL BREAKFAST!

He was young and good-looking, and the biceps of the arms that were folded over his chest were as thick as Tania's thighs.

"Eighteen," Tania said, looking calmly into his eyes. "Both of us."

A wide smile split his face and he stepped aside. "If you say so, ladies," he said. "In you go. There's always room for two more beautiful women. Have a good time, and watch out for the wolves."

Tania mounted the stone steps, keeping a firm

hold of Zara's hand as she squeezed past the doorman and towed her over the threshold and down the dim-lit red velvet stairs. In the darkness he hadn't even noticed that neither of them was wearing shoes.

"Wolves?" Zara said. "There are *wolves* here?"

"Yes and no," Tania said. "Don't worry about it. I'll explain later. But we got in, that's the main thing. Now all we have to do is pay the entrance fee and disappear into the crowds. Let's see those gray gargoyles follow us in here!"

Tania was becoming increasingly anxious. She had seen nothing of the Gray Knights as she had led the way to the nightclub, but she had the uneasy feeling that they *were* being followed, as if one or more of the knights were tracking them at a distance, shadowing their progress through the Camden night.

"What manner of place is this?" Zara asked. "And what is that noise?"

"It's a place for people who like to party all night long. It's a bit like the Festival of the Traveler's Moon, but indoors and a lot sweatier and louder. The noise is music."

Zara paused on the stairs, cocking her head to listen. She shook her head. "No," she said. "That is not music. I hear rhythm, but no melody. Rhythm without melody is but the stamping of cattle in the byre."

"There are tunes if you listen carefully, honest, but people like plenty of drum and bass these days. It's modern dance music. You'll get used to it."

"I sincerely doubt that I shall," Zara said.

The thudding of the music grew louder as they walked along a black-lined corridor.

Tania felt Zara's fingers digging into her hand as she pushed her way through a set of black swing doors. The music hit them like an avalanche.

The main club room was a huge dark area traversed by a framework of stairs and walkways and galleries of open-mesh steel. Multicolored lights spun on the high ceiling, sending rainbows of color skidding across the walls and down onto the seething mass of bodies that filled the dance floor. The room was circled by a raised mezzanine floor, filled with tables and chairs and lined with black velvet couches.

The place was packed, the high-octane music thundering out, vibrating the floor under their feet, so loud that conversation was virtually impossible.

Tania looked at Zara. The Faerie princess was staring around, her mouth twisted in a tight grimace and her eyes narrowed as though from pain. Maybe bringing her here had not been such a great idea after all. Tania had guessed it would be a culture shock for Zara but the princess didn't look so much shocked as terrified.

She put her arm around Zara's shoulders and brought her lips close to her sister's ear. "It's okay!" she shouted. "There's no need to be scared. We won't stay long. I just wanted to throw the knights off our trail. Can you put up with it for a few more minutes?"

Zara nodded and said something that she didn't catch. She held her ear to Zara's mouth, but still the music was too loud for her to hear.

"Tell me later!" Tania shouted in Zara's ear. Holding her close, she made her way around the floor, looking for an unoccupied table or couch where they could sit for a while.

They were about a third of the way around the room when Tania spotted something that froze her in her tracks. A tall, thin gray shape had come sliding in through the doors.

In an instant Tania drew Zara into the shade of a steel stairway.

It was one of the Gray Knights. But how had he been allowed into the club? Did no one see how *inhuman* he looked with his long, slithering gray cloak and his ash white face and his insane smile? And he was carrying the thin white sword openly in front of him as he moved through the crowds.

Tania stared in horror as he glided forward. She saw how the people parted to let him through, even though none of them even glanced at him or acknowledged him in any way. It was as though he was invisible to them, like a cold stirring in the air that made them shiver and move away without knowing why.

The death's head turned, the red eyes raking the room as he walked with slow purpose toward them.

Tania looked at Zara, but her sister had her eyes screwed tightly shut against the noise and seemed unaware of their danger. Taking a firm hold of Zara's hand, Tania broke cover and ran down the wide steps to the dance floor.

She edged into the dancing throng, the strobe lights flashing and swirling above her, the music pounding in her ears. She felt Zara trying to pull away from her, but she kept hold of her as she pushed through to find a place for them to stand.

She managed to take command of a small space somewhere near the middle of the dance floor. The music changed as one song faded and another came pounding out of the speakers, this time with an even faster, more frantic beat to it. Laughing and whooping, the dancers began to bounce off one another. Tania stumbled as someone bumped into her. She felt Zara's hand slip out of hers as the dancers swept them apart.

"Zara! *Zara!*" Her voice was lost in the pulsing of the music.

And then, as Tania struggled to get to her sister, Zara opened her mouth and let out a scream.

Tania had heard nothing like it in her life before. It rose high above the booming of the music, brain-numbingly loud, piercing and intense and painful. People fell against her and she was thrown to the ground. And still the scream went on, blotting out every other sound, forcing Tania to press her hands to her ears with the pain of it.

There were fizzing explosions from the ceiling. Sparks rained down. The whirling of the colored lights stopped. The music ended abruptly as the speakers erupted into crackling smoke.

And then Zara's scream faded and a stunned silence came down over the dance floor.

Tania pushed someone's arm off her legs and sat up.

Zara was standing alone in the middle of the dance floor, staring about in astonishment. All around her dancers were sprawled on the ground as if they had been thrown off their feet by a hurricane. A harsh hissing sound was coming from the speakers.

Tania stumbled to her feet. People were beginning to stir. There were groans and frightened voices calling out in the gloom of the blue wall lights—the only lights that remained now that the revolving strobes had been wrecked.

Tania looked for the Gray Knight. There he was! Standing among the fallen tables on the raised level, seemingly unaffected by Zara's scream. He began to stride toward them, the white blade of his sword shining eerily in the dim light. There was no time to waste. Tania picked her way to Zara and caught hold of her hand. She could see an exit sign on the far side of the room.

"Quickly! This way!" Moving as rapidly as they could through the mass of fallen dancers, they headed for the exit light.

A few people were on their feet now and a murmur of confused voices was beginning to rise from all over the nightclub. Unlike previously, when people seemed to make room for the Gray Knight without even realizing it, they were now milling about him too shocked to step aside, constantly getting in his way as he tried to push forward.

Tania felt a moment of terror as she imagined the

carnage that his sword could cause among those bewildered people. But he showed no sign of wanting to attack them. Perhaps the Gray Knights had instructions not to draw attention to their presence in this world. Not until their mission had been completed and the Faerie princesses were all dead.

Tania pulled Zara up the steps and shoved her through the exit door. They ran along a corridor and up some steps to a door with a bar across it. Tania slammed her hand down on the bar and pushed the door open. They came out into an alley.

"We need to get away from here," she said. "Are you okay?"

"I did not mean to cause such destruction." Zara gasped. "I only wished for the noise and the crowding people to go away!"

"I don't think you hurt anyone," Tania said. "And you stopped that knight getting to us." She snatched at Zara's hand. "We have to run now, okay?"

"Yes."

Hand-in-hand, they ran.

XVI

The night-dark blanket of clouds was just beginning to turn gray around the edges, and between buildings, the horizon glowed with a thin pale line.

Tania and Zara were still hand-in-hand, but they were walking now. They had run until a stitch in Tania's side had forced her to come to a staggering, breathless halt. She had doubled over, hands on her knees, gulping in air and trying not to succumb to the dizziness that was making the paving stones wobble under her.

After giving herself a minute or two to recover Tania had straightened up and their flight from the nightclub had continued, albeit at a less frantic pace.

Her feet were really hurting now; running hard on tarmac and stone without shoes had taken its toll. Zara walked silently at her side, her head down, her eyes hooded. Tania glanced at her every now and then, concerned by the uncharacteristically pensive expression on her sister's face.

Eventually she had to say something. "I really don't think you hurt anyone back there."

Zara looked at her. "I hope that I did not."

Tania attempted a wry smile. "That scream was amazing," she said. "How do you do that?"

"I do not know," Zara admitted. "I felt a great fear growing in me, to be surrounded by so many people. I could not breathe, and that noise like the pounding of hammers in my head—I thought that I should lose my mind." She looked at Tania, her hand touching against her own chest. "I felt the fear growing here and I had to let it out of my body or I thought I would die."

"That's some defense mechanism you've got there, Zara," Tania said, squeezing her sister's hand. "If we get into any more hot water, remind me to stick close."

"Hot water? Explain, please."

Tania smiled. "You're a good person to be with when bad things are happening. It's a pity it didn't have any effect on the Gray Knight."

"Aye, a great pity." Zara lifted her head and sniffed the air. "Dawn is near. Do we go to meet with the others now?"

Tania nodded. "We've gone a very roundabout way, but we're not far away from where Jade lives. Ten minutes, if that."

"I hope that they are safe. I am ashamed that I fled so."

"We were all frightened," Tania said. "Don't blame yourself."

Zara flashed her a sharp look. "I do blame myself," she said. "And it will not occur again." Looking into her determined face, Tania believed her.

They turned into a wide street of tall Georgian terraces, the entrances reached by flights of stone steps, the lower windows fronted by black railings. One or two lights were on in the houses, but there was no one about on the streets yet.

When occasional vehicles went by, Zara shrank away from them with narrowed, wary eyes.

"They're called cars," Tania said. "And they're harmless. Well, not if you stand in front of one. But they're just a way of getting around quickly."

"To what purpose?" Zara asked, staring suspiciously as a white van went growling past in a blaze of headlights.

"It helps people get to where they're going on time," Tania said. "And it means we can move about the country really fast. Say you wanted to go to Scotland to meet someone, you could be up there in a few hours. It would take forever to walk."

"Do you not have horses?"

"Yes, but horses aren't as fast as cars." She smiled. "And we don't have magic to help us like you do. You know, the Mystic Arts."

"Mastery of the Mystic Arts takes many long years of patient study," Zara said. "How long do humans study these . . . *cars* . . . before they are able to harness their power?"

"I think it usually takes a few months to learn to drive," Tania said. "But it's nothing like—*Uhh!*" She came to a sudden jarring halt.

"What ails you?"

"I don't know. . . ." Tania staggered, grabbing at the railings in front of the nearest house to stop herself from falling.

And everything changed.

Zara was gone. The cars that had lined the street were gone. The houses were the same except that the brickwork was of a brighter color and seemed less grimy . . . less old. And along the pavement in place of the slender concrete lampposts, she saw square gas lamps on top of solid iron columns, their light flickering yellow through sooty glass.

She was also aware that the front doors of the houses, which had previously been painted in any number of different colors, were now uniformly black, and the window frames were all white.

Something drew her up the flight of stone steps that led to the front door of the nearest house. A strange thing happened in the porch. It was as if two different realities were lying on top of each other. In one reality the black front door with its brass knocker and knob remained shut, but in the other it swung silently open into a gaslit hall with dark brown wallpaper and a red tiled floor.

Tania stepped into the hallway. The air swirled

darkly around her and suddenly she was in a warm, fire-lit room. She was sitting on a big padded sofa, snuggled up beside a beautiful woman dressed in a rustling lavender-colored gown. Golden curls hung softly around Tania's shoulders, tied with bright green ribbons. An older boy—about nine years old, she guessed—sat at the other side of the woman, and he had a lolling toddler half asleep on his lap. A boy and a girl of seven or eight—twins, perhaps?—lay in front of the fire, the boy busily engaged in cutting black-and-white pictures from a pile of newspapers while the girl sorted them and dabbed thick white paste onto their backs before smoothing them onto the blank pages of a large open book. All of the children were dressed in Victorian clothing; Tania looked down at herself to see a white shift with pleats and ruffles and frills and bows.

She felt safe and loved, and more than that she felt *happy* this time, pressed against her mother's side and surrounded by her brothers and sisters.

She gazed drowsily around the comfortable room. The ornately molded ceiling was high and the papered walls were decorated with patterns of birds and vines and scrollwork all picked out in shades of gold and ivory and brown. A warm light came from fluted glass gas mantles on the walls. A cheerful fire crackled and danced in the black hearth under a mantel topped with a gilt-framed mirror and lined with porcelain ornaments. Heavy curtains adorned the windows, drawn back with tasseled ribbons. There were upholstered chairs and footstools and an upright piano stood against one wall.

Their mother was reading to them from a hard-back book.

"Read me the part again where the cat vanishes, 'all but the grin,'" said Tania. "That's my favorite part."

"Better than the tea party, Flora, dear?"

"Oh, yes," Tania/Flora said. "The tea party is very amusing, but what I love most is to hear about the cat."

"Very well, my dear," replied her mother. "But then you must be as good as gold and go straight to bed."

"Mayn't I say good night to Papa first?" Flora implored.

"Yes, you may," began her mother. "And you may tell him that . . ." But even as she was speaking, the voice of the woman and the soft sofa and the family room all melted away in a swirling soup of darkening air.

Flora stood at the top of a long flight of stairs, illuminated by gas mantles that hung high on the walls. She was standing at a large dark brown door, barefoot now and dressed in a long white nightgown. She stepped up to the door and knocked on the panels. "Papa!" she called.

A man's voice sounded from beyond the door. He sounded tired. "A moment, sweetheart; it is not safe." A few seconds passed and the voice spoke again. "You may come in now."

Flora turned the door handle and pushed open the door. She stepped into a small, plain room filled with tables and bookcases, gaslit again but with only one small gable window and with a stained and sloping ceiling. Her father was there, standing at a table—he was a tall, handsome man with long side-whiskers and dressed in a dark tailcoat. The table was filled with odd scientific instruments, and with a clutter of jars and bottles containing colored liquids and powders, test tubes in wooden racks, bizarre devices of levers and coiled wiring and springs and gauges.

Her father stooped and opened his arms as Flora went running across the bare wood floor. She jumped into his embrace and he lifted her high, hugging her to him. He smelled of chemicals and smoke but Flora didn't mind that one bit.

"And what does my pretty little maid want with her weary old papa?" he asked.

"I am to say good night before I go to bed," said Flora, catching the sleeve of her nightgown in her fist and wiping a smudge off her father's nose. "And mother says to tell you not to spend all night with your silly experiments or you will make yourself ill."

"Then I shall finish what I am doing and that will be all for the day. How does that sound?"

"That sounds very sensible," said Flora. "Now, kiss me good night and put me down. Mother says that if I am in bed within three shakes of a lamb's tail, then she will come up and read to me." She tilted her head sideways as she looked into her father's face. "She is reading me a very good book indeed. It is about a girl named Alice. It was written by a gentleman called Lewis Carroll. According to Mother, Mr. Carroll is a mathemagician."

"Is he, now?" said her father, putting her down. "Are you sure you do not mean mathematician?"

Flora thought for a moment then shook her head. "No, mother definitely said he was a mathe-*magician*."

Her father straightened up with a smile. "Just so," he said. "Your mother always knows best."

"Good night, Papa," Flora called as she ran from the room.

"Good night, my sweet angel," called her father. "Good night."

As she began to patter down the stairs, the world was whipped again into a whirl of dark confusion until with a rush of cool, clear air Tania came to herself and found that she was outside the house and leaning against the black railings.

She gazed up the stone stairway, noticing for the first time that there was a blue plaque on the wall at the side of the door.

Ernest Llewellyn
Renowned amateur scientist
Lived here 1851–1869

"She didn't die," Tania said. "She wasn't even ill. . . ."

"Tania!" Zara's urgent voice brought her out of

her dream. "There is no time to linger here."

Tania gave a gasp of alarm. For a few moments she had forgotten all about Drake and the Gray Knights.

"What was the matter?" Zara asked. "You seemed moonstruck!"

"I'll explain later," Tania said. "Let's get to Jade's house first."

They clasped hands again and ran swiftly along the pavement with their dawn-lit shadows stretching out behind them.

XVII

"No! Get away from me! I won't go with you! I won't!"

"Tania, it's me! It's okay. It's just a dream."

Tania burst out of her nightmare as if from deep water, gasping and wild-eyed and drenched with sweat. She was in bed and Edric was sitting on the edge, leaning over her and holding her flailing arms by the wrists.

She glared into his anxious face, wanting to claw his face with her nails—to put out once and for all the evil light in his horrible silver eyes.

Silver eyes? No! No!

Brown eyes. Warm, chestnut brown eyes.

She gave a groan and lay there panting as the last remnants of the nightmare drained away from her.

"Are you going to stop trying to hit me?" he asked gently.

"Yes," she gasped.

He let go of her wrists.

"I thought you were Gabriel," she said.

"I guessed." His fingers lifted a damp lock of hair off her cheek and smoothed it back behind her ear. "It's okay now. It's over."

"Is it?" she said. "He's there, Edric, every time I go to sleep. He's there, waiting for me." She heaved herself onto her elbows, staring in confusion around the unfamiliar bedroom until she suddenly remembered that she was in Jade's room in the Andersons' house. "What time is it?"

"Just gone midday," Edric said. "You've been asleep for about six hours. I've been out for some breakfast things."

Tania looked uneasily at him. "You weren't seen, were you?"

"I don't think so," he said.

"You must tell the others to stay in the house and keep away from the windows. If any of the neighbors see people in here we'll have the police round checking it out."

"I've already told them," Edric said. He leaned close and kissed her forehead. "I'm going to make us all something to eat. Come down when you're ready."

Twenty minutes later, Tania was showered and dressed and sitting with Edric and her sisters at the stripped pine table in the Andersons' kitchen. It was a big, airy room with windows that looked out over a garden screened by tall hedges of laurel.

At first the three sisters were suspicious of the

strange foods on display and reluctant to try anything that they didn't recognize. They drank milk and ate fruit and bread but avoided most of the other things on offer. To an extent Tania could understand their unwillingness to experiment; as well as fresh fruit and bread rolls and ham and cheese, Edric had provided things that she was certain had never appeared on a Faerie table: waffles and Pop-Tarts and Hot Pockets, breadsticks and various dips, pretzels and croissants and bagels. And to drink there was fruit juice and tea and coffee.

Tania unscrewed the lid from a jar and handed it to Zara.

Zara peered into the jar. "What is this?" she asked.

"Chocolate spread," Tania told her. "Try it, it's nice."

Zara dipped a spoon in and put it in her mouth. Her face lit up.

"It is delightful!" she said. "Cordelia, you must try some." She dipped the spoon again and offered it to her sister.

Cordelia leaned across and opened her mouth for the spoon.

"It's meant to go on toast, really," Edric said.

"It is too sweet for me," Cordelia said. "I prefer this savory pale brown paste. What is it called?"

"Hummus," Tania said.

From that moment on Cordelia and Zara seemed determined to try everything, randomly sampling food from the cartons and packets and pots and jars and serving plates. Only Sancha seemed unwilling to join in the feast.

"Are you okay?" Tania asked her. "You're not eating much."

"I have eaten sufficient for my needs," Sancha said. "This beverage is very pleasant—what is it?"

"Coffee with cream," Tania said. "You see? Not everything in this world is nasty. There's good stuff, too." She smiled, feeling herself unwinding a little for the first time in days.

They had already exchanged stories about how the two parties had got to the house. Edric's journey had been less fraught than that of Tania and Zara. He had led the princesses down a side alley into the back garden of a house farther down Eddison Terrace, and they had gone over fences and walls from garden to garden until they had come to the end of the street. Luck had been with them; they had managed to jump on a night bus that had taken them to the end of the road where the Andersons lived. Then it had just been a case of keeping under cover until they had seen the Andersons' car drive away in the predawn darkness. Shortly afterward Edric had led them up the drive and they had slipped into the house undetected.

"Zara's scream was unbelievable," Tania told Edric. "It knocked an entire roomful of people off their feet, not to mention zapping all the electrics. It's just a pity it didn't seem to have any effect on the Gray Knight."

"They are wound about with protective incantations," Sancha said. "Not so easily will they be defeated." She looked thoughtfully at Zara. "We already know that Zara can sing enchantments. Her scream came from the same source, I do not doubt."

"It came from being fearful for my life in that dreadful place!" Zara said, her words slightly muffled by a bagel.

"You took her to a *nightclub*?" Edric asked Tania in obvious surprise.

"It seemed like a good idea at the time. I had a feeling that we were being followed. And I was right; the knight came in after us." Tania frowned. "It was the weirdest thing," she said. "He just strolled through there and no one batted an eyelid. And you know how freaky they look. It's not like you wouldn't notice one of them in a crowd. Are they invisible to humans or what?"

"Not invisible," Sancha said. "Say rather that mortal folk *choose* not to see them. I have read many books on the customs and manners of mortals. They seem to have a great capacity for ignoring those things that do not conform to their narrow system of beliefs."

"They're really not that bad," Tania said.

"Indeed, they *are* that bad!" Cordelia said. "They wield power without thought or responsibility, and that is ever the act of a wayward child."

"What power do you mean?" Tania asked.

Cordelia gestured toward the light fitting in the ceiling.

"Electricity isn't dangerous," Tania said. "Well, it *is*, but we've learned how to keep it under control. So long as people don't act stupidly with it, it's really useful. In fact in a society like this, I'm not sure we'd be able to survive without electricity."

"And that does not concern you?" Cordelia exclaimed. "That you are beholden to a power that you do not understand and over which you have no control?"

"We can control it," Tania said. "We can switch it on and off whenever we like. And as for not understanding it—well, okay, I don't know *exactly* how electricity is made, but it's like that for a lot of things. I don't know how to fly an airplane or how to do open-heart surgery or make a pair of shoes, but I don't need to. Other people do those things for me."

"And that is the peril," Cordelia said. "To rely on others for your survival is foolhardy. Were I cast from the palace in nothing but my shift, I would endure and thrive. I know how to make fire for warmth and light; I know how to defend myself against danger. I know how to seek for fresh water, and what is good to eat in the forest and what must be avoided. I can grow grain and roots, and I know the seasons to sow and to harvest. Can the same be said for the beings who inhabit this rat's-warren of a city?"

"Well, no, I don't suppose so," Tania admitted. "If something goes wrong and you have an electrical blackout, then you're kind of . . . helpless."

"Helpless, indeed," Cordelia said. "But we are not

helpless, not even against the peril that has come upon us from Lyonesse. Not while we have our wits and our swords."

"I keep telling you," Tania said. "I don't know how to use a sword."

"Then you must practice and remember," said Cordelia. "Come, I shall give you a lesson. Do not fear, I shall not prick you more often than the need for sharp lessons dictates."

"If it's all the same to you, I think I'd rather have Edric give me a lesson," Tania said, unsure of submitting herself to Cordelia's idea of suitable teaching methods. At least she knew Edric would do his utmost to avoid hurting her. She looked down the table at him. "If that's okay?"

"I can do that," he said. "Princess Cordelia, can you fetch the swords? Then we need to find some space to work in."

"There's a big room at the back," Tania said. "They use it as a dining room on special occasions. If we move the table and chairs, there'll be plenty of room."

"So be it," Cordelia said, getting up. "Let the lessons commence!"

"Watch your footwork!" Edric called. "You have to stay balanced and you have to be thinking two moves ahead. You're holding the sword too low. If I aimed a cut at your neck, you wouldn't be able to parry in time." He made a startling sideways leap, ducking in under the wild swing of Tania's sword and aiming a slicing sweep at shoulder height, then jumping backward again so that he was beyond her reach almost before she knew what was going on.

"There you are," he said, hardly even out of breath. "I've just cut off your head. Now what are you going to do?"

"Cancel my next hairdressing appointment, I guess," Tania responded gloomily.

They were in the sunlit back lounge of the Andersons' house. The long dark-wood table had been put against the wall. Cordelia and Zara were sitting on it, Cordelia cross-legged, bent forward, watching intently; Zara more carefree, leaning back, letting her legs swing. Sancha was watching quietly from a chair.

So far, Tania hadn't remembered a single thing about how to use the sword that she had been given. It felt clumsy and unwieldy and despite Edric and her sisters' best efforts to instruct her in the basics of a fighting technique, whenever Edric lunged at her everything went clean out of her head and all she could do was to stand there swiping randomly with the blade.

"Tania, you do but swat at flies!" Cordelia shouted. "Parry, thrust, riposte! It is all in the wrist and the feet!"

"Not helping!" Tania growled—but at least Cordelia wasn't laughing like Zara or looking increasingly worried like Sancha.

Cordelia jumped off the table and came over to where Tania was standing.

"The truest and surest blow is from above," she said, taking Tania's sword arm and lifting it, angling her wrist so the point of the blade was aimed toward the center of Edric's chest. "But to make the approach you must first draw your left foot close to your right foot and lunge forward as forcibly as you may, ending in the low ward."

"Ending in the *what*?"

"If your opponent moves to the right, follow through with a slash to the head," Cordelia continued, ignoring her question. "To defend yourself against the same blow, stand in the low ward, take the coming blow by the edge, and push your enemy's sword to the right, stepping in all the time. Keep the point of your sword down toward the enemy, so that with luck he will impale himself on your blade as he follows through."

"What's a low ward?"

"High ward is with the arm raised and the sword pointing down," Zara called. "Low ward is with the arm lowered and the sword pointing upward."

"We could take a break if you like?" Edric said.

"No way!" Tania said. "I'm going to get this right. Come at me again with that head-slicing thing."

He lunged toward her, his sword arm up, the point down. She took a deliberate step back, her own blade in the low ward position.

She tried to do as Cordelia had suggested, stepping

suddenly toward him, coming in low, bringing her blade up against the side of his and pushing it away. But she had misjudged his speed and strength. Her sword slipped and they crashed together; she felt a sharp pain in her wrist as his sword-point nicked her skin.

Tania's reaction to the pain was immediate and instinctive. She spun her sword up across his, knocking his blade cleanly to the right; then she took a long step backward with her right foot, shifting her balance and coming in easily on his undefended left side, lunging and thrusting solidly at his stomach, knowing that the rising blade would push up under his ribs and pierce his heart.

She stopped the move with perfect precision, the point of her sword only an inch away from his body. And then, before he could react, she took a well-balanced bound backward and came to rest in a poised, defensive posture.

"A hit!" Cordelia cried, clapping loudly. "A thrust to the very heart!"

Edric stood grinning at her. "That was amazing," he said. "I'm dead and I didn't even see it coming."

"The old skills return anew," Sancha said, smiling now. "It is good."

Edric's face fell as he saw the spot of blood on her wrist. "I hurt you," he said.

"It's nothing," Tania said. "And it helped." It was as if a long-closed door in her mind had been kicked open. She knew how to use the crystal sword. She knew how to attack and how to defend herself. And it had all come back to her in that instant of pain. Only one question remained in her mind now—and it was not one she felt like sharing.

If it did come down to a life and death face-off between her and one of those Gray Knights, would she really be able to use the sword on him? Even if it was to save her own life, did she have it in her to kill?

It was a little while later and they were all gathered in Jade's bedroom. Tania was sitting in front of the computer. She had opened the Pleiades website to the page that showed the photo of Lilith Mariner.

"It is our mother indeed," Zara said, her trembling fingers reaching out toward the computer screen. "Oh, how it fills my heart to see her beloved face again after so long a time." She looked excitedly at Cordelia and Sancha. "Do you see?"

"I do," Sancha said. "It is a blessing to know that five hundred years in the Mortal World has done no harm to the Queen—none that can be seen, in any hap."

"How was this likeness created?" Cordelia asked, peering over Tania's shoulder. "I see no brush work, yet it has the look of oil and pigment in the hands of a master artist."

"It's a photo," Tania told her. "It's another bit of gear that I can't really explain," she said with a half-smile. "It comes from a small metal box. You point it at someone and press the button, and there you are. An instant picture." She looked at the empty digital camera cradle at the side of the computer. "I'd be happy to show you how it works, but Jade's taken hers on holiday."

"At another time, perhaps," Zara said. She grimaced at the computer. "The noise of this machine makes my head hurt," she said. "Thank you for showing us our mother's likeness, but with your leave I will await you below."

"As will I," Cordelia added. "In truth, your *con-tutor* buzzes like a nest of summer wasps!"

"Computer," Tania said quietly. "Sorry, I'll turn it off now." She was surprised that the low humming was bothering them so much—she was hardly even aware of it.

"I'll put the kettle on," Edric said. "Sancha? Coffee?"

"That would be kind," Sancha said.

A few moments later Tania was left with only Sancha standing at her side as she closed down the computer.

"I saw that there were words on the machine," Sancha said, staring at the blank screen. "But I cannot *feel* them; they are not real to me."

"How do you mean?"

"A word written in a book has texture, it has form, it is a thing of ink, a real thing, a thing with substance. But I can feel nothing within your machine. It is as empty to me as the face of the moon." She touched a very tentative finger to the top corner of the screen. "No, I see nothing."

"That's because I've switched it off."

"You do not understand," Sancha said. "Remain seated, and I shall explain my meaning to you." She moved away so that she was standing behind Jade's desk, facing Tania. She lifted her hand and made a small twirling movement of her fingers.

Tania heard a soft sliding sound. She turned her head and saw one of Jade's books slip off the shelf and float toward her. Sancha's fingers moved again. The book hung in the air in front of Tania and opened itself, its cover toward Sancha so that she could not see the pages.

"Behold words of ink," Sancha said. "Words on paper. Look to the top of the left-hand page. 'David was back within ten minutes. "All done," he said. "We've got the whole place to ourselves now. Come on, let's see if we can find out anything about that White Lady."'"

They were the exact words that Tania's eyes were following in the book. She glanced at Sancha. Her sister's face had gone blank, save for two deep lines between her eyebrows. Her eyes were half closed, the irises hidden under the fallen lids so that only a thin white line was visible.

"How are you doing that?" Tania asked. "You know what's written in the book without reading it, don't you?"

Sancha opened her eyes. "It is part of my gift," she said. "I can feel the substance of written words even if they are not visible to me. In a library as vast as the one in the palace, it is a useful ability, would you not say?"

"Extremely useful, I should think," Tania said.

Sancha pointed to the computer. "But I see nothing in the machine. There is no life in there, no depth."

"I wish we'd had you with us when we went to the place where Titania works," Tania said. "You could have just read her telephone number and her home address from their personnel files." Her voice trailed off.

"What is the matter?" Sancha asked.

"I've had an idea," Tania said, springing out of the chair. She ran from the room and bounded down the stairs. "Edric! Cordie! Zara!"

"In here," came Edric's voice from the kitchen.

Tania ran in with Sancha close on her heels. Edric was standing by the kettle. Zara was at the table, spooning up the remnants of chocolate spread from the jar. Cordelia was at the window, gazing into the garden.

"Sancha can read things from a distance," she announced. "Without having to see them."

"This is known to us, Tania," Zara said with a puzzled frown.

Tania looked at Edric. "What information did we want from that man at Pleiades?"

"Lilith Mariner's phone number, for a start," Edric said. His eyes sparked with understanding. "You think Sancha might be able to read the number off her file?"

"Her phone number, her home address, the lot."

Tania turned to Sancha. "If we take you to the place where Titania works, could you do that? Could you read her file?"

"If ink has been applied to paper, then time and silence are all the tools I will need," Sancha said.

"We have to go there," Tania said. "We have to go there right now!"

XVIII

It was mid-afternoon. Tania and Edric and the three princesses were standing in the paved courtyard outside unit five of the Spenser Road Forum. Banners of thin white cloud straggled across the sky, but it was warm when the sun broke free, although in the shade a keen east wind took the edge off the summer heat and more than once Tania had felt a chill on her neck that made her think that Gray Knights were near. Not that they had seen any sign of them on their way here from the Andersons' home.

Tania had not been looking forward to getting her three sisters all the way to Richmond, especially not since the quickest and easiest route was via the Underground. She had feared that the noise and the crush and the claustrophobic nature of a tube train might freak them out, but they had endured the journey in tight-lipped silence, keeping close together, braced against the cacophony as the carriage had rattled its way through the tunnels.

Surprisingly to Tania, Zara had showed the least fear. She had sat between her two sisters, holding their hands and, when the noise levels permitted, comforting them with quiet words. Cordelia had been the worst affected, flinching away when other passengers passed by her in the aisle, jumping at the hiss and clatter of the doors.

Sancha and Zara had stayed on either side of her when they had finally come up out of the Underground system and had begun the brief walk through Richmond to Spenser Road.

"The animals are strange here," Cordelia had remarked at one point. "In the song of the birds I can hear lamentations for the loss of the wildwoods. Although they are drawn to this place, they say that the mortals who dwell here are wasteful and dangerous. Many birds die by mischance and cruelty in the brick and stone canyons of the city, but those that live grow fat on discarded mortal food. And I sense foxes and squirrels and other small beasts, although they are hidden now from the sun. But they smell strange to me, tainted by eating mortal food and walking mortal streets, and they have lost the ways of the wood. But other beasts thrive and are merry, rats and spiders and the animals that live on shadows and decay. And the insects care nothing for mortals, for they have been here since before time began, and they will be here still when even the memory of this place and of the race that built it has been dust for a million million years."

Shortly afterward, they had arrived at the wrought-iron gateway of the Spenser Road Forum. They had stepped into the sunken courtyard and walked across it to stand together outside the red-brick facade of the Pleiades Legal Group.

Shining images of the cloud-striped sky filled the tall windows. The sun reflected off the steel-and-glass doors that led to the reception area.

Cordelia was staring into the sky and frowning.

"All will be well," Zara said, taking her hand. "We will be with our mother soon."

Cordelia looked at her, but to Tania it seemed that her sister's clear blue eyes were still full of the sky. "The birds are uneasy," she said. "They smell evil moving on the air."

"Is it the knights?" Sancha asked. "Are they near?"

Cordelia lifted her head. "I smell horses that are not horses," she said. "Their breath is cold; their brazen hooves strike sparks on the stones. They draw closer." She looked at Tania. "Do your business in this place as swift as you may. We should not have left our swords behind."

Cordelia had argued for them to come here armed, but Tania and Edric had convinced the others that it would be impossible to carry their swords through the city without being arrested.

"Will you stay out here with Cordelia and Zara?" Tania asked Edric. Sancha had already told her that she would need to be inside the building in order to be able to seek out Lilith Mariner's records.

"Of course. Be as quick as you can."

Tania nodded.

She walked toward the glass doors, tucking loose strands of her hair under the black cloche hat that she had borrowed from Jade's wardrobe. She had tied her hair back into a long, thick ponytail, and the hat hid the rest. She had also brought sunglasses with her—the idea of this simple change of appearance being to stop the receptionist from recognizing her and immediately calling security to have her thrown out.

She put on her sunglasses and pushed through the doors, leading Sancha to the low seats in the waiting area.

"You sit there," she told her. "I'll keep the receptionist busy while you do your thing, okay?"

A wry smile lifted Sancha's lips. "Oh-kay," she said. "And pray that Cordelia is wrong and that I shall have time to . . . do my thing . . . ere the Gray Knights fall upon us."

"Here's hoping," Tania muttered as she turned and walked toward the high-fronted reception desk. One problem disappeared as she leaned over the counter. The woman seated behind was not the same one as before—she was a small, thin, dark-haired woman in her midthirties. At least Tania was not going to be recognized and asked to leave—not unless Mr. Mervyn turned up.

Tania took off her dark glasses. "Hello there," she said.

"Hi, can I help you?" the woman asked with a professional smile.

"I hope you can," Tania said, leaning on the counter to try and stop her legs shaking so much. "I was wondering whether Lilith Mariner had come back from Beijing?"

"I'm afraid not," the receptionist said. "But I believe she's due back in London any time now."

"Really?" Tania asked, her heart jumping a little. "Do you know exactly when?"

"I don't, sorry. She's not expected back in the office till later in the week."

"Oh, that's a pity," Tania said. She got ready to spin the story that she and Edric had been rehearsing on their way over here. "The thing is, I was hoping to have a very quick word with her. I plan on studying law at university and I was hoping that Ms. Mariner might be able to provide me with some work experience over the summer holidays. I've been told that she's very keen on assisting women who want to get into the legal profession."

"We do take on students as clerical assistants," the receptionist said. "But Ms. Mariner doesn't usually organize it personally, and I think you might be a bit young for our program. I'll give Ms. Mariner's office a call. One of her assistants may be free to come down and have a quick word with you."

"That would be brilliant," Tania said. She didn't mind who she spoke to—short of George Mervyn—so long as it gave her an excuse to stay here long enough for Sancha to locate and read the personnel files.

The receptionist picked up the phone and punched in a number.

Tania shot a quick glance over to Sancha. She was sitting ramrod straight on the low chair, her hands clasped together on her knees, her knuckles white. She was frowning and her eyes were half closed. Her lips were moving, as if she was reciting something in her head.

"You're in luck," the receptionist said. "Ms. Mariner's legal secretary says she can give you a couple of minutes. If you'd like to go and sit over there, I'm sure she won't keep you waiting long."

"Great," Tania said. "Thanks. Is there a coffee machine or anything?"

"Yes, of course." The receptionist stood up, obviously intending to point out where Tania should go to get refreshments, but something caught her eye, something that she could see through the windows behind Tania. "It's getting very dark out there," she said. "Looks like we're in for a storm, and the weather girl said on TV this morning that it'd be a sunny day."

A cold fist clenched in Tania's stomach. She snapped her head around. The day had grown suddenly dark but Tania did not think it had anything to do with gathering storm clouds.

An oncoming movement swelled behind the tinted

glass, like a gray wave beating its way across the courtyard. And there was noise: the clatter of hooves, the swish of sharp swords slicing the air, the rattle of harness, the slap of leather.

A moment later the glass doors were flung open and Edric and Cordelia and Zara burst in, running for their lives.

"They are upon us!" Cordelia screamed.

The gray wave hit the windows. There was a tumultuous crash as four mounted knights plunged through the windows, sending thousands of fragments of glass exploding across the reception area. Tania threw herself over the reception desk, pulling the receptionist down as shards rained over them.

A wild neighing tore the air and the four knights began to shout in shrill, cruel voices. Tania heard Cordelia shouting, her voice thin but brave in all the tumult.

"Gray steeds! Gray steeds! Harm us not! I have the power of love over you! I have the power of light over you! I have the power of the sweet white water over you! I have the power of lush spring grasses over you! These powers I have over you. Go back! Harm us not. Go back!"

Tania pushed the terrified receptionist under the desk. "Stay there," she said. On her knees, surrounded by broken glass, Tania looked around for some kind of weapon.

There was nothing. She lifted her head and peered over the desk.

Sancha had been thrown to the floor by the assault of the four horsemen, but her chair had tipped over on top of her and seemed to have shielded her from the flying glass. Zara and Edric were leaping this way and that, their arms up to ward off the lashing hooves of the horses. Only Cordelia was standing still in all the mayhem, her arms stiff at her sides, fists clenched, out-staring the horses as they reared and bucked around her.

It looked to Tania as if at any moment, Cordelia would be struck down and trampled but for some reason the maddened horses never touched her as they plunged around her. One of the knights swung out sideways from the saddle, clinging grimly to the reins with one hand and aiming a long, sweeping blow at Cordelia's head.

"No!" Tania screamed. She snatched up the keyboard from the desk and flung it at the knight with all her strength. It struck his sword arm, jolting the blade from his grip, sending it spinning in a white blur through the air as he howled in rage.

Tania scrambled onto the top of the desk. With a wild yell she flung herself at the nearest of the knights. But he spurred his horse forward and Tania missed him by inches, her momentum sending her hurtling to the floor.

She sprawled on her face, all the air driven out of her lungs, colored lights flashing in the darkness that swam in front of her eyes.

She was vaguely aware of Edric's voice. "Zara! See

to Sancha!" And then a wild shout. "Tania! Tania!"

She managed to drag herself to her feet. She saw a sword slicing through the air toward her, the slender white crystal carving the gloom. A razor's edge come to spill her blood.

She even had time to regret that she would never see her Faerie mother. So sad that it would all end like this.

And then a second blade cut the darkness, blocking the first.

And then the black cloud was gone and the fog cleared from Tania's brain. Edric stood between her and the Gray Knight, fighting grimly, a sword rising and falling in his hand as he forced the dismounted knight back. He must have snatched up the blade that she had knocked from the other knight's hand.

Edric lifted the sword into the high ward and drove the blade down into the creature's chest. The Gray Knight's body exploded into dust. His clothing fell empty to the floor, his sword ringing on the tiles, his long glistening cloak settling like a shroud over the scattered ashes.

And as the creature died, his horse reared, screaming aloud as the flesh shriveled on its bones until it was nothing more than a skeleton hung with shreds of dried skin. The crazed red light went out of its hollow eye sockets and it fell onto its side, crashing to the floor and shattering to dust like its rider.

The three remaining horses reared away, letting out ear-splitting screeches of terror.

"Tania, run!" It was Edric's voice, and it was Edric's hand that caught her arm and pulled her away as another sword slashed the air where she had been standing.

She saw Zara ahead of them, running down one of the corridors that led from the reception area. She had Sancha with her. Cordelia was only half a step behind.

"Get them out of here!" Edric shouted to Tania, letting go of her arm and turning to confront the first of the oncoming riders. He lunged with his sword at the first knight. With a fierce snarl, the creature deflected the weapon with his own blade.

But even as he bore down on Edric, his horse swerved under a rising stairway, and the knight was knocked out of the saddle. The horse spun on its haunches, its head dragged around by the reins that were still clutched in the fallen knight's fist. The other two horses crashed into it and for a few moments everything was pandemonium as horses and riders fought to stay upright.

In those few precious seconds Tania hurled a pair of swing doors open and shouted for everyone to follow. They came tumbling through after her: Zara and Sancha first, then Cordelia and last Edric. Tania and Edric slammed the doors closed but there was no catch, no lock. Edric stared around for something to block the doors.

Tania saw that they were on the landing of a stairway that zigzagged up and down, but to one side she saw an elevator, and the door was open.

"In here!" she shouted and her sisters plunged in after her. "Edric! Quickly!" He leaped across the landing, slipping through the doors just as they were closing.

Tania hit the lowest button and the elevator began to descend. She guessed that down would be safer than up. Down might lead to a way out; up could only trap them in the building.

They dropped three levels. The elevator came to a smooth halt and the doors opened. They were in a large underground parking lot, the low roof held up by rows of square concrete pillars.

The place was illuminated by yellowish strip lighting, but through the ranks of parked cars they could see a haze of white sunlight that filtered down from a ramp at the far end.

They ran toward the ramp, but at the top they found that the rising roadway was blocked by a steel grid. Edric led them to a narrow doorway and a flight of plain stone steps. They went through another door and came into an alley blocked off by a wrought-iron gate.

"Do they pursue?" Zara gasped, staring back the way they had come.

"Not yet," Cordelia panted. "But I would put distance between us ere we take rest."

Edric rattled the black gate. It was padlocked. "Up and over," he said. He sprang onto the gate and climbed to sit astride it. He reached down a hand. Cordelia took it and jumped easily down on the far side.

It was not long before all the princesses were on the pavement on the other side of the gate. Tania didn't recognize where they were, but she knew it wasn't Spenser Road; they must have emerged on the far side of the Forum. Still, it wouldn't take long for them to find their way back to the main streets and get the first tube train out of here.

Sancha was leaning against the wall, looking dazed.

"Are you okay?" Tania asked, putting her arm around her sister's shoulder. "Did you have time to find anything out before the knights came?"

"I am unhurt," Sancha said. "The knights were swift upon our heels, but I did manage to glean some knowledge before the sky fell on me!"

They all stopped, turning to look at Sancha.

"What did you learn?" Zara breathed.

"All that you would wish!" Sancha said. "I learned where the woman named Lilith Mariner lives. I know where our mother has made her home!"

XIX

The summer afternoon had given way to a warm, shadowy evening. The cloudless sky was a grainy gray-blue and seemed to shimmer like water reflecting off a shield of brushed steel. Tania and Edric and the princesses were standing in the shade of a long brick wall, gazing across the road at a four-story block of flats set back off the street behind tall poplar trees and hedges of privet and fuchsia and yew.

The elegant block was of warm brown brickwork, with balconies and angular bays and wide white-framed windows.

Traffic moved steadily along the road. A sign stood above a low brick wall that fronted the hedges and trees.

> *Dover Court*
> *Park Lane*

If Sancha was right, then Lilith Mariner owned flat 7 in this block.

They were very close to Hampton Court Palace—the diminished mortal echo of the great Royal Palace of Faerie—but they had not come here via the direct route from Richmond. Once on the Underground they had headed north, taking the first train and changing three or four times, moving from the District Line to the Piccadilly Line to the Northern Line and then doubling back and heading south of the Thames to Waterloo, where they caught an over-ground train to Hampton Wick, a five-minute walk from where they were now standing.

Their travels had taken several hours, but they had to do everything they could to try and throw the Gray Knights off their track.

"A grand house, indeed," Sancha said. "A worthy residence for a Queen of Faerie."

"She won't own the whole place," Tania explained. "Just one flat."

Sancha gave her a puzzled look. "One *flat*?"

"Lilith Mariner's apartment will be only a few rooms in one part of the block," Edric said. "The rest will belong to other people."

"Servants and attendants and courtiers, yes?"

"No, people don't live like that here," Tania said. "At least hardly anyone does these days. I think we should go over there and check whether she's home yet."

"And if she is not?" asked Zara.

"Then we'll leave her a letter," Edric said.

"And trust that her response is swifter than the steeds of Lyonesse," Sancha murmured. She turned to where Cordelia stood, slightly apart from them, her fingers tight around the black iron bars of a gate set in the long wall at their backs. "Cordelia? Come, we are departing now."

Cordelia pulled her gaze with obvious reluctance from whatever she had been looking at through the gate, and Tania saw that tears had left shining pathways down her freckled cheeks.

Tania was the first to move toward her, but the others were close behind.

"Cordie? What's wrong?" She peered through the gate's filigree of twisted and shaped wrought-iron, seeing a wide flat area of rough grassland traversed by paths and scattered with slender trees. "It's Bushy Park," Tania said. "Why has it upset you?"

Cordelia wiped a sleeve across her eyes. "Do you not recognize where we are? In Faerie it is upon this very ground that the menagerie stood. Here I tended the hounds and gave food and shelter to the animals that chose to dwell with me: The otters and the swans and the deer and the unicorns and ravens. All the houseless creatures of Faerie." She turned her face away. "I cannot bear it," she said quietly. "Where the clamor and filth of mortals hold sway, there I see no image of Faerie, but here, where some small part of nature is allowed to survive in chains and fetters of concrete and iron, that is when I see a glimpse of home, and it pierces my heart."

Zara turned to look across the road at Dover Court. "And it is here that our mother chose to dwell," she said thoughtfully. "So close to home, but yet so very far away."

They crossed the road and walked through a gap in the low wall that surrounded Dover Court. They made their way down wide steps into an attractive sunken garden circled with shrubs and flowering plants and containing wooden benches and a stone fountain. The noise of the traffic seemed less intrusive down here behind the screen of trees.

They walked through the garden and came to the main doors leading into the apartment block. They were white with frosted-glass panels.

Edric gave them a push. "Locked," he said.

Tania was standing to one side of the entranceway, running her finger down a series of labeled buttons on the brass plate of an intercom system.

7. L. MARINER.

She pressed the button. An electronic buzzing came from the slotted grid at the top of the intercom.

"Yes?" A metallic, rasping voice; the speaker was female, but that was all Tania could tell.

"Ms. Mariner?"

"Yes."

Tania's mouth was suddenly bone dry. "It's Tania. . . ." she croaked. She brought her mouth closer to the microphone. "It's *Tania*."

There was no response.

She looked at the others. "I'm not sure. . . ."

An electronic growl sounded from the doors. Edric pushed at them and one swung open. He walked through, followed by Cordelia, Zara, and Sancha. Tania followed, not quite able to believe that this was really happening. The door swung shut at her back and the lock clicked.

They were in a clean white vestibule. Corridors stretched off to the left and the right. To one side a stairway led up. A sign fixed inside the doorway showed on what floors the various flats could be found. Flat 7 was on the fourth. Directly ahead of them was an elevator. Edric pressed the small square panel and a white triangle lit up above the door. A few moments later the metal door slid open and the five of them stepped inside.

Tania pressed 4 and the door glided closed.

She didn't look at the others—they all seemed enclosed in private bubbles of silence, as though they were afraid that if they spoke of their hopes, it might somehow ruin everything.

The elevator came to a halt. The tension was unbearable.

The door swished open.

A woman stood facing the elevator, bare-legged and barefoot, wearing a knee-length, dark green suit skirt and a lime green blouse. Her long curling red hair was tied back off her face. Her hands were up, almost as if in prayer, covering the lower half of her face, but above her long, elegant fingers finely sculpted cheekbones and wide green eyes were visible. The expression in her eyes was both eager and wary, as though she feared to trust the truth of what the opening elevator door might reveal.

For a moment there was a silence so profound that Tania could hear the blood beating in her head. Then Edric stepped forward and fell to one knee at the woman's feet, his head bowed.

"Your most gracious Majesty."

His words shattered the airless silence.

"My daughters!" The woman gasped, reaching out her arms toward the girls, her face full of an impossible joy. "My beloved daughters!"

Zara, Sancha, and Cordelia ran from the elevator and fell into their mother's arms with sobs and muffled cries.

Tania hesitated, stepping out of the elevator as the doors closed but holding back, staring in confusion and uncertainty at the Queen of Faerie. It was not that Titania resembled her so closely—she had been prepared for that, up to a point. What pulled her up short was the heart-wrenching realization that she was finally face-to-face with the woman who was her Faerie mother, the woman who had given birth to the Faerie part of her nature as surely as Mary Palmer had brought her mortal half into this world.

Tears of pure joy were running down Titania's face as she hugged and kissed her daughters. And

Tania was suddenly aware that warm tears were running down her own cheeks and that her chest hurt and her throat was full and that a bird seemed to be fluttering wildly in her heart.

Titania lifted her head from her other daughters and looked at her—and in her face was such devotion and relief and happiness that all doubt and fear drained from Tania's body and she found herself stumbling forward.

"Tania! My darling child!"

Tania came into her mother's embrace, pressing her face into the warm neck, breathing in the Faerie scent of her.

"Why did it take so long?" Tania sobbed. "Why so many years?"

"Ah, I don't know, my beloved girl. I don't know why," Titania murmured, kissing Tania's face and caressing her hair. "It's been such a long journey for the two of us. But it's all done now. All done."

"Oh, mother," cried Sancha. "Would that this moment could be perfect, but we bring terrible news!"

A spasm of pain crossed Titania's face. "I felt there was something wrong," she said. "Three days ago I had a sense of some evil thing coming to life, but I didn't know what it was." She looked at Edric, who had risen to his feet and was standing quietly to one side.

"Well met, Master Chanticleer," she said. "Is it by your master's Art and charity that I am reunited with these four of my children?"

Edric looked up at her. "I am no longer in Lord Drake's service, Your Grace."

Titania's eyes narrowed. "I see," she said. "Come, we can speak more freely behind closed doors. It seems there is a lot that I need to know."

Lilith Mariner's living room was airy and clean, but strangely impersonal. The walls were white, and the floor stripped pine. The furniture was elegant but functional and there were no ornaments, nor pictures on the wall, nor any other objects that might give any hint as to the character of the woman who lived there.

Titania sat on the couch with Zara at her feet, Sancha and Cordelia to either side, and Tania in one corner, holding tightly on to her Faerie mother's hand. Edric was perched on the edge of an armchair facing them. Tania could hardly bear to look at Titania's face as the long, terrible story of the past few weeks was revealed to her.

Her eyes closed tightly as she was told of Rathina's treachery, a single tear escaping and running down her cheek. "Poor child," she whispered. "The poor lost child."

"You cannot feel sympathy for her, Mother," Cordelia said. "She betrayed us all of her own free will. I will never forgive her. Never."

"No, no, Cordelia," Titania said sadly. "Rathina is my daughter. I still love her, even though I hate what she has done."

"It may be that a mother must love her children, even though they become demons," Sancha said. "But

Rathina's actions have loosed a great peril both to our own Realm and to this world. The great traitor Drake has led Gray Knights here, and they are pursuing us with a deadly loathing."

Titania looked at Edric. "Your former master has become a dark and corrupt being," she said. "I'm glad you parted with him."

"I had to, Your Grace," Edric said. "For Princess Tania's sake."

"And for the sake of the love that has grown between you," Titania added. She squeezed Tania's hand. "You can tell me more about that later but first we have to decide what to do next."

"Can you guide our footsteps back into Faerie?" Zara asked. "We hoped that you might be able to teach Tania how to break the iron barrier that Lyonesse has raised between our worlds."

Titania shook her head. "I don't have those kinds of skills," she said. "I can't help Tania turn her gift into a weapon against the Sorcerer King's enchantments."

Tania felt all her hopes shriveling away as Titania gently eased her daughters aside and stood up. The Queen walked to the window and stared out into the gathering night.

"I chose to live here because from this window I can see the Palace at Hampton Court," she said. She pointed. "The towers and roofs are visible over there, beyond Bushy Park." She sighed. "After five hundred years in the Mortal World, I was afraid that I might forget my real home . . . and maybe even forget who I really am."

"Could you not have made a water-mirror and viewed it from afar?" Sancha asked. "Has your gift deserted you?"

Tania remembered Sancha mentioning that Titania had the gift to see faraway things by looking into pure, still water.

Titania gave a sad smile. "There is no water in this world pure enough to form an image," she said.

"I do not doubt it," said Cordelia. "How have you survived for so long in this benighted world, Mother? We have been here but a few hours, and already the horror of it gnaws at my heart."

"And how have you survived the touch of Isenmort?" Zara asked. "We carry jewels of black amber with us at all times, but what protection have you used against the poison of metal?"

Titania opened the collar of her blouse and drew out something that spun slowly at the end of a long fine chain. She held it up for them to see. It was a ring of white crystal, and set into it was a black jewel that flashed in the light.

"Your father gave this ring to me on our wedding night, as a token of his undying love," she said. "The stone is black amber. Don't you remember it?"

"Yes, of course," Sancha said. "The Troth-ring of Tasha Dhul."

"It protected me from Isenmort," Titania said. "And as for all the other dangerous things in this world, I used my knowledge of herbs and healing to fend off the worst diseases, and I was lucky not to suffer any life-threatening accidents." Her eyes took on a faraway look. "I was probably in the greatest danger of death when the Great Plague hit London in 1665. A lot of people died then—a third of the population— but I couldn't just run away and hide. I knew enough about medicine to be able to help some of them. And I was lucky; I never caught the disease."

"But how have you hidden your true identity for so long?" Sancha asked.

"It was never easy," Titania replied. "A few years would pass, and the friends that I had made would start commenting on the fact that I never seemed to grow any older. And then in time, the comments would change to suspicion and fear and I would have to disappear and reappear in another part of London with another name and another trade. It was hard in the early times, having to start from scratch over and over again, building a life, losing it, always on the move, or that's how it felt at the time." She smiled. "But these days that is less of a problem. I have been Lilith Mariner for almost thirty years and the only thing people ask about the way I look is the name of my cosmetic surgeon."

"But why did you choose to live in this dreadful place?" Cordelia asked. "Were I lost in this world, I would seek out the remote wildernesses where I would be free of the clamor of mortal-kind."

Titania came back from the window. "I had to be

within reach of your sister," she said, taking Tania's hand again. "It took me a while to find her. For two years I roamed the city in search of her, and then one day I finally came close enough to be able to sense her Faerie Spirit. It was like a warmth in my heart when I felt she was near to me, even though the Spirit was trapped in the body of a sickly mortal girl."

Tania stared at her. "Was her name Ann Burbage?" She remembered her Elizabethan flashback—five hundred years ago she had been called Ann, and her father had been called Richard Burbage. Was she the sickly child that Titania meant?

"How did you know that?" Titania asked, frowning at her. "I didn't think you had any memory of your previous lives once you were born again."

"I didn't," Tania explained. "It's only been happening recently. I get these brief flashbacks. I was Ann Burbage, and I was a little girl called Gracie, and I was Flora Llewellyn. My father was a Victorian inventor called Ernest."

Titania nodded. "Yes, I remember all those children," she said. "And I remember the girl you were before you became Anita Palmer. Your name was Barbara and you were born twenty-seven years ago in Dulwich." She gave a deep sigh. "But you were run down by a car on your way home from school when you were eleven years old." Sadness filled her voice. "I read the details of it in the local newspaper. It took me eighteen months of searching before I discovered you again in the body of a baby girl called Anita Palmer. In

Faerie the gifts of the Royal Family come alive at the age of sixteen. I was sure that if only you could survive for sixteen years in a mortal body, then the Faerie part of your nature would wake up and you would know who you were."

"And that's why Your Grace sent Tania's Soul Book to her," Edric said.

"That's right," said Titania. "I became more and more excited as Anita Palmer got closer to her sixteenth birthday, although my work prevented me from watching as constantly as I'd have liked." She looked quizzically at Edric. "Otherwise I would certainly have recognized Lord Drake's servant when he appeared in London disguised as a mortal." She turned to look at Tania. "I posted the book to you so that you'd get it on your birthday, and once you'd had a chance to read some of it, I was going to come to your house and speak to you."

"And you did," Tania said. "But by then I was gone."

"When I heard that you'd gone missing, I was certain that you must be dead." She shuddered, gripping Tania's hand fiercely. "I thought I'd lost you again, and I thought I'd also lost the only real thing that linked me to you, your Soul Book." She sighed. "I can't begin to tell you how I've ached for this moment, how I've longed to be with my children again."

"And we with you, Mother," Sancha murmured.

"I must have faith that Hopie and Eden are alive and well," Titania said. She hugged the girls to her. "I wish that our reunion could have been under better circumstances, and I wish I knew how to defeat the evil of Lyonesse. But I don't know how to fight the Gray Knights, and I don't know how to get us back to Faerie."

Zara's eyes widened in alarm. "Then are we trapped here forever?"

"Not forever, I fear," Sancha said. "For how long may we escape the Gray Knights of Lyonesse?"

"We can't just run and hide from them," Edric said. "We have to fight back."

"And we have to find a way of getting into Faerie," Tania said. "I could try again. Perhaps now we're all together, it might work."

"I do not think so," Sancha said. "Faerie lies behind a barrier of Isenmort. The Sorcerer King's enchantments cannot be so easily broken."

"Black amber is ever a protection against Isenmort," Zara said. "Could it not be turned into a weapon? We have your crown, Mother. There are yet eleven black amber stones upon it—can they not be used against Lyonesse?"

"A blade shaped from black amber might be sharp enough to cut a way between the worlds," Sancha said.

"Black amber can be melted if it's heated carefully," Titania said. "But even then, a knife forged from molten amber would be too small to cut through into Faerie."

"Your Grace, what if we could melt it so that it made a coating over a crystal sword?" Edric asked.

"The princesses brought four swords into this world. Could one of them be used?"

"It's possible," Titania said. "A crystal sword coated with a layer of black amber might be powerful enough." She looked at Tania. "If it was in the hands of the right person. But it takes a lot of heat to melt black amber, more than we could create without finding a furnace or something similar."

"How about an oxyacetylene torch?" Tania asked. "Would that give a hot enough flame?"

"I should think so," Titania said.

"What is this of which you speak?" asked Sancha.

"It's an apparatus that allows you to make a very small, very hot flame," Tania explained. She looked at Edric. "Do you remember what Jade's dad's hobby is?"

He frowned. "Messing about with old motorbikes, isn't it?"

Tania nodded. "Their basement is full of bits and pieces of old bikes. He's forever cutting up bikes and welding them back together, and sometimes he uses an oxyacetylene torch. I've seen it down there."

"But have you seen him use it?" Titania asked. "Do you know how to work it safely?"

"Not exactly, but he's the kind of person who'd keep the instruction manual," Tania said. "We'll be able to figure it out from there."

"Must we then return to your friend's house?" Cordelia asked. "Is that not perilous?"

"All choices are fraught with peril," Zara said. "But inaction is the most perilous of all. At the very least, we shall put up such a fight that any Gray Knights that outlive us will long remember the battle."

"Pray that it does not come to that," said Sancha. "Mayhap it were safer for only one or two to go to the house and for the rest to remain here?"

"No," Titania said. "We have to keep together now, whatever happens. My car is in the underground parking lot. I'll drive us all over there, if you'll tell me the way, Tania."

"I think I can do that," Tania said.

"Ere we depart, let me learn the lie of the land," Cordelia said. She got off the couch and walked to the window. Edric went with her and undid the latch.

Cordelia threw the window open. A gentle breeze wafted into the room.

"Can you smell the stink of the Gray Knights?" Zara asked.

Cordelia took a long, deep breath. "Nay," she said. "They are not near." She leaned out of the window and let out a series of whistles.

Tania got up and stood behind her, peering out into the night. She heard a distant whirring and fluttering sound that grew nearer and louder—and soon dark shapes began to swoop through the darkness toward the window.

Birds. Scores of birds, coming from every direction at Cordelia's call. Swifts and swallows and tits and sparrows and rooks came in wheeling formation, darting this way and that across the glass, circling in front of the window. A flock of pigeons flew noisily over the rooftops. Some birds landed on the sill, jostling for space as more and more arrived. Starlings and blackbirds and jays and magpies sped through the air. An owl flapped slowly up, landing heavily on the sill, dislodging most of the others as it caught its balance and folded its great brown wings.

Tania gazed into the eerie luminous eyes of the owl as it bobbed its round head and ruffled its feathers.

"My friends," Cordelia called. "A dreadful evil is at large in this place. Twelve gray monsters upon twelve undead steeds. Have any of you seen these creatures, or do you have any knowledge of them?"

The air was suddenly full of the voices of birds, whistling and cheeping and trilling and chirruping and croaking. The owl hooted several times.

It sounded chaotic to Tania, but Cordelia listened intently.

"Thank you, my friends," she said when the noise died down. "Do not put yourselves in peril. If you chance upon these creatures, flee them. Go now, and the blessing of all good things be upon you."

The owl bobbed its head again, then turned clumsily on the sill and launched itself off. It dropped like a stone for several yards, then its wings spread and it was suddenly elegant, brushing the treetops as it soared away and was lost in the night. All the other birds scattered, too, filling the air with noise and hectic motion as they went, gliding and swooping, high and low, until they spread out across the dark sky and were gone.

Cordelia closed the window. "Many of them have smelled the creatures on the air and some have seen gray shapes, like shrouds of walking mist in the streets. But there are no Gray Knights near this place."

"I suggest we stay here and rest for a few hours," Titania said. "Then I'll drive us to the Andersons' house. Maybe the Gray Knights will be less alert when the night is at its darkest."

"Let's hope there won't be any Gray Knights between us and Jade's house," Tania said, tightening her fist around an imaginary hilt. "I want to have a sword in my hand next time we meet up with them!"

XX

Titania parked her dark blue BMW about fifty yards down the street from the Andersons' house.

"That wasn't so bad," she said.

The journey from Hampton had passed without incident. There had been no sign of the Gray Knights and Cordelia had not been able to sense the presence of their steeds in the air. They arrived in the Kent House area of London in the small hours of the night. The street where the Andersons lived was quiet and empty and shrouded in darkness, save for the pools of orange light that cascaded from the streetlamps.

"Wait here till I beckon you," Tania said, peering through the windshield. "Then come one at a time. If you hear anyone or see any movement from the other houses, just walk straight past, okay?"

She got out and walked alone along the pavement. There were no lights on in the neighboring houses;

the street was deserted. At the gate of Jade's house Tania turned and raised her hand as a sign for the next person to follow. Then she slipped in through the gate and sprinted up the path to the door.

Standing under the shadow of the porch, she watched as Sancha appeared. She heard the clump of fast-moving shoes—not Sancha's. Someone on the pavement. Obeying Tania's instructions, Sancha walked on past the gate. A few moments later a young man went past, plugged into an iPod, walking quickly with his head down and his hands in his jacket pockets. Fifteen seconds later Sancha reappeared and this time she came in through the gate and ran to join Tania.

Gradually they all arrived unseen at the house.

"No lights," Tania warned them. She looked at Titania, suddenly realizing she had no idea how to address her. "Titania" didn't sound quite right in the circumstances, "Your Grace" was too formal, but "Mother"? No, it was far too soon for that. "The others will show you where the kitchen is," she said, managing to avoid calling her anything. "Maybe you could make us all some drinks? I'm going down to the basement with Edric. I won't be long."

At least in the windowless basement room, they were able to put on some electric lights. The basement was mostly filled with the usual piles of household items and discarded junk, but one large corner was given over to Mr. Anderson's hobby. There were three complete motorbikes there, as well as a wide scattering of parts: Wheels and shafts and engine parts and mudguards and handlebars and other miscellaneous chunks of metal. A locked and bolted door at the far end of the basement led to a concrete ramp that Jade's father used to wheel his bikes to and from ground level.

The oxyacetylene equipment was carefully stacked in a corner, and in the top drawer of a nearby cabinet they found an instruction and safety manual. Edric started reading it while Tania went back up to check on Titania and the princesses.

Tania sat on the living room carpet, her ankles crossed, her knees drawn up to her chest, her arms wrapped around her shins, and her chin on her knees. She watched her Faerie mother and her three sisters sitting close together, talking about past times in Faerie.

"Do you remember the morning of Cordelia's sixteenth birthday?" Sancha said. "How she came running to the breakfast table in her shift to tell us that a linnet had flown in at her window and wished her a happy birthday!"

Zara clapped her hands. "Yes!" she cried. "And she would not be persuaded to dress, but insisted on going out into the gardens as she was and speaking to every animal she met."

Cordelia smiled at the memory. "I did not understand more than a few words of their languages," she said. "They must have thought me a great fool!"

"Do all the different animals have their own

languages, then?" Tania asked, eager to find a way into the conversation.

Cordelia nodded. "Some have only a few words, but others speak a language even richer and more varied than our own."

"And you know them all?"

Cordelia laughed. "Indeed not," she said. "That were a study of ten thousand years. But I can understand many of the beasts and birds of Faerie—those that will speak with me—and I know at least enough of their tongues to bid them good day and to ask after their well-being. And that is sufficient. I would not tame them with familiarity. They must remain true to themselves—they must remain . . . wild."

Tania lapsed into silence. Things weren't going quite the way she wanted. She had hoped that finding Titania might have helped her to find the lost part of herself. She had imagined that her Faerie self, all her Faerie memories, would come flooding back into her mind the first time she saw the Queen.

It hadn't happened.

A peal of laughter from Zara broke into her thoughts. They were discussing a picnic by the lake that lay north of the palace, the lake where Oberon had built Titania's mausoleum. Zara had been a toddler; she had tried to ride a swan, but the bird had swum away and she had been reduced to tears.

"And although Eden was but green in the Mystic Arts," Zara continued, "she used such powers as she had to form the reeds into a boat shaped as a swan and I paddled my swan-ship on the lake till long after nightfall."

"And you wouldn't come when you were called," Titania said. "I remember it very well." She looked at Tania, and her eyes were troubled. "Is something wrong, Tania?"

Yes! Why don't I remember any of this!

She managed a smile. "I was just wondering how Edric was getting on," she said, getting up. "I think I'll go and see if he needs anything."

She opened the basement door. A sharp smell hit her, along with a wave of hot air and a fierce hissing sound.

Cautiously she walked down into the basement. The hissing noise got louder, becoming an intense roar.

Edric was crouching with his back to her in a cleared space on the concrete floor. He was wearing protective goggles and his body was in deep shadow, lit up all around by a corona of intense blue-white light that made his hair shine like spun filaments of silver. A metal cylinder stood a little way off with tubes leading from it. Plumes of gray smoke rose above him and coiled across the ceiling.

The crystal sword and the black amber stones lay nearby. It didn't seem like a good time to disturb him. She walked quietly back up the stairs and came into the darkened hallway again. She could hear Titania and the princesses talking from the living room.

She had a sudden desperate urge to phone her

mum and dad. To hear their voices, to reach out and make contact with something that made absolute sense to her.

Mum? Remember when . . . ?

Yes, of course, dear.

So do I! Isn't that wonderful! I remember it, too!

But she couldn't call them, because then they'd know she wasn't in Florida. For a moment, Tania felt more alone than she had ever been in her life. . . .

She listened to the Faerie voices. Wishing . . .

Wishing without even knowing what she was wishing for.

To be Anita Palmer again?

No, not that.

To be Princess Tania?

"No!" she said under her breath. "That's not it, either. I don't know what I want."

She ran up the stairs. In the dark of the upper landing she opened the door to Jade's room and went in. She sat at the desk, pressing the button that would start up the computer. She felt that her sense of her own identity was somehow slipping away from her.

Crazy, really, she thought, *considering I've had more lives than anyone!*

But she wanted those past lives to become more real to her. Maybe she'd have a firmer grip on her own identity if she could find out about her previous selves. And she thought she had a way into at least one of them.

She went into a search engine and typed: ERNEST LLEWELLYN.

She gave a breathless laugh of surprise as the results showed over two hundred thousand hits.

"What are you doing?" The voice startled her. Sancha was standing in the doorway.

"I told you about the flashback I had of the Victorian family when Zara and I were on our way here," Tania said. "I'm seeing if there's anything about them on the Net."

Sancha moved into the room and stood behind her, her hands on Tania's shoulders. "I see," she said. "And this 'Net,' will it help you to catch this family as the net of a fisherman catches the fish in the sea?"

Tania smiled up at her. "That's exactly how it works, like a big electronic fishing net."

"I would learn more of this *electricity*," Sancha said. "It is strange and perplexing, but you do not fear it, so neither shall I." She took the chair from in front of Jade's dressing table and drew it up to the computer desk. "Show me wonders, Tania; teach me how this mortal marvel fishes for knowledge."

"Okay," Tania said. "First of all I'll have to narrow the search parameters." She typed ERNEST LLEWELLYN LONDON and pressed SEARCH.

95,7001 hits.

"See that?" she said, pointing to the top of the page. "That's how many times those words have been found."

"It is a vast ocean, indeed," Sancha said.

"And getting bigger all the time," Tania said. "But I think this might be the one we want." She moved the curser to the third name down on the list.

A new page came up. White with blue writing.

Ernest Llewellyn
1831–1869

There was a block of text alongside a faded black-and-white photo of the man in the attic room. In the photo the man's face was set and severe, and he was holding a stiff, unnatural pose, but she could tell it was the same warm-hearted man who had swung little Flora up into his arms.

"That's him," she said breathlessly. She began to read aloud.

"Respected amateur scientist and inventor. Born the son of a blacksmith in North Wales, Ernest Llewellyn had little formal education, but his family moved to Kent when he was ten years old where he became apprenticed to a London chemist. He acquired a store of scientific and chemical knowledge by voracious reading and by attending the lectures of the prominent men of science of his day. Llewellyn's experiments yielded some of the most significant principles . . ." She turned to Sancha. "There's a lot of stuff about his work and all that, but I really want to know more about the family." She scrolled down the page, ignoring the line drawings of various strange scientific devices and bypassing boxes that contained complex chemical formulas.

"There!" she said. "That's them." It was a family portrait. Again, the people were posed in a slightly awkward and very formal way, but they were all there, photographed in what looked like their very best clothes against a painted backdrop of trees and fields. Ernest stood with one hand clasping the lapel of his frock coat and the other on his wife's shoulder as she sat in front of him with a toddler in her lap. The oldest son stood in front of his father—he had been the boy that Tania had seen on the couch with the sleeping toddler across his knees. Two younger children stood side by side on the other side of the mother's chair—the boy and girl who had been lying in front of the fireplace.

Sitting cross-legged in a foam of white lace at her mother's feet was little Flora Llewellyn, staring intently into the camera with her hands clasped in her lap, her impish face full of life and curiosity. It felt strange to see her from the outside, knowing how it had felt to be behind those sparkling eyes.

"Yes, that's exactly how they looked," Tania said.

"Tania?" Sancha's voice was subdued. "Have you read the words beneath the picture?"

"Not yet."

"Read them," Sancha said. "Read of the fate of this family."

Puzzled by the tone of Sancha's voice, Tania tore her eyes away from Flora's face and read the caption below the photograph.

*The Llewellyn family, a portrait taken in the
studios of Laporte & Hudson in July 1869. It
shows Ernest; his wife, Charlotte; their eldest
son, George; the twins, Arthur and Dorothy;
their younger daughter, Flora; and the baby,
Henry. This was the last photograph taken of the
family before the tragic house fire that claimed
all of their lives. It was believed that the fire
started late at night in Ernest's attic laboratory,
but so ferocious was the blaze that his sleeping
family were unable to escape, and all perished.*

A biting coldness seeped into Tania's chest.

No! They couldn't have died. Not *all* of them.

"You knew the child could not have lived to adult-hood," Sancha said gently. "Do you not recall what our mother said? That you had never before reached the age of sixteen."

Tania's throat hurt and tears were stinging her eyes. She slammed her hand on the computer's main control button, so upset that she didn't even bother to shut it down properly. The soft hum of the machine died instantly and the photograph vanished as the screen went blank.

"Not all knowledge brings joy," Sancha said. "But in the Mortal World is death not made endurable by new birth?" She lifted her hand to Tania's cheek and gently turned her face toward her. "That child needed to die so that you could be born." She gave a faint, sympathetic smile. "I would not have you different from who you are now, sweet sister, and you are only that person because of what happened in your past—both the good and the bad, the joyful and the sorrowful."

"But they were so happy," Tania whispered. "It's horrible to think that they all died . . . maybe only a few days or weeks after I saw them." She stared in horror at her sister. "Maybe even on that same night. If Flora had been able to persuade him to stop his work, the fire might never have happened."

"My poor sister," Sancha said. "Such a burden you bear! Such a heavy weight!"

Tania threw her arms around Sancha's neck and buried her face in her dark hair, sobbing and sobbing as the agony of her past lives broke out of her like a great churning flood of dark water. All those children! Weak, sickly Ann Burbage. Poor drowned Gracie. Flora Llewellyn with her golden hair and her angel face. And how many others? How many more lives had been lost before Anita Palmer had been born?

In time Tania's tears had finally dried up. Sancha had suggested that she might sleep for a while. But sleep wasn't any kind of comfort to her, not with Gabriel Drake lurking in the darkness behind her eyelids.

She was in the basement again now, sitting with Edric on a pile of old carpets. She had made him a sandwich and they were talking as he ate.

"You look tired," he said. "Why don't you get some sleep? I'll wake you when we're ready."

She shook her head. "Everyone's telling me to sleep," she said. "Bad dreams, remember? Anyway, I want to be with you. I want to help."

He smiled. "I thought you'd want to be with the Queen. Can you get your head around that yet, having two mothers?"

"I've stopped trying," she admitted. "It's too weird. I suppose it's a bit like finding out you've been adopted, that there's a whole other family out there that you don't know about. Except that it's worse, because they keep talking about things I was involved in, but I don't remember any of it." She leaned forward and kissed Edric's dirt-smudged cheek. "At least I have you," she said, wrapping his arm in both of hers and resting her head on his shoulder.

"You know what's weird?" she said quietly. "I was so intent on finding Titania that I never actually stopped to think about her . . . as a person, I mean." She looked up at his face. "She's been alive in London for five hundred years. She was here when they cut off King Charles the First's head; she was here when half the city burned down in the Great Fire. She was here when Nelson defeated Napoleon at Trafalgar. When Queen Victoria came to the throne, and through two world wars, and the millennium, and . . . and everything else. And for all those years, all those hundreds of years, she was just waiting for the chance to be with me." She pulled away and sat up. "And now we're together, and I don't know what to say to her. Do I say, 'Hello, Mum, thanks for not giving up on me'? Or do I say, 'It's really nice to meet you, Your Queenship, but I already have a mum, thanks'?" She looked at him. "Have you any idea how freaky all this is for me?"

"No," he said. "I don't. I'm not torn apart like you are. I know where I want to be."

"In Faerie, you mean."

"No—with *you*."

"So, if we survive all this, if we defeat the Gray Knights and save Oberon, if, after all that, I decide I want to live here rather than in Faerie, do you mean you'd be prepared to stay here with me?"

Edric gave a weary smile. "Let's work on staying alive for now. If we can't find a way to beat Lyonesse, choosing a place to live isn't going to be an issue." He stood up. "Okay," he said, picking up the crystal sword. "Let's get this finished."

"What do you want me to do?"

He pointed. "There are spare goggles and protective gloves over there," he said. "Put them on and bring over the tongs you'll find with them. You'll need them to hold the sword steady."

She pulled the goggles over her head and tightened the leather strap. The round lenses of the eyepieces were scratched and smeared, but she could see well enough through them. She drew on the heavy leather gauntlets and stooped to pick up the long metal tongs. She walked back to where Edric was crouching, goggles covering his eyes and the torch in his hands.

She knelt in front of him and watched as he fired

up the torch. The flame was like a slim white leaf in the heart of a hissing blaze of bright blue light.

Edric laid the sword on the concrete floor between them and carefully placed one of the black stones onto the blade.

"Okay," he said. "I'll need you to use the tongs to keep the stone still. Can you do that?"

"Yes." Tania opened the tongs and carefully brought the heavy metal jaws down on either side of the jewel. She closed the jaws so that the stone was held between them.

Slowly, Edric brought the roaring flame onto the black stone. When the hissing tongue of flame hit the stone, it jerked out of the tongs, bouncing off the sword blade and rolling across the floor.

"Sorry, *sorry*," Tania muttered, annoyed with herself. "Give me a moment."

"Don't worry about it," Edric said gently.

"I wasn't holding it tightly enough." She took the stone between the jaws of the tongs and replaced it on the sword. "It'll be okay now."

Again, he brought the flame onto the stone. This time the metal jaws held it steady. She watched the fierce white flame as it played over the black amber jewel.

For a long, long time, it seemed as if nothing was happening.

"Is it working?" Tania asked.

"I don't know. I think it's going to take a while. Are you okay holding it like that?"

"I'm fine." Tania's arm and wrist muscles were

beginning to ache from the strain of being in the same position for so long, and of maintaining the grip of the tongs on the stone.

Long minutes passed. Tania saw that the metal jaws were beginning to glow red—but still there was no sign of anything happening to the stone.

And then she noticed a thin stream of black smoke rising from the stone.

"Carefully now," Edric warned above the roar of the flame. "I think it's going."

It happened in an instant. Tania felt the stone dissolve away from between the tongs, the black jewel turning all at once into a thick, shining liquid that slid like oil over the crystal sword.

She lifted the tongs away and watched as Edric used the flame to guide the molten amber so that it spread smoothly over the blade.

Edric took the flame away. A section of the sword about the length of Tania's hand was coated with a shining layer of blackness. She leaned in closer. The surface of the melted amber was alive with tiny ripples and puckers, like the skin that forms on hot milk.

"Should we let it cool?" she asked. "See if it's going to work?"

"No, it'll take too long." Edric took a second stone and placed it on the blade an inch or so from the glistening pool of black amber. He looked at her. "Ready?"

She nodded. Ignoring the aching of her arms and hands, she closed the tongs around the second stone.

"How's it going?" Titania's voice sounded from the head of the basement stairs.

Tania jumped up and walked to the foot of the stairs. "Good so far," she called up. "We've done one side already and it seems to have worked really well. We're just waiting until the amber cools enough for us to turn the sword over and do the other side. Then we'll be ready." She smiled up at her Faerie mother. "How are things up there?"

"Cordelia is getting a bit edgy. She's spending most of her time out in the garden, getting news from the birds."

"She's being careful not to be seen, isn't she?"

"Yes."

"So? What are the birds telling her?"

"That there's something nasty heading this way," Titania said.

"The Knights?"

"It has to be."

"Does Princess Cordelia know how long we've got, Your Grace?" Edric asked, joining Tania at the foot of the stairs.

"It's about an hour till dawn," Titania said. "Cordelia says we should definitely *not* be here when the sun comes up."

"One hour, Your Grace?" Edric said. "Yes, we should be finished well before then."

"And then we just cut our way into Faerie," Tania said.

"That's the plan," Titania said. "But not here. I've been discussing it with Sancha and she doesn't think this is the best place to try and break through."

"Why not?" Tania asked.

"The Sorcerer King's enchantments are very powerful. But in some places his power won't be quite so strong. Eden understood that—that's why she broke through into this world in Bonwn Tyr, in the brown tower that shares the same space in Faerie as your bedroom does in this world."

"So you think we should go back to my house to break through? Is that safe?"

"No, it isn't *safe* at all," Titania said. "But we may only have one chance of using the sword; when it clashes with the Sorcerer King's barrier, it may be destroyed. We have to be in a place that gives us the best chance of success. The Oriole Glass in Eden's sanctum would be our first choice but we can't risk it. Lyonesse will have put a heavy guard on it and we'd almost certainly be walking into a trap. There are other places—Crystalhenge in the West and Castle Ravensare to the North and Tasha Dhul itself—but those places are too far away from the Palace. We can't risk a long journey across country, we have to enter Faerie as close to the Palace as possible so that we can make our way to the dungeons and free Oberon before Lyonesse can act against us. Your bedroom is our best choice."

"Okay," Tania said uneasily. "Let's just hope that Gabriel hasn't figured that out, too."

"Is it ready?" Tania asked. "It looks ready to me."

The oxyacetylene torch was quiet now. The black blade lay smoking on the concrete floor. Edric was hunkered down in front of the sword, staring intently at it, watching for the moment when the liquid amber would have solidified enough for it to be picked up.

"I'm not sure," he said. "Let's give it a few more minutes."

"Do we have a few more minutes?"

Tania was standing behind him. Sancha was sitting on the bottom step of the stairs. Zara and Titania were about halfway down the staircase, Zara leaning against her mother's knees, Titania's hands resting protectively on her shoulders. The basement room was stiflingly hot from the blasting of the torch. Moisture was running down the walls and threads of steam were still curling in the corners.

But the job was done. It was just a case now of watching and waiting, and hoping they would have the time to get out of there before the Gray Knights arrived.

The news wasn't good. With every passing minute Cordelia's birds were becoming more agitated. The knights could not be far away. Tania was so apprehensive and on edge now that even with her eyes open, she could see their pale grinning faces looming toward her. And more frightening than that, she could see Gabriel's smirking face floating in the air in front of her, and the triumphant look in his silvery eyes seemed to suck all the courage and strength out of her.

And his voice whispered constantly in her ears, like the raging of a distant sea. *You will never be free of me! Did you not know? We are bonded for all time!*

For . . . all . . . time!

"The car's ready," Titania said. "It's parked right outside the house. The moment you're ready we can be gone."

"A minute or two more, Your Grace," Edric said. "I can't risk moving the sword until the amber has set."

A voice sounded from the head of the stairs. "I fear you will have to take that risk, Master Chanticleer," Cordelia called down. "We have no more time. The Gray Knights are here."

XXI

"Which direction are they coming from?" Titania asked.

"Over the gardens," Cordelia said.

"Will you have the birds attack them?" Sancha said.

"No! I will not ask for such a sacrifice again. Come, we have swords. It is our battle. They are but five: We can defeat them."

"Is Gabriel with them?" Tania asked, her voice cracking with fear.

"I know not. The birds told me that five monsters were approaching, that is all." Cordelia vanished from the doorway.

Tania turned to look at Edric. He was crouching over the steaming sword, his hand extended toward the hilt.

"Is it ready?"

His mouth set in a determined line. "It'll have to be!" He gripped the hilt and lifted the black sword into the air. The amber shone like oil. It held on to the blade. He turned, brandishing the sword.

"Let's get out of here," Titania said.

Cordelia was in the hall, staring through the open kitchen door, the remaining swords in her arms, the backpack with Titania's crown in it hanging from one shoulder.

The first faint hint of dawn light was gleaming beyond the kitchen windows. The wall clock showed ten to five.

Sancha and Zara took swords.

"Tania, you're the most important one of us," Titania said. "You keep in the middle. Edric, we'll go through the front door first. The car is by the gate. Stick by me in case we're attacked. Zara, stay on Tania's right side and protect her at all costs. Sancha, guard her left side. Cordelia, watch our rear."

"I can fight, too," Tania said.

"I know. But not yet. If you're hurt, none of us will get away."

"But—"

The crash of breaking glass cut short Tania's protest. One of the kitchen windows burst inward in flying fragments. A slender white shape rode on the air like a long sharp finger, pointing directly toward her.

Someone's hand dragged her to one side. The razor-sharp blade of a long white spear sliced through the air half an inch from her face. There was a booming thud. The spear shivered, its point embedded deep in the front door.

The air was suddenly full of ululating cries and furious neighing. A madly grinning, ghost white face appeared at the broken window. Blows rained down on the garden door.

"Go!" Cordelia shouted.

Edric ran to the front door. Titania snatched the backpack from Cordelia's shoulder and followed him, pulling the pack onto her shoulders as she went.

A second spear cut through the air with a sound like a sigh, gouging into the floor between Cordelia's feet. Tania backed away down the hall, Sancha and Zara at her sides, their swords ready.

Cordelia snatched up the spear and threw it back with a shout. The face disappeared from the broken window and there was a high-pitched cry.

Edric threw the front door open, the black sword shining as he leaped over the threshold.

"It's safe!" he shouted. "Quickly!"

Tania turned, running with her sisters flanking her. She heard the splintering crash of the garden door being broken down. The neighing and the howling of the Gray Knights grew louder, the horrible noise clawing at the inside of her skull.

She heard a skirling shriek from her left and the sound of thudding hooves. One of the Gray Knights emerged from the side of the house, one hand gripping the reins, the other arm lifted, aiming a spear.

In a moment the spear arm jerked and the slim

shaft was thrumming through the air toward her. Sancha grasped her sword in both hands, spreading her feet for balance, her black hair flying. The blade rang as it hit the spear, sending it spinning up into the air. It made a long arc against the dawning sky and thudded into the ground a few yards away.

The horseman was almost upon them now. The wild-eyed Gray Knight had drawn his sword and was hanging half out of the saddle, sweeping the blade before him in a low arc as he urged his horse on toward the princesses.

Sancha stood firm, parrying his blow. But the impact jarred her off her feet and she sprawled on the path, the blade skidding from her hand. Tania threw herself to one side as the hideous steed bore down on her. She felt its foul breath on her face and her eyes were filled with the sight of flying hooves as it thundered past.

She was aware of a blur of movement behind her. The Gray Knight gave a single screech, cut off short as Tania whipped around to look. The creature's severed head leaped high as Zara's sword flashed and whirled.

But the head turned sharply in the air, slowing and turning back on itself to come hurtling down toward Zara, the eyes still blazing red and the open grin of the mouth once again emitting a deadly, piercing shriek.

Zara swiped wildly at the plummeting head, but she was too shocked to be able to aim her blows and the head beat off her chest like a cannonball, driving her to the ground with a cry of pain.

The great gray horse reared, its lips foaming as it neighed. The headless Gray Knight was still in the saddle, still holding the reins, still wielding the sword. And even as Tania watched in growing horror and disbelief, the screaming head of the knight leaped high into the air again and came down upon the waiting shoulders with a triumphant screech of manic laughter.

She heard Edric's voice calling. "The heart! Strike to the heart!"

Cordelia's sword sang as it spun through the air from behind Tania. The blade entered the knight's thin body between the folds of his cloak. He clutched at it for a moment with bony fingers, then there was a gust of gray ash where his face had been, and a second later the empty clothes crumpled and fell loosely out of the saddle.

Tania didn't wait to see the horse fall. She scrambled to where Sancha lay sprawling and helped her to her feet.

Cordelia leaped forward as the emaciated horse plunged to the ground, hurdling the hollow rib cage, snatching up her sword as she ran.

Zara was on her feet, too, and they were all running now, running for their lives as a second and a third horseman came wheeling around from the side of the house, spurring their horses onward, swords shining and mouths grinning.

The car's doors were open. Titania was in the driver's seat, gunning the engine. Edric was standing by the open back door, urging the sisters in. Zara was first, Tania and Sancha tumbling in after her in a tangle of arms and legs and white blades.

Cordelia was only one step behind.

The first of the knights urged his horse up and over the front wall. As Tania stared out and up through the back window of the car, it seemed to her as if the huge gray horse filled the entire night.

Edric vaulted the hood of the car and threw himself into the front passenger seat. Cordelia slammed the back door behind her. The car lurched forward, the four princesses tangled up together along the backseat.

Tania saw another horseman looming ahead. With a shout of defiance Titania drove straight for him. Tania was thrown back in her seat as the car accelerated. All she could see through the windshield were insane, blazing red eyes hurtling toward them. A sword. Hooves. The swirl of a glistening gray cloak.

The horse reared and leaped. The car bucked like a boat on a stormy sea as the great hooves came crashing down on hood and roof with a noise like iron hammers beating on an anvil.

Then the horse was behind them, the knight fighting to turn the animal.

"Go! Go! Go!" Edric shouted.

The knight gave chase, howling as the car sped away from him. He galloped after them for the length of the road, but gradually he fell behind, disappearing from the back window as they negotiated the long curve.

Tania gasped. "We got away from them!"

"There were but five," Cordelia said grimly. "Ere we dance a jig, think on where the others may be."

"Aye," Zara said. "And their fell captain with them."

"Waiting for us at journey's end, belike," said Sancha. She looked at Tania, and there was fear in her dark eyes. "The rising sun may yet see bloodshed. Our troubles are not over."

With a groan, Tania closed her eyes—and from far away in the darkness she was sure that she could hear the sound of Gabriel Drake laughing.

The journey from Jade's house to Eddison Terrace was not much more than a mile, and even in the tangle of the North London streets, it was only a few minutes later that the Queen, following Tania's instructions, brought the car to a halt at the far end of the street where the Palmer family lived.

The fringes of the sky were gunmetal gray, although the night still flowed through the streets and made caverns of deep darkness in porches and behind walls. A handful of houselights were on, making little yellow squares in the bleached grays of the housefronts.

Cordelia opened the car door a fraction. She leaned her head toward the crack, listening carefully.

"Do you hear?" she asked, her face grave.

"There is no sound," Zara said. "What can you hear, Cordelia?"

"I hear nothing," Cordelia said. "'Tis dawn—why do the birds not greet the rising sun?"

"The knights are here," Zara said breathlessly.

"So we have to assume the house will be held against us," Titania said, turning to look over the back of her seat. "How many of them, do you think?"

"Thirteen stones in Oberon's crown," said Sancha. "Two of the knights have been destroyed. We left four behind us so we must assume our foes number seven: Six knights and the traitor Drake at their head."

Tania shuddered.

"We can't take it for granted that the ones from Jade's house won't get here in time to be a problem," Edric said.

"So eleven, then," Cordelia said. "Eleven monsters and four Faerie blades."

"Tania should have the black sword," Edric said. "She and Her Grace the Queen *must* get through into Faerie. The rest of us have to do everything we can to make sure that can happen."

"Even if we must sacrifice ourselves in the attempt," Zara said.

"No!" Tania broke in. "No sacrifices. We all get through, okay? All of us."

"The knights will be lying in wait for us," Sancha said. "They are not fools; they will have the house surrounded. How are we to break through?"

"They'll be expecting us," Edric said. "So there's no point in trying to take them by surprise."

"There might be a way of surprising them," Tania said. "There's a walkway that runs along the bottom of all the gardens in our street. It's not meant for cars, but I'm sure it's wide enough to drive a car down if you had to."

"They'll have the garden covered," Edric said. "We'd have to climb the fence and then make it all the way to the house. We'd be cut to pieces."

"Not if we stayed inside the car," Tania said. She looked at Titania. "If you got up a good speed along the walkway, then veered off when I told you and crashed straight through the fence we could probably get right up to the house."

"We'd be inside before they knew what hit them," Edric said.

Cordelia grinned. "So we will drive our attack home in a chariot of Isenmort. 'Tis well! Let's to it!"

Tania sat between her sisters in the back of the car. She was holding the black sword in both hands, the blade vertical in front of her, point upward. Now that the amber had hardened it didn't reflect any light at all. In fact, as Tania gazed at the slender black blade, it was as if she was staring into a slim crack in the world, looking into absolute nothingness.

The jolt of the car lifting over a curb brought her out of her trance. Titania had come to the entrance of the back alley. Zara's face wore a fixed and resolute stare, the sky blue eyes as hard as stone. Sancha's eyes were closed and her lips were moving. Cordelia was smiling, but there was dark hatred in her eyes and her thumb was running slowly back and forth along the edge of her sword blade. Tania had the feeling that Cordelia was remembering the starlings that had died in their escape from Tania's house and relishing the chance to even the score with the Gray Knights.

Tania's gaze switched to Edric in the front passenger seat, and as though he sensed her looking at him, he half turned toward her and smiled.

She couldn't think of a single thing to say to him; she wasn't even sure that she could have coughed up any words from her dry and constricted throat. She forced a smile in response to Edric's.

"Once we're in the garden, just concentrate on getting up to your room," he said, and the fear that scratched in his voice made her glad she hadn't tried to speak. "You'll be fine."

She nodded.

"Everyone ready?" Titania asked. "Let's go."

She revved the engine until it roared, then she slammed it into gear. It leaped forward, pushing them all back into their seats.

It was a tight fit in the walkway, and in places where rogue bushes and saplings had taken root, branches clawed at the windows like skeletal fingers. Tania counted the houses just visible above the tall fences.

She couldn't afford to get this wrong.

The car was moving fast now.

Five houses to go.

Faster.

Three.

"Now!"

Titania spun the wheel.

They were all thrown to one side as the car veered toward the fence. There was a bone-jarring impact and a loud bang as the right-hand wing of the car struck the wood. The entire fence panel came loose, tipping forward, blinding them all for a few moments, then sliding sideways off the hood and crashing to one side.

Tania stared into her garden. The car was jolting over a flower bed, skimming between the hawthorn tree and her father's shed. The lawn lay straight ahead, leading to the patio and the back of the house. The back door that led into the kitchen was missing. It had been wrecked on the night of their escape. She could see her own bedroom window up there, the glass reflecting the grainy sky.

So close now . . . If only she had wings . . .

Four Gray Knights barred their way. They sat in a row astride their wasted horses, as still as gray statues, each holding a spear, each wearing a fixed, joyless grin. The four heads turned as the car bumped onto the lawn and it seemed to Tania at that moment that the whole world was drowned in shades of gray and that the only color that still existed was red, as if all the fire in the universe was concentrated in those four pairs of deadly staring eyes.

As the speeding car bounced over the lawn, the four horses plunged to either side, the riders screaming in rage as they struggled to keep in their saddles and regain control of the panicking animals.

But they were adder-quick in their movements. It was only a split second before the air was shrill with the whine of hurtling spears.

Three of the spears pierced the car, two punching holes through the windshield, the third bursting through the side window, scattering glass pebbles.

Tania reacted with pure instinct, her arm moving almost before her brain had registered the danger. She flicked her sword up in front of her face and the spear that was flying directly at her head was deflected so that it passed right through the car and went crashing out of the back window.

The second spear had come to a thudding halt between the front seats, its haft still sticking out of the windshield.

Tania heard a stifled cry at her side. The last of the spears had come in at an angle, breaking in through the side window and plunging into the backseat between Tania and Cordelia. Cordelia's hand clutched her arm and Tania saw blood welling between her fingers.

Titania spun the wheel again, slamming her foot on the brake as the car swerved. Tilting dangerously, the vehicle bumped up onto the patio, skidding sideways across the stones as the back wall of the house came rushing toward them.

There was a reverberating clang as the back of the car struck the wall.

"Out!" Titania yelled.

Cordelia wrenched at the door handle and kicked the door wide. The passenger side of the car was hard up against the wall and those doors could not be opened. Cordelia stumbled out of the car. She stood spread-legged on the patio, her left arm hanging limp, but in her right she brandished her sword, shouting defiance.

Tania was right behind her, her ears still ringing from the impact of the car against the wall.

The Gray Knights had rallied. They were charging, their white swords spinning, their voices as harsh and sharp as carrion birds.

Tania ran to stand at Cordelia's side. She was vaguely aware of Sancha beside her, and of Zara scrambling up to take a vantage point on the roof of the car.

"No!" Cordelia spat, glaring at Tania. "It is for us to do the fighting. You must get into the house."

Tania ignored her, widening her stance for balance, crouching in the low ward, her eyes fixed on the closest of the onrushing knights. She had no intention of deserting her sisters.

But someone had other ideas. She gave a furious shout as she was dragged backward.

It was Edric. "Get inside!" he shouted. "Save Faerie!"

He spun her around and almost threw her through the broken doorway. She stumbled onto her knees, only just managing to keep her grip on her sword.

She got to her feet, intending to run back out into the garden. But Titania was in the doorway, her face frantic.

"Go!" she said, panting.

Beyond her mother Tania could see Edric and her sisters battling with the horsemen.

Tania ran across the kitchen. The floor was sticky with bloody feathers and dotted with the corpses of the birds who had died to help them.

She braced herself for more knights. There were only four in the garden—where were the rest? Was there no one inside the house? She raced along the hallway and snatched hold of the banister rail, pivoting around to face the stairs.

She could see her bedroom door now. So close. Only fifteen steps away.

She darted up the stairs.

A shadow broke free from the deeper shades of the landing.

A blade glinted.

Silver eyes flashed.

A figure stepped up to the head of the stairs.

"Well met, my bride," Gabriel said, his voice as smooth as a sliding snake. "Long have I pined for your presence."

Tania crashed down onto her knees on the stairs. Her arms fell limp to her sides as she stared up at him.

"Come, my lady," he said, beckoning to her. "I have a gift for you, the gift of a loving husband."

Tania felt herself getting to her feet. She struggled to regain control of her body, but so long as she was held by those silver eyes, she had no strength to resist. She could do nothing as her legs bent and her body carried her up the stairs toward the Faerie lord.

Gabriel stepped back from the top of the stairs, smiling as she came up and stood in front of him. Their bodies almost touched; her head tilted up slightly, her eyes fixed on his. Pools of shining silver. They were all that existed now. Everything else went spinning away into a great empty void. No other sound but his voice. No other sight but his eyes.

She was aware of the black sword falling out of her fingers and clattering as it tumbled down the stairs. She had a faint, nagging feeling that there was something she should be doing, but she had no idea what.

Nothing important.

Pools of silver light.

A warm, soft voice.

"Would you like your gift now, my lady?"

"Yes . . . please . . ."

On the edge of vision, she saw his white sword move between them. She felt the point prick against her stomach through her clothes.

She felt peaceful. Untroubled. Hanging in space. Held by his eyes. His mouth moved forward to kiss her as the blade pressed harder against her flesh.

And then the tranquillity was shattered by a scream of agony as a splinter of shooting darkness came stabbing forward past Tania's head and sank into Gabriel's shoulder.

"Leave my daughter alone!"

Tania saw Drake fall away from her, his face twisted in pain, his hand clutching at his wounded shoulder. She reeled and might have toppled over backward if Titania hadn't been right behind her, still gripping the black sword that she had used to stab Gabriel over Tania's shoulder.

"Which is your room?"

Still groggy from Gabriel's enchantment, Tania pointed. Titania pushed her toward the door.

Gabriel had crumpled to the floor, his right arm hanging, his left hand pressed to his bleeding shoulder. Titania kicked his sword out of his limp fingers.

"I wish I had the time to thank you properly for what you've done," she spat. "Just remember this: I'll do everything in my power to bring Rathina back to us and to rid her of your influence."

Drake stared up at her, his handsome features contorted with pain. "Make no such vain promises, Your Grace," he hissed between gritted teeth. "Not while your husband lies in bonds of Isenmort and the King of Lyonesse sits upon his throne."

Titania smiled coldly. "With your leave, my lord, my daughter and I are about to do something about that."

Tania opened the door. The curtains were open and the first pale gleam of morning was filtering into the room. Far away, the sun was climbing over the horizon and the sky was flooding with a wash of fresh blue light.

Tania turned, looking at her Faerie mother. "What do I do?"

Titania handed her the sword. "Walking between the worlds is your gift, Tania," she said. "I can't tell you how to do it."

"What about the others?"

Almost as the words left her lips she heard the commotion of feet coming rapidly up the stairs. Zara burst into the room first, a wild, exultant light in her eyes.

"Two are slain!" she said, panting. "Cordelia is hurt—Edric holds the rear!"

A moment later the two other princesses appeared, Sancha supporting Cordelia, whose clothes were laced with cuts and spattered with blood. There was a cut along her cheek and blood trickled down to her chin, but her eyes still blazed defiance.

Edric came last, bounding into the room and snatching the door closed in the face of a pursuing knight.

"Quickly, Tania!" Titania said.

Edric put his back to the door, digging his heels into the carpet to hold it shut as it shivered with repeated blows.

"I saw . . . two more of them. . . ." he said. "Coming in from . . . the front. . . . We won't . . . be able to hold them off . . . for long. . . ."

Tania turned toward the window, trying to clear her mind of fear and panic—trying to lock out the screeches of the Gray Knights and the hammering of fists and sword hilts on the door.

She lifted the black sword in both hands, picturing in her mind the curved stone walls of that small circular room in the brown tower in Faerie.

She walked forward, the sword held up in front of her.

She took a side step.

Her mouth filled with the foul taste of iron. She felt a swarm of unseen creatures beating at her with leathery wings, raking her skin with needle-sharp claws, screaming demonically in her ears.

She swung the sword, and the creatures fled.

But a blistering pain was growing in her forehead. Burning pincers of agony gripped tight around her chest and her waist and her hips, as if bands of hot iron were being bent around her body, holding her fast, imprisoning her in rings of smoldering metal.

She heard Edric's voice calling as if from a million miles away.

"The sword! Use the sword!"

But the sword seemed to weigh a thousand pounds, the point dragging her arms downward as she struggled to raise it above her head. Using every ounce of strength in her body, she fought to lift the blade through the unyielding air.

At last she held it poised above her head, gripping the hilt in both hands. Straining forward, as though walking into a hurricane, she brought the blade slashing down.

A sparkling white cut opened up in front of her.

The slash widened and through it she could see the arched window of Bonwn Tyr and the tops of the aspen trees and the clear blue Faerie sky beyond.

A sweet waft of Faerie air came through the gap, filling her head with its enchanted scent, taking away the taste of iron from her mouth.

She stepped over the V-shaped threshold of the shimmering rift, one foot in Faerie, one foot in the Mortal World. The black sword had evaporated from her hand—utterly destroyed in the opening of the portal. Straddling the worlds, she turned back, reaching out urgently.

Speechless, and with wonder-filled eyes, her mother took her hand and stepped through into Faerie. Cordelia came next, her arm over Sancha's shoulders as they crossed the sparkling threshold between the worlds.

Zara followed. She looked into Tania's face, her hand coming up to caress her cheek. "My wondrous sister!"

"Edric, quickly!" Tania called. The door was being slowly beaten open from the outside. Another second or two and the Gray Knights of Lyonesse would be in the room.

Edric sprang forward. The door burst open, the swords of the howling Knights hacking the air at his heels as he sprinted toward Tania.

A sword flashed through the air, turning end over end—aimed at her head.

She flinched away from it, losing her footing and

falling heavily onto her back on the bare wood boards of Bonwn Tyr.

Now that she was no longer bridging the gap, the sizzling gash between the worlds began to close.

"No!" she screamed.

Edric was still in the Mortal World.

The white heart of energy shrank and dwindled— but at the last possible moment, when she thought the circle of light was already too small, Edric came diving through headfirst into Faerie.

A crystal sword-point followed him. But while it was still only halfway through, the ball of white light shriveled to a pinpoint and vanished. The blade hung for a split second in the air, cut clean through halfway to the hilt. Then it fell to the floor and shattered into white powder.

Tania scrambled across the floor to where Edric lay, panting and dazed.

"Are you okay?"

He blinked at her and smiled. "I'm fine. I think."

They helped each other up, clinging tightly, as Titania and the three princesses crowded joyfully around them.

Outside the window the Faerie sun was rising on a new day. Birds sang in the aspen branches. The scented breeze blew warm air in from the northern downs. For the first time in five hundred years Titania, Queen of Faerie, was home.

Watch for Tania's next journey
between the Realms in

The Sorcerer King

Book Three of *The Faerie Path*

Tania has brought the long-lost Queen Titania back to
Faerie from the Mortal World of modern London. But
when they cross between the worlds, they find only dev-
astation. The Sorcerer King of Lyonesse—ancient
enemy of the Faerie Court—has been released from his
amber prison. As the wicked Sorcerer regains his power,
King Oberon, Tania's father, is imprisoned and the
Faerie Court is being destroyed. Tania and her true
love, Edric, must travel the Realm to try to find and rescue King Oberon, who is their only hope for defeating
the evil King. And Tania must prepare for battle . . . and
to fight a war that she may not survive.